Little Black Girl Lost

Little Black Girl Lost

Keith Lee Johnson

Little Black Girl Lost
Keith Lee Johnson

Urban Books
74 Andrews Aveune
Wheatley Heights, NY 11798

ISBN 0-9747025-5-2

First Printing February 2005
Second Printing April 2005
Third Printing October 2005
Printed in United States of America

10 9 8 7 6

This is a work of fiction. Any references or similarities to
actual events, real people, living, or dead, or to real locals are
intended to give the novel a sense of reality. Any similarity in
other names, characters, places, and incidents is entirely
coincidental.

Dedication

To my darling mother, Rose Marie Murray, thanks for
your invaluable wisdom and for always being there for
me and beating my behind regularly, which kept me out
of prison.

Part 1
Innocence Lost

Chapter 1

"All women go through this."

Johnnie Wise was just fifteen years old when her mother sold her virginity to an unscrupulous white insurance man named Earl Shamus. Stunningly beautiful, with long, naturally wavy black hair, she possessed the voluptuous body of a thirty-year-old woman. Her skin was the color of brown sugar. Johnnie had heard about Earl Shamus and his escapades among the poor black women in New Orleans, but what she didn't know was that Shamus had quietly made several of the neighborhood girls his reluctant concubines after their youthful bodies ripened. She was next!

Shy and religiously chaste, Johnnie was a shining example of obedience, modesty, and compliance. She learned this at Mount Zion Holiness Church where she sang in the choir and played piano. People from affiliate churches came from as far away as Baton Rouge, Morgan City, Venice, and some even traveled from Shreveport just to hear her sing and play. However, a conflict raged within Johnnie. She wanted to become a traveling evangelist someday yet she wanted to sing what the church called "the Devil's music" and become rich. In her mind, there was no way she could do both and still call herself a good Christian. It must be one or the other.

Johnnie was reading in her room, which served as a secluded retreat from Marguerite, her domineering mother, whom she loved with a familial kind of love but didn't like for a number of reasons. Marguerite, equally stunning, had always been the center of attention from the time she was a child. However, as Johnnie blossomed, Marguerite became more jealous of her, insisting that Johnnie be nearly perfect at everything, which meant she had to do and say the right things to make Marguerite look like the perfect mother when nothing could be further from the truth.

Marguerite was very demanding, expecting Johnnie to do almost all of the cooking and cleaning. She often told her daughter she wanted her house cleaner than a spotless Marine Corps barracks. To make matters worse, Johnnie was the daily butt of cruel jokes because her mother was a prostitute. Kids talked about each others' parents all the time. The jokes about Marguerite wouldn't have hurt nearly as much if they weren't so penetratingly true. When Johnnie attended church, which was every Sunday, Reverend Staples delivered fiery sermons that constantly stressed the vices of Marguerite's lifestyle, but she was never there to hear them. Nevertheless, Johnnie loved her mother. She just didn't like her very much.

The weather was bitterly cold that Christmas Eve in New Orleans, which was unusual for the Crescent City. It threatened to snow on several occasions, but never did. Instead, it rained constantly. Johnnie heard someone knocking at the front door and wondered who would be out in a thunderstorm. The knocking was only a minor distraction, but the voices she heard downstairs in the living room piqued her curiosity. It was her mother and what sounded like Mr. Shamus. She stopped reading and listened closely, hoping it wasn't him. *He's a fornicator and an adulterer, bound for the hottest part of hell.*

"Johnnie!" her Creole mother shouted. Marguerite, forty-three and shapely, was the offspring of a married wealthy Frenchman named Nathaniel Beauregard, and Josephine Baptiste, a black prostitute he'd fallen in love with. Marguerite's voice was silky smooth and refined. She could sound sophisticated when white folks were around, an art she learned from the women in the brothel where she was reared. The white men of New Orleans who frequented seraglios expected the women to be cultured. In the downtrodden neighborhood where she lived, the people considered her the white man's whore. "Come on downstairs, girl."

"Okay, Mama," Johnnie said obediently.

While humming "I Love the Lord," her favorite spiritual, she walked down the stairs with the grace of an Egyptian queen. Courtbouillon emanated from the kitchen, reminding her she hadn't eaten. When she reached the bottom of the stairs, she saw Mr. Shamus standing near the spectacularly decorated eight-foot Christmas tree. She stared at him and intuitively knew something was amiss. As she lowered her eyes, which was expected of Negroes when they looked at a white person, she could see his privates bulging outward and throbbing at regular intervals.

"Johnnie," Marguerite began. "This is Mr. Shamus. He's responsible for the presents under the Christmas tree and all the food in the refrigerator." In French, Marguerite continued, "So I want you to be very nice to him, you hear?"

Something about what she heard unnerved Johnnie. What did she mean, be very nice to him? "What do you mean, Mama?" Johnnie asked in French, unable to accept what she was thinking.

"You know what I mean, girl," Marguerite said, frowning. "You're of age."

4

Now it was clear to Johnnie what she meant. She looked at Mr. Shamus. He had a twisted grin on his face. "Mama, no. I've never known a man before. Besides, it is a sin to—"

"Are you sassin' me, girl?"

"No, Mama, but . . ."

"Ain't no buts, girl."

A tear rolled down Johnnie's cheek. "But why, Mama? Why I gotta do this?"

"How you expect us to live if you don't? Huh? How you expect us to live?"

"The Lord will provide." Johnnie sobbed.

"And he has. He's providin' through Mr. Shamus, girl. Don't you see that? Why, it's as plain as day."

"But, Mama, it's wrong," Johnnie pleaded.

"All of your other friends have done it already. You the only one left."

Overcome by lust, Earl Shamus took Johnnie by the hand and dragged her into Marguerite's bedroom. She looked back at her mother over her slender shoulder. A waterfall of tears ran down her innocent face.

"It'll be okay," Marguerite said. "All women go through this."

That was the same thing Marguerite's mother told her the day she sold her virginity to a white man.

Chapter 2

"Next time, it'll be easier."

When they entered the bedroom, Shamus undressed hurriedly as Johnnie watched him, almost panic-stricken. The look on his face was like a man in the Sahara Desert desperately in need of water. While Earl Shamus stripped down to his boxer shorts, Johnnie stood there watching, unsure of what to do. Shamus turned around and saw Johnnie standing there, still fully dressed and staring at his protruding organ. She could see a small wet spot in the front of his shorts where the semen had already begun to seep out. Johnnie looked him in the face and wondered what he expected her to do. *I've never done this before.*

"What are you waitin' for, girl?" Shamus asked, impatiently. "I don't have all night. I have to get home. My wife is holding dinner for me. Now get undressed!"

Oh, my God! Suddenly it became clear to Johnnie that not only would she be fornicating with Earl Shamus, but she would also be an adulterer—just like him. She wanted to get out of that room and out of the situation altogether. *But how?* "Yo' wife know you be in the colored neighborhood spreadin' yo' sap around?" Johnnie asked, hoping the

6

question would be enough to jar his conscience.

"What's it to you? You just take them clothes off. I've been waitin' a long time for you and I mean to have you. Do you have any idea how much money it cost me to get you? Plenty, that's for sure."

Is there no shame in you? She wished her big brother Benny was home, believing that if he were there, Earl Shamus wouldn't dare try this. But Benny had a family of his own now, and was living in San Francisco with Brenda, his wife, who had just given birth to Jericho in October.

"Come on, girl," Shamus ordered.

Reluctantly, Johnnie undressed. Shamus watched her every move as if she were doing a striptease just for him. His mouth watered when she took off her blouse. He knew she had a nice shape, but hadn't fathomed how well put together she was. Johnnie's measurements were 40-24-38. Her delectable breasts spilled over her bra, revealing lots of cleavage. She had a trim waist, and her pear-shaped derriere sat atop slim, muscular thighs and calves. There wasn't a hint of fat on her.

Johnnie could see the eagerness in his eyes. He looked like a ravenous lion that hadn't eaten in weeks, which terrified her. She slid out of her skirt and stood before him wearing a white bra and panties. Black pubic hair was visible at the outer edges of her panties.

"The rest," he demanded.

Johnnie reached around, unhooked her bra and slid each arm out. The tears flowed again. She looked at him, praying he would have mercy and let her go.

Looking at her large breasts, Earl Shamus couldn't wait to fondle and suck them. Somehow, the whole idea of seeing her half naked made him even harder, and he wanted to see more. "The panties too." It was more of a request than a demand this time. The sight of her nakedness made the

7

anticipation of being inside her all the more stimulating.

Johnnie slid out of her panties one leg at a time and stood motionless before him, attempting to cover herself. Shamus took off his boxers and she looked at his stiff penis, semen still oozing. She'd never seen one before. It looked gigantic. She saw a thick vein sticking out and wondered if an erection hurt. With him being as big as he was, it would certainly hurt her, she thought. She had heard how the first time was very painful from some of the sexually active girls at school.

As Johnnie contemplated what was about to happen to her, Shamus grabbed her and threw her on the bed, recklessly squeezing and sucking her breasts. His hands were still cold and damp from being outside. His groans sounded like a wounded animal. Then he kissed her lips. The smell of wine on his breath made her nauseous. Johnnie wondered what her mother was doing out there in the living room. And what did she mean when she said all women had to go through this? *Was Mama raped? Or did grandmama sell her too?*

Johnnie could hear him lapping at her breasts, and those terrible animal sounds he made. When she felt him touching her genitals, she wanted to scream in horror but clenched her teeth instead. He pried her legs apart with one of his knees and positioned himself to enter her.

"Oh, Jesus! Sweet Lord! Don't let this happen to me! Please God! No! No! No! No! No! No!"

Earl was so overcome by lust, so blinded by wanton desire that he couldn't hear her supplication. He moved his organ around until he found the opening of her extremely tight vagina.

Suddenly, without warning, she felt the piercing pain of the violation taking place.

"Ooooooh, God! Nooooo!"

With each violent thrust, she cried louder and louder. "Stop it . . . Stop it . . . Stop! Please stop!" And as suddenly as it began, it was over. She could feel him slipping out of her. Exhausted, Earl Shamus rolled off her. Then he looked at her and kissed her cheek.

"Thank you. That wasn't too bad, was it?"

Not knowing what to say, Johnnie, still whimpering, shook her head no. She was frightened and confused. Only minutes ago, she was upstairs reading in her secluded retreat. The next thing she knew, she was being sold to a white man for Christmas presents and food.

"Next time, it'll be easier," Shamus told her.

"Next time? You mean I gotta do this again?" Johnnie wondered how many times she would have to do this to pay for the gifts and the food.

"Yeah, girl. You might even learn to like it." Shamus chuckled, feeling like a stud. He got out of bed and put his clothes back on. He put five dollars on the pillow. "Buy yourself something. See you next week."

Chapter 3

"It's up to you."

Sobbing softly and curled in a fetal position, Johnnie thought about what happened to her. The pain subsided, but she could feel the warm blood between her legs and on the bed. Johnnie lost something vital to her sense of being, something essential to her sense of self-worth, something she could never have again. Then she realized that Earl Shamus would be back and he expected her to do it again. The thought of him touching her made her skin crawl. Suddenly, she could smell the wine on his breath and hear his animal-like groans of ecstasy again. She felt her stomach heave, but there was nothing to throw up.

Johnnie could hear Earl Shamus and her mother talking in the living room, but she couldn't understand what they were saying. Moments later, Marguerite walked into the bedroom. Johnnie wore a vacant look on her face. Marguerite could see that her daughter's mind was in another place. Marguerite understood how Johnnie felt because she had been through it too. *I got over it and so will she.* "You a woman now, girl," Marguerite said, attempting to comfort her.

Johnnie didn't say anything. She was extremely quiet, still unable to believe what had happened to her.

"And ain't no need in frettin' about yo' virginity. I did you a favor. You was gon' lose it someday anyway. Probably to some good for nothin' nigga who ain't got nothin', ain't never had nothin', and ain't gon' never get nothin'. All men are the same, girl. They all want what you got between yo' legs. And they'll do anything to get it. That's for sure. You might as well get somethin' for it. Ain't no need in blamin' 'em for the way they is. That's how they made. That's somethin' all women eventually realize. Trouble is we always think if we love 'em enough, this one'll be different, but they ain't. They all the same. Even yo' brother, Benny, is the same. Now, you got a choice, girl. You can either give it away for free and hope his love will be enough, or you can take advantage of his weakness. It's up to you."

"Mr. Shamus say I gotta do this again, Mama. Is that right?"

"For a little while, just until we get on our feet. But the next time it won't be as bad. Now get up and take a hot bath and you'll feel a lot better."

"I don't think I'll ever feel better, Mama."

"You will in time, child. You will in time."

Chapter 4

"Let the redeemed of the Lord say Amen!"

The following Sunday, Johnnie walked through the doors of Mount Zion Holiness Church. Service had already begun and she was late. She skipped choir rehearsal the previous day and contemplated skipping Sunday morning service altogether, but felt the need to go. In order to sing on Sunday morning, she had to go to rehearsal on Saturday. Johnnie never missed a rehearsal prior to losing her virginity. Singing on Sunday morning was something she looked forward to. Worship service offered her the opportunity to hone her singing skills as well as sing the Lord's praises. Now the thought of singing spiritual songs made her feel like a hypocrite; especially since she knew that the man who had deflowered her would return so she could pleasure him again.

Worship service was in full swing when Johnnie walked into the sanctuary. The church was packed with members, singing and praising the Lord. The whole building seemed to sway with the gospel rhythm. "Hallelujah!" Johnnie heard Reverend Staples shout. Shortly after that, she heard, "Holy, Holy, Holy, is our God," followed by, "Rose of Sharon, bright and morning star, King of kings, Lord of lords, we give you the highest praise." The woman next to her lifted her hands

12

and shouted "Hallelujah!" Then from the back of the church, someone shouted another hallelujah, and another and another until it seemed as if the entire church was caught up in the spirit of the service. Conviction consumed Johnnie when she heard such high praise. She never considered herself a sinner even though she believed all human beings were born sinners. Johnnie knew she wasn't perfect, but she believed she was closer to it than anyone at Mount Zion— Reverend Staples being the only exception, and she wasn't sure about him.

The fact that her mother had sold her virginity so callously removed the veil of innocence and stripped her of any semblance of perfection, reducing her to the status of an ordinary sinner. Ever since Johnnie was a little girl, she had been taught that sin separates people from God. Now that she had consented to sexual sin, she was separated from God, and therefore, no longer a Christian.

After the announcements were read, Reverend Staples stood up and said, "Let the redeemed of the Lord say Amen!"

"Amen," the members said and took their seats.

"Turn with me in your Bibles to Jeremiah 17:9," Reverend Staples continued. "When you find it, say Amen."

"Amen," the members said in unison a few moments later.

Reverend Staples read, "The heart is deceitful above all and desperately wicked." Johnnie thought he was talking to her as he spoke, like he was standing right next to her, speaking directly in her ear. "Some of us are so self-righteous that it's going to take a lifetime to discover the truth of this verse so that we might be truly saved," Reverend Staples went on. "If you're lookin' around at your neighbor . . . If you're thinkin' of your husband or your wife . . . If you're thinkin' of anyone other than yourself . . . this message is for you."

13

Johnnie found his words to be both penetrating and prophetic. Something within her told her to run to the altar, but she resisted. Her mother needed her to "be nice'" to Earl Shamus. Yet, somehow she knew that her refusal to go to the altar would alter the course of her life for years to come—perhaps forever. *If I'm going to continue having sex with Mr. Shamus, what's the point in confessing my sins? I'll confess when I know I won't have to do it with him anymore.*

Chapter 5
"The best laid plans"

Earl Shamus, now forty, average height and build, graduated from high school, but never attended college. He didn't have any money saved, and not even a penny in his pockets yet he always believed that one day his ship would come in. It did, in the form of a woman named Meredith Buchanan, daughter of West Buchanan, the insurance tycoon. Earl was the concierge of the chic Bel Glades Hotel when he met Meredith, who was attending a wedding reception there.

Meredith was twenty-two when she met Earl, who was twenty-four. She was sheltered all of her young life, had never even been on a date. No one ever asked her out except the shy boy who lived next door. He asked her if he could take her to the prom and she turned him down immediately as there was nothing about him that appealed to her. To Meredith, it was better that her father, whom she was very close to, take her rather than settle for the bookworm next door.

Meredith was very bright and found college to be a bit boring. She loved to read and learn new things, but no one asked her out. She hoped college would offer more opportunities to meet interesting men who would appreciate

15

her chaste attitude and change her into the swan she knew she could be—with the right man, of course. While other college girls were going on dates and to football games, Meredith went to the library and read the classics with her free time, which she had plenty of. She dreamed about the knight in shining armor who would one day come along and sweep her off her feet.

When Earl opened the glass door of the Bel Glades for Meredith, she believed her knight had finally come to rescue the lonely damsel who wanted nothing more than to be seen as a desirable woman. Earl looked dashing in the gray doorman's suit with its shiny brass buttons and burgundy braids, which were attached to the shoulder strap of his uniform. He almost looked like a West Point graduate. Meredith offered him an inviting smile. She felt a little electricity between them when he smiled at her.

Earl, however, wasn't the least bit attracted to Meredith, even though he sensed she was attracted to him and was quite possibly an easy lay. He didn't think she was anything special until one of the desk clerks told him her father was West Buchanan. The clerk went on to explain that West was a former salesman who defied the odds and built Buchanan Mutual Insurance Company. When the clerk said that Meredith was the sole heir to his fortune, suddenly Meredith became very attractive—at least her money was.

Meredith was sitting in the reception hall bored to tears. She couldn't help thinking of the charming doorman with the kind face. She wondered if he was still in the lobby at the door. She left the reception and entered the lobby to see if he was there. She saw him standing near the door with his dark gray doorman's uniform on. She walked near the door to get his attention.

"Leaving the party so soon?" Earl asked when he turned around.

"Yes, it's quite boring in there," she told him. "I'm Meredith Buchanan. Pleased to meet you."

"Earl Shamus. Pleased to meet you also."

The two of them talked for hours in the lobby. She gave him her telephone number and told him she'd love to talk again some time. Earl wanted to talk again too, but not for the reasons she wanted to. He saw dollar signs when he looked into her plain Jane face. There was nothing physically attractive about Meredith, but she did have a wholesomeness about her that made her the sort of woman men brought home to their mothers.

Earl began formulating his plan to seduce and marry Meredith. He believed that if she were pregnant with his child, her father would be forced to take him and the baby into the fold. What he didn't know was that West didn't have anything against him and his lowly stature in life as a doorman. West didn't like rich people. He thought they were self-righteous and they tended to look down on the people who made it possible for them to have the wealth they enjoyed. He hoped Meredith wouldn't fall in love and marry one of the sons of those affluent bigots.

West wanted Meredith to marry a working stiff, someone more like himself. He wanted her to be with someone who knew what it was like to be poor and not have ends meet. His plan was to have one of her sons take over the family business. When he found out about Earl, he had him investigated. The investigation showed him to be a modern day nomad. Earl couldn't seem to keep a steady job and he had a problem with authority.

This was definitely not the man for Meredith, West thought. She could certainly do better than him. Unfortunately, it was too late. Meredith was pregnant and she had her heart set on marrying Earl. West strictly forbade her to marry Earl, promising he would take care of her and

17

her child and they wouldn't want for anything. West even offered Earl ten thousand dollars to leave Meredith.

But Earl wanted it all, so he gambled on West's love for his daughter. He assumed West would take care of them because Meredith was his flesh and blood. West knew this and promptly disinherited Meredith. Earl and Meredith hoped West would change his mind when the baby came, and he would have if the baby had been a boy. But it was a girl. They named her Janet, now sixteen.

The couple kept trying, but ended up with two more girls, Stacy, fourteen, and Marjorie, thirteen. They weren't able to have a boy, West Buchanan Shamus, until twelve years later. Only then did West end the cold war between the couple.

West was quite fond of his grandson. He called him Little Buck, short for Buchanan. He treated Little Buck like he was his own son. He couldn't stand having him live just a notch above the indigent, so he bought Meredith and Earl a sixteen-room home in an exclusive area of New Orleans called Rivera Heights. The home had six bedrooms, four bathrooms, living room, formal dining room, island kitchen, den, library, laundry room, full finished basement, and a three-car attached garage. West even gave them both brand new Cadillacs.

After Little Buck's birth, West hired Earl at Buchanan Mutual. He told Earl he was grooming him to take over the company, but in reality, West only wanted Earl to run things long enough for Little Buck to take over. After all, Little Buck was blood; Earl wasn't. He was just an opportunist who took advantage of a young woman who didn't know any better. Most importantly, West knew Little Buck needed a role model in the home to look up to.

Therefore, grooming Earl to run the company was not just a shrewd move. It was essential for Little Buck to see his father running a business and to hear business conversations at the dinner table. West wanted Little Buck to be thoroughly ingrained in business during his formative years so that it would become a part of his being.

Little did West know that his granddaughters would learn to detest him for the way he made them live when they were their brother's age. They also resented Little Buck because of all the attention West lavished on him. Whenever West visited, and he visited often, he would spend virtually all of his time with Little Buck, telling him how handsome and how smart he was.

Janet, Stacy, and Marjorie felt like the family mascots. Meredith didn't help matters as far as the girls were concerned. She was so passive that the girls didn't bother to tell her how they felt. Instead, they talked among themselves and their jealousy began to fester. They often found themselves wishing something terrible would happen to their baby brother.

Chapter 6

"Was I not a good Christian?"

At first, Earl Shamus was in a hurry to have sex with Johnnie and get home to his family. His lust demanded immediate satisfaction. He had been coming to the house two, sometimes three times a week. But after a few months of unbridled passion, he began to stay longer and longer, talking to Johnnie about his dreams of running the family business. Eventually, he'd end up telling her how he wished he could leave his wife but couldn't because he would be out in the cold without a cent to his name. Meredith was an albatross hanging around his neck, he told Johnnie.

Each time Shamus left Johnnie, he placed conscience money on the pillow. Johnnie refused to spend it, believing that the moment she spent it, she would be the whore that Earl Shamus and her mother had made her. She toyed with the idea of putting the money in church, but if she did, she thought it would be like giving money stained with sin to God. So, she just kept putting the money in her dresser drawer, occasionally counting it to see how much was there, and to keep track of how many times Earl Shamus had violated her.

There was no longer any pain when he entered her. Johnnie was feeling pleasure now. She felt ashamed of herself for feeling pleasure with him, albeit brief. She began wondering what it would be like to do it with boys her own age. That made her feel ashamed, too, but the more she tried not to think about sex, the more she thought of it. Guilt consumed her. She felt like a hypocrite for continuing to go to church, singing, and playing the piano.

Everything changed. Nothing was the same. And where was God in all of this? Johnnie wondered. Why had he let all of this happen to her? *Was I not a good Christian? Was I not chaste and faithful before Mama sold me?* She began to pray that God would stop her from having sexual feelings and thoughts, but the more she prayed, the more the thoughts increased, until finally she stopped praying.

It was bad enough that Earl Shamus was having his way with her, but it was worse when Johnnie realized that everyone in the neighborhood knew her shame. What she found particularly bothersome was that she had put other young girls down for being fornicators. She preached righteousness, and now she was practicing what the elders of the church called "the Devil's work." *How can this be?* To combat these thoughts, Johnnie read the Bible. She read how almost all the great men of the Bible had fallen into some sort of sin from time to time. She read how Joshua spared the life of Rahab, the whore who hid the two spies, and she found solace.

Solace aside, her sexual urges grew as the months passed. In all that time, Johnnie still had known only one man, though she fantasized about others. She had learned to accept her situation and made the best of it. In those months, she became skilled in the art of making love—so

21

much so that she began asking Earl, as she now called him, for more money, which he willingly paid. He had fallen in love with her. In addition to the extra money, Earl bought her fine dresses, shoes, and jewelry. Johnnie decided to continue saving her money so she could leave New Orleans one day. She wondered how Earl would feel if she left, and decided to ask him the next time he came over.

Chapter 7

"Do you love me, Earl?"

Choir rehearsal ended promptly at 6 p.m. Johnnie was on her way to the restroom when she heard a few teenage girls say, "Why we always lettin' her lead songs on Sunday morning? Everybody knows she's a whore now." Johnnie heard them laugh. The comments hurt, but the laughter brought the tears. Johnnie believed that she wasn't a whore as long as she went to church and sang in the choir. If she was going to get understanding and mercy, the church was the only place in the world to get it, but now she knew differently. Instead of going to the restroom as she planned, she left the church and headed home. Although she had just suffered one of the most humiliating moments in her life a moment ago, Johnnie still had to get home and be further humiliated by her only paying customer.

It was about 7:00 in the evening when Earl arrived. Johnnie knew his habits now. He was going to come in and have a glass of red wine with the andouille she made for him. Earl would tell her about his day then he would complain about his wife. After that, he'd want her to make love to him as only she could. But today was different. Earl came in, gave Johnnie a big kiss and told her he had good news, but first he needed a quickie. He took her clothes off

23

right there in the living room. He licked her luscious, dark nipples. Johnnie moaned. Then he buried his head in her crotch.

After Earl's lust was satisfied, he said, "I got promoted today, Johnnie. I won't have to go door to door selling insurance anymore. I'll have my own office downtown."

"So, you won't be comin' around no more?" Johnnie asked sarcastically.

"Yeah, I'll still be coming around." He rolled over and faced her. "Why? You don't want me to?"

Johnnie turned over onto her side to hide her face from him. "Well . . . I've been thinkin' about leaving New Orleans."

"Really?" he said skeptically. "Where will you go? How will you live?"

"I'll do just fine," she said confidently. "I've been saving my money."

"You have, have you?"

"Yes, I have."

"Why don't you put the money in the bank or invest it in stocks and bonds?"

"Is that what you do with your money?" Johnnie asked.

"Yes, but my wife is rich, as you know. When her father dies, I'll be taking over the company." He turned her over so he could see her face. She wanted to leave their arrangement and it bothered him. "You should let me invest your money in the company for you. How much have you saved?"

Johnnie stared at him for a moment or two then turned her back to him again. Johnnie wondered if she could trust him with her money. It had been almost a year since he took her virginity, and now he wanted to help her make money? It didn't make sense. *Why would you want to help me?*

"Are you still seeing other women, Earl?"

"Why? Would it bother you if I did?"

Sensing his vulnerability, Johnnie asked, "Do you love

24

me, Earl?"

He was silent. *Do I dare admit that I've fallen in love with this young black girl, this beautiful vixen who drains my strength from me?*

Johnnie looked him in the face. She climbed on top of him and moved back and forth on his soft penis until she felt him stiffen. When he was fully erect, she slid down onto him. She moved up and down until he made those animal-like groans.

"Do-you-love-me-Earl?" she repeated through clenched teeth with each impassible thrust.

"Yes, oh yes," he said desperately. "I do love you, Johnnie."

"Can-I-trust-you-with-my-money-Earl?"

"Yes, you can," he said, gasping for air.

She looked down at him, sensing he was on the verge of orgasm. So, she pumped faster and harder until his eyes rolled back into his head. Then she said, "How-do-I-know-that-Earl?"

No longer able to control himself, he rammed himself inside her as fast and hard as he could. Seconds later, he came harder than he had ever come in his life.

Catching his breath, he said, "I'll tell you what. Tell me how much you have, then I'll tell you how I can prove it."

"Okay."

She slid off him and ran up the stairs to count her money. She had $870, a fortune to a teenager. She ran downstairs and climbed back into bed with Earl.

"I've got almost nine hundred dollars."

"Nine hundred?" he repeated, obviously stunned.

"Yeah, you started off by giving me five, then ten. And now you give me twenty."

"And you haven't spent any of it?" Earl frowned.

"Nope, not even a penny."

"Okay, give me half of it, and if I don't double it, I'll give you the money back out of my own pocket. How's that for trust?"

"Yeah, but I still have to trust you to give me back the money if you lose it, Earl."

"Johnnie, you have to learn to take chances in life. That's the only way to get ahead." Johnnie was lying on her back, looking up at the ceiling. Earl rolled onto his side and looked down into her face. "You are so beautiful," he whispered as sweetly as he could.

"Okay, Earl. If you lose my money and you don't pay me back, then you cain't have me no more. Now, that way you either make me money or I buy my freedom."

"Is sex with me really that terrible, Johnnie?"

After all this time, she still didn't find their relationship fulfilling and it hurt him. The lust he felt for Johnnie was so overwhelming that he actually believed he had found love for the first time. And even though she was just sixteen, Earl convinced himself that Johnnie embodied all he wanted a woman to be. Johnnie was a beautiful young woman who made him feel like a man. She was sweetly obedient, did as he asked, was a good cook, and now he knew she had good business acumen. As his feelings for Johnnie grew, Meredith, who was on the homely side, became less and less appealing, to the point that he was no longer sleeping with her or anyone other than Johnnie.

"Is it a deal, yes or no?" Johnnie demanded.

"Deal."

"Swear, Earl."

"I swear."

"No, Earl, say it all."

"Okay, I swear if I lose your money, I'll either pay you back, or I'll leave you be, okay?"

"Okay."

"Now, is it really that bad with me?" Earl asked anxiously.

"Don't you worry none how bad it is for me. You just worry about what you gon' be missin' if you lose my money." And with that, Johnnie climbed on him, and the animal groans filled the room once more.

Chapter 8
"Anything botherin' you?"

Marguerite came home about twenty minutes after Earl left. She had been at Shirley's house, a friend of hers who lived two doors down. They were playing spades for a nickel a game. She waited until the game was over even though she'd seen Earl's Cadillac pull off. Upon entering the house, Marguerite smelled the food Johnnie was preparing and walked into the kitchen, where Johnnie was sitting at the table about to eat. Marguerite pulled a chair back and sat down. She put some of the red beans, rice, and plump spicy sausage on her plate. She was just about to dig in when she noticed Johnnie had something on her mind.

"What are you thinking about so hard?" Marguerite asked in French.

Johnnie was quiet for a moment, trying to figure out what kind of mood her mother was in. One moment she could be friendly, and the next she would snap at her like a vicious dog.

"Mama," Johnnie said, also in French. "Did you love my daddy?"

"Yeah, I suppose so. Why?" she asked while cutting up her sausage.

"I don't remember him. I guess I wanna know what happened between y'all to put us in this situation, Mama."

"It's a long story, girl," Marguerite said gruffly. "Maybe I'll tell you about him someday."

"You promise?"

"Yeah, I promise." Marguerite put some more food into her mouth. As if it were an afterthought, she said, "Anything botherin' you?"

"Yeah."

"What?"

"I don't know . . . I guess it's the way people look at me now."

"They just jealous of you, girl. Women always have been jealous of us Baptiste girls 'cause we's pretty."

"Really?"

"Yeah, girl. They was jealous of my mama. They was jealous of me. And they sho' as hell gon' be jealous of you. I remember when I was about twelve years old. My mama was attractin' all the men, especially the white ones, and all the women got mad at her and put us outta the house. We didn't have nowhere to go, but my mother got one of her suitors to get us a place of our own, and that's where we lived for a while. Then I met Michael, Benny's daddy, and like a fool I ran away with him."

"Was he colored?"

"Yeah, he was colored. You don't think a white man is goin' to marry a colored woman in the South, do you?" Marguerite didn't bother to wait for an answer. She just continued talking after a brief pause. "Let me tell you somethin' about white men, girl, and don't you never ever forget it. A white man got to have his brown sugar. That's just the way he is. It's in his blood now. See, girl, ever since slave time, the white man has been havin' his brown sugar. He creep his ass out to the slave quarters at night, havin' his way with the colored women. Then he go back to the big house with his family. The same shit Earl is doin' today.

"Now, his white sugar is for show, see. They need the white woman for respectability, but what they didn't know is, all them years of sneakin' down to the slave quarters and sportin' with the colored women give him what they call a predilection for us. And a lot of his offspring end up havin' the same penchant. That's why colored women, like my mama, always had it better than white women did. And that's also why white women and colored women don't like each other too much.

"It's all about what we got between our legs. And how we use what we got between our legs usually determines our lot in life. We womenfolk like sex, too, so now it comes down to who gon' have a man. You see how we women compete with one another for a man's attention. How you think a white woman feels, knowin' her husband is doin' to us what she wants him to do to her?"

"But if white women like doin' it, cain't they get the same . . . what's that word again?"

"Predilection toward colored men? Yeah, and many do. White women either love colored men or they hate 'em. And even when they hate 'em, I have to wonder why. Most of 'em think a colored man wants to rape 'em. Colored men know not to even look at a white woman, let alone rape one. They know if they do, the white man will string 'em up and cut off their plows."

"How old was you, Mama?"

"How old was I when?"

"When you ran away."

"Oh, about sixteen or seventeen."

Marguerite looked into her daughter's eyes. In them, she

saw the flicker of young love on the horizon. Intuitively, she asked, "You like some boy at school or somethin'?"

"Yeah, Mama," she said, her fondness of the boy gushing forth. "His name is Lucas Matthews, and he likes me too, Mama. I see 'im watchin' me all the time."

"Girl, don't you get yo'self in trouble with that boy," Marguerite snapped. "How we gon' live if you get yo'self with child?"

"Cain't Earl get me with child?" she asked flippantly. "And if he do, how we gon' live then, Mama?"

Marguerite reached across the table and slapped the triumphant grin off Johnnie's face. "Don't you get snippety with me. I'm still yo' Mama and I expect you to show me some respect in my house. You understand me, girl?"

"Yes, Mama."

"And don't think you too old for me beat the black off you neither!"

"I'm sorry, Mama."

"You better be." Marguerite frowned. "Now finish your dinner. You got homework to do before you go to bed."

Chapter 9
"The Savoy"

Marguerite bathed and prepared herself for a rendezvous with a married preacher named Richard Goode, who also served as the Grand Wizard of the Ku Klux Klan. She usually met her clients, as she called them, while Johnnie was in school or after she went to bed. Goode had been paying for her sexual expertise for years, unbeknownst to the Klan for obvious reasons. Their sexual liaison was a closely guarded secret, but like most secrets, word leaked out. The few colored folk who knew about it kept quiet for various reasons. Most of them feared repeated reprisals from the Klan, but Robert Simmons had his own reasons for keeping it quiet.

Simmons was a black man who owned the Savoy Hotel. His family owned it since he was a little boy. Now, he managed the hotel's daily operations and often greeted guests at the main desk. The hotel earned its reputation for allowing mixed couples to check in several years earlier when Simmons let one of his friends bring a white woman there to make love.

Simmons was against it at first, fearing the white populace might burn down his hotel if word ever got out. Slowly, the news spread that it was okay to bring white women to the Savoy. Late one night, Richard Goode brought Marguerite to the hotel. He was surprisingly cordial, but he made Simmons promise to keep it quiet. If he agreed, Goode promised he would see to it that nothing happened to his hotel. When Simmons asked how he planned to do that, Goode told him he would simply tell the Klan that any white woman who would sleep with a nigger was trash and was of no use to the white race. It would be best to let the degenerates leave the race so the pure white women would remain.

Simmons agreed. Since then, mixed couples had the freedom to go to the Savoy to indulge their carnal appetites. Strangely enough, racial problems continued to pervade the city. The Savoy was the only safe haven in New Orleans for such activity. Simmons, as did many of the black men who worked there, hated the idea of black women sleeping with white men. Nevertheless, Simmons allowed it to go on in his hotel because these illicit affairs made him a lot of money.

It had been hot all day, but now it was quite cool. The wind felt good on Marguerite's skin at first, but she was getting cold. She folded her arms to keep from shivering. She was standing at the corner of Waite and Henry Streets just two blocks from where she lived, wearing a short black skirt and pumps. She wasn't wearing any panties because Goode loved to feel her up as he drove down the street, grinning.

She heard a car coming. *It's about time.* She thought it was Mr. Goode, as he demanded she call him, arriving to pick her up, but it wasn't. It was Sable Parish Sheriff Paul Tate, who was a regular client before his wife found out. He stopped the black and white, then rolled down the window.

"Now, what's a fine thing like you doing out here, Marguerite?"

Sheriff Tate got out and leaned against the patrol car with his arms folded. He was wearing a beige uniform and a black wide-brimmed Mounty hat. He was tall and slender and sported a thick mustache.

Marguerite walked over to him, feeling sexier with each step, and said, "Hi, Sheriff Tate. How you doin' tonight?" She reached out and patted his beer belly. She could smell beer on his breath. "Still drinkin' in the squad car on lonely nights, huh?"

"You gettin' beside yo'self, woman. Don't think you can talk to me any way you want. I'm still the fuckin' sheriff."

"I know you the sheriff, Paul, honey. I know," she said, rubbing her hands across his chest.

"You waitin' on the preacher to pick you up for one of his late night snacks?"

"Uh-huh," Marguerite said, sliding her hand down to his crotch. She could feel him stiffening in her hand. "You need a snack tonight?"

Sheriff Tate couldn't contain his lust. He never could with her. She was the sexiest woman he had ever known. He couldn't be in her presence two minutes without wanting to take her. He tried for years to leave her alone, but his lust kept him coming back for more. He grabbed her shoulders and kissed her deeply.

"Now, Paul honey, you know I have a date tonight," Marguerite said, pulling away. "If you want to see me, all you have to do is call."

"You know I shouldn't be seeing you, Marguerite. Why do you torture me so?"

"Am I torturin' you?" Marguerite teased.

"You know you are," Tate said and kissed her again.

Marguerite could see Goode's dark blue Chevrolet out of the corner of her eye, just down the street. She knew he was watching. She pulled away and backed off, then she folded her arms and smiled. "Yo' wife still houndin' you about seein' me?"

Tate told her that he promised his wife he wouldn't see her again, but Marguerite wanted to keep the money coming in. She had a nice little nest egg saved up. "Let's leave my wife outta this."

With a serious tone, Marguerite said, "Sheriff Tate, are you going to arrest me tonight or what? 'Cause if you are, go ahead and arrest me. If you're not, then you need to let me handle my business with the preacher."

"Marguerite, you know I'm not going to arrest you. I just don't understand why you would take that hypocritical Klan leader as a client."

"Oh please, Paul. Where you get off callin' anybody a hypocrite? Look at you. You're the parish sheriff and you drink on duty. You pay me to have sex and you're married."

"Yeah, well, at least I'm not a redneck racist."

"You're not, huh?"

"No, I'm not."

"So, you don't call us niggas?"

"Hey, I only call the bad ones that."

"Just the men, you mean. Yet you wanna fuck me every chance you get."

Sheriff Tate got back in the car and started it. He looked at her again, and said, "Put me down for tomorrow night." Then he drove off.

Chapter 10

"I'm ready!"

Richard Goode waited until Sheriff Tate was out of sight before starting the car and turning on the lights. He pulled up to the corner where Marguerite was waiting, then rolled down his window and yelled, "Get your black ass in the car!" Marguerite laughed. His verbal abuse was part of his mating ritual. Goode always wanted oral sex, and while she gave it to him, he would call her a dirty black Jezebel. During intercourse, he whispered, "I hate you for making me do this."

Marguerite dutifully walked around to the other side of the car and got in. Goode turned on the ceiling light. She pulled up her skirt so he could see she wasn't wearing panties. As he looked intensely at her luscious crotch, she often wondered what was going through his demented mind. She spread her legs for him. He put his hand there, attempting to feel her heat, which made him long to taste her sweet nectar. When he found her spot and Marguerite began to lubricate, an inane grin emerged on his face and he pulled off.

Whenever Goode had an appointment with Marguerite,

he would call Simmons so that he would take the proper steps to insure secrecy. Simmons would register them under a phony name and sneak them in through the back door. He always gave them the same room close to the exit to make it as convenient as possible. One night, as Simmons was going out the back door to smoke a cigarette, he heard the strangest thing going on in the room and began listening to them.

Simmons couldn't believe what he was hearing. He had to see what was going on in there for himself. After they left, he drilled a small hole in the wall of the next room. When they came back, he would check them in, get a clerk to cover the desk, then go to the room he prepared to watch what was going on.

When they arrived, Simmons checked them in and gave the Klansman time to finish his business, as he wasn't interested in seeing a live sex act. Simmons was interested in what they did when the sex was done. He went to the kitchen and made himself a turkey sandwich with Monterey Jack cheese, bacon, lettuce, and tomatoes, with a pickle and chips on the side. He grabbed a bottle of Rolling Rock beer out of the refrigerator and went to his perch for a bird's eye view.

Simmons could still hear the creaking of the bedsprings when he arrived. He took his time walking over to his stool, where he watched the show. Even though he wasn't interested in the sex, he peeked in early anyway to see. Goode was pumping her hard, saying, "You goddamn gorilla. You beast of the field! You fucking animal! Oh, it's so good. Lord in heaven, why do you make me do this? I'm coooomiiiing!" Simmons shook his head.

Later, Marguerite came out of the bathroom wearing nothing but a black bra. Goode was naked and lying on the bed. Simmons took a bite of his sandwich and watched

Marguerite, who seemed to be beside herself with glee. Simmons could tell she enjoyed this part. Perhaps this was the reason she consented to the name-calling, he thought, and took a swallow of the beer.

"Do it, you evil black bitch!" Goode demanded.

Marguerite rubbed her hands over the back of his head and smiled. She grabbed a hunk of his thick hair and snatched his head back. His neck reddened as she pulled.

"You like that, Richard?"

"Yes, Mommy. I've been a bad boy. I deserve a whipping."

Simmons put his hand over his mouth to muffle his laughter. He had watched the scene a hundred times. It became more hilarious each time he saw them.

"Good, because that's exactly what you're going to get."

Marguerite went over to the mirrored dresser and picked up the black riding crop. She put her hand through the noose-like strap and went back over to the bed. She looked down at his vulnerable, pale body and proceeded to beat him mercilessly. Goode put his face in the pillow to squelch his cries. With each blow, a red welt appeared on his milky white buttocks. The beating was so fierce that Marguerite began to perspire.

Simmons sat there watching, shaking his head. A part of him was disgusted by this act in their sordid play. Another part of him enjoyed watching the leader of the Klan taking the kind of vicious beating he no doubt doled out to black men time and again; not to mention the random castrations and hangings that went on. Another part of him thought this was certainly God's divine justice in a world where justice was seldom realized.

"I'm ready!" Goode shouted.

Catching her breath, Marguerite grabbed the black dildo off the nightstand and inserted it in him.

Chapter 11
"Whose money is this?"

While making a pot of jambalaya, Johnnie found herself daydreaming more and more about Lucas Matthews, wondering how sex would be with him instead of Earl. When Earl came by, she made passionate love to Lucas Matthews. The daily fantasies about him fueled her lust, and the ruggedly handsome Lucas stayed on her mind like an incurable plague. Although they hadn't said anything more than hello to each other, she wondered how his lips and tongue would feel against her breasts and what it would be like to have his bronzed, naked body against hers. Johnnie often pictured Lucas coming over and taking her the way Earl did.

Instead of feeling guilty about it afterward, Johnnie believed she wouldn't feel any shame with Lucas. To Johnnie, he was her only true freedom from what her mother and Earl expected of her. With Lucas, she was free to run away from New Orleans and be a singer, even if it was only in her mind. As her fantasies about Lucas Matthews raced, she could feel moisture in her panties.

Johnnie was awakened from her lust-filled interlude with Lucas when she heard a key enter the lock of the front door. She knew it was Earl. After turning off the stove, she walked into the living room. The door opened and Earl entered, smiling broadly. Having seen that look on his face before, Johnnie knew he would recklessly invade her young body soon. She also knew he was going to want to share his day and whatever good news he had. She had come to understand Earl. All he needed was good sex on a regular basis, and a listening ear. That and a good home-cooked meal. In Johnnie, he had everything he wanted, except her love. And he would never have that.

"Hi!"

"Hello, Earl." Johnnie yawned.

"Well, don't get all excited," he said with a chilly tone.

"Earl, I'm tired. Don't expect me to get all excited just because you is."

"Well, maybe this will excite you," he said, reaching inside the breast pocket of his suit. He pulled out a white envelope and handed it to her.

"What's this?" Skeptically, Johnnie opened the envelope. To her surprise, there was a check for almost four thousand dollars. Overwhelmed, she said, "Whose money is this?"

"Who do you think?" Earl beamed. "Read the name on the check."

She looked at the check again. Even though she saw her name, she still couldn't believe all that money was hers. It had been four months since she'd given Earl half of her money. He had kept his word.

Earl was rapidly moving up the corporate ladder, which was to be expected, being married to the boss' daughter. He wasn't a financial wizard by any stretch of the imagination, but Buchanan Mutual was growing by leaps and bounds. He simply bought her stock in the company. Everything was going according to plan.

Johnnie wanted to please Earl for making her all that money. She took off the red silk robe he'd given her on

Valentine's Day, standing before him completely naked. Earl gazed intensely at her dark nipples, the contours of her body, then at her thick bush. The sight of her nakedness caused him to throb.

Johnnie undressed Earl, beginning with his jacket, then his shirt, leaving only his T-shirt on. She dropped to her knees and unbuckled his pants. They fell to the floor. She could see his hardness through his white underwear. She pulled them down and took him into her mouth. Earl placed his hand behind her head and moaned uncontrollably. She stood up and kissed his thin pink lips as if they belonged to Lucas Matthews.

Chapter 12

"What does that mean for me?"

"You want me, Earl?" Johnnie asked, feeling sexy.

"Yes," he said desperately. "You know I do."

She climbed on top of him, positioning his engorged member to enter her. When she found the opening, she forced herself downward onto it while imagining that Earl was Lucas Matthews. Johnnie closed her eyes and saw him in her mind. She moaned and moaned like never before; so much so that she couldn't hear Earl's wounded animal groans. Her movements became rapid and uncontrolled. Her moans were loud and fierce.

Earl stopped moaning and opened his eyes, staring into her contorted face. For the first time, he believed he was actually pleasing her. Suddenly she convulsed and fell forward, panting. She sat on him, relaxing as her breathing returned to normal. Earl enjoyed the moment.

"I love you, Johnnie," he said and kissed her on the neck.

"Do you have more good news for me?"

"Oh, yeah. I almost forgot. You know I've been moving up in my father-in-law's insurance company the last six months as a junior executive, right?"

"Yeah, Buchanan Mutual, right?"

"Right. Well, West just put me in charge of the financial division. He thinks I should know where the money is and how each dollar is spent. A year or so from now, I expect to be promoted to senior executive status, which means more money, not that I need it."

"That's good for you, Earl, but what does that mean for me?"

"I've been thinking about that, Johnnie. How would you like to move uptown in your own place?"

"Uptown? Where the white folks live?"

"Well, not that far uptown, but close."

"I figured as much." She frowned.

"Well, at least think about it, okay?"

"I don't know, Earl. Are you going to be coming around every day or what?" She was thinking about how often she could sneak Lucas Matthews over if he was willing. She knew he was; at least that's what she told herself.

"Probably not as often as now. I'm going to be really busy. But I'd say once or twice a week."

"Well, what about my privacy? Will I have any?"

"What do you mean privacy?"

"I would just want to know when you're coming by so I'll know to cook your meals, run your bath water for you and have the place ready. I don't have much privacy here. I just want some there. If you gave me some privacy, it would be much better between us."

"Okay, Johnnie," he said, eager to please her. "If it'll make it better between us, fine."

"You mean it, Earl?" she asked excitedly. Her smile always made it hard to refuse her.

"Yes," he said, as though he were a father talking to his favorite daughter.

Suddenly, she kissed him again. It wasn't long before she felt his hardness returning.

Chapter 13
"What's the matter?"

"Listen, Johnnie, I've gotta go. My wife is expecting me home early tonight. I hadn't planned on staying this long. I just wanted to drop off this check and ask you how you felt about getting your own place."

Johnnie was quiet for a moment. She thought about what Earl had said about having her own place. She bowed her head and frowned.

Seeing the disenchantment in her eyes, Earl said, "What's the matter?"

"Do you even care, Earl?" she asked, looking into his eyes.

"Of course I do, Johnnie. That's why I want you to have your own place."

"My own place, Earl?"

"Yes, your own place."

"Right, Earl."

"What's the matter, Johnnie, really? I don't understand what this is all about. I said I would get you your own place, and I will."

"How can it be my own place, Earl, when you're the one who owns it?"

Now he understood. "What exactly are you worried about, Johnnie? Me leaving you? Is that it?"

"You act like I shouldn't be worried, Earl. Look at you now. You come over, throw money in my face, have your way with me, and then you're out the door. And I shouldn't be worried? What if I do move out? Then when you've had enough of me, what do I do then? Move back home with my mama? You know what, Earl, I really don't think I can do this. I mean, it's a big risk. You say you love me, but you're married. You can change your mind anytime you feel like it. And if you do, where does that leave me? Out on the streets?"

"Johnnie, I wouldn't do that to you. I do love you, but who do you think is paying for all of the stuff I promised you? The check you have is from them. The clothes and jewelry I buy you is paid for with their money. What do you expect me to do? Buy you a house or something?"

Johnnie just looked at him and raised her eyebrows.

"So, you want me to buy you a house, is that it?

"Why not, Earl? What if your wife finds out about us? What she gon' do, say it's all right? You just said it's her money. She find out about this, and won't neither one of us have a place to stay."

"Dresses and jewelry is one thing, Johnnie. Houses are expensive. How am I supposed to get the money without her finding out about it?"

"You smart, Earl. Figure it out. You got six months before your promotion, right? Get a little at a time." She paused for a moment. "What about your stock in the company? And don't say you don't have none. Ain't no way you gon' bring me a check for four thousand dollars and you don't have no stock in the company."

Earl grinned.

"So, you do have stock in the company, huh? How much did you make? I bet it was a lot more than what I made."

"Johnnie, do you expect me to buy you a house with my own money?"

"If you love me, you will. I cain't believe you're so greedy. You have all that money, plus you get a salary and a check from the company. You already live in a mansion. Look at where I live. See, Earl, this is why I want my own place. You say you love me, but you're unwilling to part with what's yours. What do you make as a junior executive?"

Earl was quiet.

"What do you do with all that money? Save it? I bet you have more than enough to get me a house, don't you?"

"Johnnie, if I buy you a house, it would wipe me out. I'd have to start all over again."

"So what, Earl? Are you going to leave your rich white wife for a sixteen-year-old black girl who doesn't have anything but the clothes on her back? And you have the nerve to ask me what I'm worried about? I'll tell you what. Let's just forget the whole thing," she said, turning away from him.

"Okay, okay. I'll get you the house."

"I don't want no run-down shack either, Earl. I want a nice place."

"Listen, I gotta go now, okay?"

"Okay. Bye, Earl."

"Don't be that way. I said I would do it for you, and I will, okay?

"We'll see."

Earl started for the door, then he turned around and asked, "Do you want me to reinvest your dividend check for you?"

"Why? So you can buy me a house with my own money?

No thank you."

"Okay. Whatever you do, don't spend the money. Buy some more stocks in the company while you can."

"How do I do that?"

"I'll call my broker at Glenn and Webster. He's a good friend. I'll let him know you're coming. He'll take care of you. His name is Martin Winters. Now, I really gotta go, Johnnie."

After seeing Earl walk out the door, Johnnie wondered why he even bothered with his wife. He didn't love her. *What is the point?* She promised herself she would only marry for love, and when she did, it would be someone like Lucas Matthews. For her, there wasn't enough money in the world to marry someone for it.

Chapter 14

"You must be a mind reader, Mr. Winters."

The next day, Johnnie, impeccably dressed and stylish, walked nervously into the downtown office of Glenn and Webster Financial Services. She was wearing a low-cut lavender dress with a white belt, a matching two-toned hat, shoes, earrings, purse, and dark sunglasses. As she walked to the secretary's desk, she could feel every eye on her. She liked the attention. It gave her a sense of power, especially over men—white men in particular. It wasn't just her beauty that captivated the people in the office. She was a black woman, expensively clad from head to toe.

When she reached the desk, the secretary said, "May I help you?" There was a hint of superiority on her face and in the tone of her voice. Her nameplate read CYNTHIA LAMAR. She was pretty, petite, and shapely with blond hair. Instantly, Johnnie knew Cynthia thought she was better than she was; even though Cynthia had no idea who she was or why she was there. Johnnie knew she had to play the part she was dressed for, or she would never get past Cynthia for the appointment she had made. She looked down at the woman and smiled warmly. "My name is Johnnie Wise and I'm here to see Martin Winters, my stockbroker. He's expecting me."

Skeptical, Cynthia said, "I'll check. Have a seat." She picked up the telephone and dialed a number. "Mr. Winters, I have a Negro woman out here claiming to be a client of yours. What do you want me to do, sir?"

"I'll be right out."

While sitting in one of the comfortable leather chairs, Johnnie looked around the classy office and admired the decor. She wanted a cup of the coffee she smelled brewing over in the corner just five or six steps from where she was sitting, but she was afraid to ask. Cynthia Lamar's constant stare made her uncomfortable. Johnnie looked at the glass table, which was covered with magazines, and saw a picture of Marilyn Monroe on the cover of *Life*. She was about to pick it up when Martin Winters came out.

"Hello, Ms. Wise. I'm Martin Winters."

Earl Shamus had told him she was beautiful, but he was absolutely floored when he saw her. She had high cheekbones, naturally arched eyebrows, and no makeup to speak of. Earl had bragged about having sex with her whenever he felt like it. He went on and on about the way she sounded in bed. Without realizing it, a prurient grin emerged on Martin's face.

Johnnie looked up and saw him for the first time. Martin Winters was a handsome man, she thought. Tall, thin, but muscled. He wore a gray suit with black wing-tipped shoes. He had an inviting smile and polished teeth.

"Hello," Johnnie said, extending her hand as she stood.

"Would you like a cup of coffee or tea or something?"

"You must be a mind reader, Mr. Winters," Johnnie said, smiling. "I was just thinkin' how nice it would be if someone showed some southern hospitality and offered me a cup of café au lait." She looked at Cynthia.

"Please, call me Martin. Let's go over your investment portfolio in my office." He turned to his secretary and said, "Cindy, bring me and our new client a cup of coffee."

"Right away, Mr. Winters," Cynthia said then looked at Johnnie, rolling her eyes.

"Cream and sugar, Ms. Wise?"

"Yes, please."

"Right this way, Ms. Wise," Martin said, gesturing with an open hand in the direction of his office.

"Please, call me Johnnie," she said. She looked at Cynthia and smiled triumphantly.

Johnnie sensed something more than racial bigotry going on, and wondered if Cynthia and Martin were involved. She wondered if Martin was married. *A good-looking white man like him has to be.* She looked at his left hand and saw a shiny gold wedding band on his ring finger. As far as she was concerned, the ring was all the evidence she needed to confirm that he was seeing Cynthia. Judging by the way Martin looked at her, Johnnie could tell that, given the opportunity, he would be with her too, which confirmed her mother's philosophy about men.

When they took their seats, Martin handed her a black vinyl portfolio with her name stenciled on it in gold lettering. Johnnie smiled when she looked at it. It made her feel like a small child on Christmas morning. She had come a long way in a short time.

"If you open the portfolio," Martin began, "I think you'll find everything in order. What I'd like to do, with your permission of course, is diversify your investments so you won't be stuck if one of your stock investments plummets."

Although Johnnie was an A student at her under-funded high school, complete with hand-me-down books from a privileged white high school, she had no idea what "diversify" meant. She decided to nod her head and look the word up in the dictionary later. But she liked the way Martin talked to her. He seemed to respect her, or so she thought.

"So, what do you suggest I invest in, Martin?" Johnnie asked flirtatiously.

Martin noticed the sexy tone in her voice. He was staring at her breasts and was so into the moment that he didn't realize she was aware of his gaze. Not that it bothered her. In fact, she leaned forward a little and showed him a lot of cleavage. His eyebrows rose.

Hmmm, if I pretend to be interested in him, Martin Winters is a man I can learn a lot from. And if I have to flirt, or even sleep with him to learn how the stock market works, that's what I'll do.

When he didn't answer, she said in the same flirtatious tone, "Martin, you're staring, dear."

Snapping out of it, his eyes rose to her face. "I'm sorry, but you are a very attractive woman. I hope I haven't offended you."

Seeing his embarrassment, she said, "No, but I will be offended if you refuse to share your knowledge of the stock market with me."

"It's a little complicated, but I'll be glad to come by and explain the intricate details at a later date. Right now, I'd like to show you what I want to do."

"I'm not opposed to a later date, Martin," she said, stringing him along. "But I want to know and understand everything, okay?"

"No problem," he said eagerly. "Now, I thought we'd start with some relatively safe stocks. If you look on page two, you'll see I've chosen General Electric, General Motors, Ford, Coca-Cola Corporation, and Sears department stores."

Chapter 15

"Hey man, leave her be!"

"There she goes! There goes the white man's whore," someone shouted as Johnnie walked past a group of students on the way home from school.

Johnnie pretended not hear what was said. It hurt her deeply, but she maintained her dignity and continued walking, head held high.

"How could you do it with the white man?" Billy Logan yelled. "How could you give yourself to the white man after what he's done to us?"

Johnnie walked faster. The crowd followed, still taunting her. Then Billy Logan yelled, "My mother said she's a whore! She comes from a long line of whores! What do you expect a whore to do? She probably sucks his dick too! Don't you, whore? Don't you suck his dick?"

Johnnie burst into tears.

"That's what I thought, ya tramp," Billy Logan said, continuing his tirade.

"Hey, man, leave her be!" Lucas Matthews intervened.

Lucas was the high school football star who blew his

chances of getting into Grambling University because of inadequate grades. People thought he wasn't very bright because of his poor reading skills. At the time, no one knew what dyslexia was. Lucas had to work hard just to remain eligible for the high school team, but the season was over and the reality of poor grades finally set in.

Coach Mitchell told the handsome and well built high school football star that he couldn't endorse a letter to Grambling University because he feared that Blacks would be exploited forty or fifty years in the future by white coaches who would not put a premium on education. Coach Mitchell gave Lucas the same advice he received and heeded. He repeatedly told Lucas to develop his mind so he would have something to fall back on after his football days were over. Unfortunately, Lucas didn't take his advice to heart, and was in danger of flunking out his senior year.

Having been teased early on by his classmates about his poor test scores, Lucas learned to use his fists and had whipped several grown men. But none of that mattered to Johnnie. She found him very attractive—all the girls did. Now that he was defending her honor, she liked him all the more. She began to see Lucas as her rescuer, her protector, and her soon to be lover.

"Or what? You her guardian angel or somethin'?" Billy asked Lucas.

Billy Logan was sort of a tough guy too. He liked Johnnie, but when he found out about Earl Shamus, he just didn't see her the way he once did, high on a throne. If Johnnie would give it up to the white man, she would give it up to anybody. And if she would give it up to anybody, she couldn't be special no matter how pretty she was. But still, he was deeply infatuated with her. He couldn't help himself. She was that gorgeous.

"Or I'ma kick yo' ass," Lucas blared.

The crowd oohed and ahhed, egging the two boys on. Billy didn't want to fight Lucas because he knew of Lucas' formidable reputation for kicking ass and taking names. Nevertheless, he knew he couldn't back down, not in front of the crowd, and certainly not in front of Johnnie. He had to show her he was man enough to back up his words with his fists. If it came down to fighting Lucas, he would.

"Are you her guardian angel?" Billy repeated. He wanted to get out of the situation before it got out of hand. "If you're a relative or something, no problem."

Lucas, sensing his vulnerability, decided to press the issue. He liked Johnnie too. All the boys did. He believed he could take Billy in a fistfight, and if he did, he would have a chance with Johnnie. He wanted to impress her with his fighting skill. Other than football, fighting was the only other thing he was good at. Lucas believed that if he beat up Billy over Johnnie, word would get around and everybody would know she was his girl, eliminating the competition.

"Yeah, I'm her guardian angel. If you don't believe me, all you have to do is call me a liar."

Still looking for a way out, Billy said, "If you say you're her guardian angel, fine. No problem."

Johnnie watched Lucas with admiring eyes. She liked the idea of him defending her. No one had ever defended her, not even her own mother. From what she read in her bible, she believed a loving God should have done what Lucas was now doing, the night Earl Shamus stuck his tool in her private place. And since not even God had protected her from evil men, if Lucas fought for her and won, he would become her new god and she would worship him forever. She would freely give him what Earl had to pay for and much more. She would give Lucas her very soul if he desired it.

"No, there is a problem," Lucas growled. "Apologize or

I'ma kick yo' ass."

"Ain't that much ass kickin' in the world, nigga," Billy felt compelled to say. It was a cliché in the neighborhood whenever one was challenged to a fight.

The crowd gathered around, still egging them on. Both boys had their guards up, looking for an opening. Johnnie watched with eager anticipation.

"Get 'em, Lucas," Johnnie yelled.

That was all Lucas Matthews needed to hear. He went right after Billy. He hit him with a left jab and a right cross which staggered Billy, but didn't make him fall. Billy came forward, faked with the right and connected with a lightening quick left hook that shook up Lucas. It felt good to connect against such a well-known fighter. It gave him confidence to continue being aggressive, but it was a mistake.

Billy was over-confident now. He'd gotten a lucky punch in and thought he had a chance to win the fight. He faked with the right again. He thought if it worked once, it would work again. Lucas knew the left hook was coming next and waited on it. Just as Billy was about to throw the left hook, Lucas stepped in and threw a right cross of his own. It hit Billy flush on the chin. He staggered and took a few steps backward. Lucas moved in quickly and hit him with a left right left combination that put him on his ass. Billy shook his head, trying to clear the cobwebs.

Standing over him, Lucas yelled, "You ready to apologize now?"

Billy stood to his feet and shouted, "Hell naw! Don't nobody knock me on my ass and get away with it." He charged Lucas and tackled his legs. The two boys rolled on the ground while the crowd cheered the combatants on. Lucas ended up on top of Billy, but neither of them had an advantage. Their bodies were tangled together. Neither boy could get a blow in. Then Lucas noticed some water from the previous night's rain within arms reach. He broke free and put his hand in the water. Quickly, he flicked the dirt-filled water into Billy's eyes. Billy panicked and let go to rub his irritated eyes, leaving himself vulnerable. He couldn't see as Lucas pounded his face with both fists. Hurt, Billy was bleeding from the mouth and nose. Both eyes were swollen.

Lucas stopped the beating and screamed, "You ready to apologize to her, or you want some more?"

Lying prostrate on his back, Billy said, "I'm sorry," through a bloodied mouth.

Lucas, who was standing up, said, "Hell naw, muthafucka. On your feet and say that shit like you mean it."

Billy stood up. "I'm sorry."

"Muthafucka!" Lucas yelled. "Didn't I say to say that shit like you mean it?" He hit Billy with three wicked left hooks. The first one dazed him, the second staggered him and the third put him on the seat of his pants again. "Now, say that shit like you mean it. And do it from there. Better yet, say it on your knees."

Humiliated to tears, Billy Logan said, "I'm sorry, Johnnie. I didn't mean it. You're not a whore, okay?" Then he cried out loud.

"See, muthafucka," Lucas said softly. "That's how she felt when you said that bullshit to her." Lucas folded his arms and looked at the crowd. "If I ever hear about any of you bitches and bastards saying some shit about her again, ya ass is grass and I'm the lawnmower. Spread the word. Now take ya asses home."

Chapter 16

"I'm a lady, in my own way."

Now that he had beaten Billy Logan into submission, Lucas Matthews believed the spoils belonged to him. "Can I carry your books home for you, Johnnie?" Lucas asked, feeling like he could do no wrong.

"Yes," she said with a smile.

By the time they got to Johnnie's house, Lucas' jaw was swollen from the one punch he'd received from Billy Logan. Johnnie invited him in so she could put an ice pack on his jaw. It was the least she could do since he defended her in front of a crowd of kids who were hurling insults at her. The house was quiet when they entered. Johnnie knew Marguerite would be at Shirley's as usual. Lucas was almost glad he'd caught a punch. He hadn't hoped to get this far this fast. He was in her house and felt like he was on top of the world.

"Have a seat," Johnnie said. "I'll get you some ice for your jaw."

Lucas sat down. He looked around the house, admiring the way it was arranged. There were family pictures on the wall across the room from where he sat. He got up and walked over to the wall to get a better look at the pictures of Johnnie when she was a baby. She was even cute then.

57

She still had those alluring eyes and those dimples that made his heart melt. He could hear Johnnie coming back into the living room.

"Here," she said. "Let me put this on your jaw." When the ice, wrapped in a towel, touched his jaw. Johnnie could feel his body shake. "How does that feel, Lucas?"

"Cold."

"Hold the ice on it and the swelling should go down."

"Okay," he said. His hand touched hers when he put his hand to his jaw. He felt the warmth of her hand. They looked into each other's eyes for a moment.

When Johnnie removed her hand, she felt herself becoming aroused by the momentary touch and the wanton looks. She wanted him inside of her, but she didn't want him to think she was the whore everyone made her out to be. *I'm a lady, in my own way.*

"So, who are these people in these pictures, Johnnie?" Lucas asked. He wanted to kiss her while they were staring at each other, but thought better of it. To Lucas, pretty girls were good girls, and good girls didn't give it up the first time they had you over. Nevertheless, his erection was harder than a brick. He was hoping she couldn't see it.

"Oh, these are pictures of me, my mother, and my brother."

"I can tell which one of these baby pictures is you, Johnnie."

"You can? How?" Johnnie smiled.

"Your eyes and your dimples are still the same."

"You really think so?"

"Yes, I do. You're the prettiest girl in school and the prettiest girl I've ever seen. Everybody says it, even the girls. That's why they don't like you. 'Cause they know you better lookin' than they is. That's why they call you a whore. But you ain't no whore. Not to me."

Johnnie turned away from him. She was a whore—at least she felt like one. The proof of her whoredom would be walking through the front door in a few hours, expecting her to put out for him. It didn't matter that she was forced into this kind of life. Besides, she liked sex now. She learned to please herself by touching her privates when she was in bed. At first, she was embarrassed when she masturbated to orgasm, but now she thought of Lucas Matthews when she did it. And now he was in her house and they were talking about her whoring. In those seconds that she'd turned from him, she toyed with the idea of telling all but dismissed it. It was too soon. He thought too much of her.

"Johnnie, what's wrong?"

"Nothing, Lucas. You just been so kind to me. I feel like I don't deserve it," Johnnie said, looking into his eyes.

At that moment, Lucas wanted to ask her if she would be his girl. He didn't know if she was being nice or if she really liked him. All he knew was that he really liked her and he wanted her to be his. He decided he would take the chance.

"Johnnie," he said, nervously. "Will you—"

The front door opened and Marguerite entered the living room. "What the hell is goin' on up in here?"

Chapter 17

"I'll let you know after I move."

"Nothin', Mama," Johnnie said, feeling guilty even though she hadn't done anything wrong.

"Nothin', huh?" Marguerite repeated. "Nothin' my ass!"

"Ma'am," Lucas interceded. "We wasn't doin' nothin', honest."

"You wasn't doin' nothin'?" Marguerite mocked. "You mean you didn't have a chance to do nothin'. You ain't foolin' me, boy. You cain't wait to get yo' dick up in her. If I hadn'ta come in here, who knows what woulda been goin' on."

"Mama!" Johnnie shouted, feeling totally embarrassed. It was bad enough that she had to have sex with Earl. Now that she liked a boy her own age, her mother was ruining it for her.

"And don't Mama me," Marguerite exploded. "You know I don't allow no boys in this house, girl. You can get mad all you want, but you know that."

"Johnnie, I better go," Lucas said, bowing his head. "I'm sorry I caused trouble, ma'am."

"You goddamn right you better go," Marguerite yelled. "And don't let me catch you here again. You hear me?"

"Yes, ma'am," Lucas said and started walking toward the

door.

"Let me see you out," Johnnie said, still embarrassed. She opened the door and they went out on the front porch. "I'm sorry, Lucas. I'll be gettin' my own place soon. I can have you over then, if you still want to see me."

"I do, Johnnie. I want you to be my girl. Will you?"

As much as she wanted to say yes, Johnnie knew not to, not yet anyway. She had too much going on in her life right now. She had to please too many people. She had her mother, Earl, and now Martin Winters wanted in.

"We'll see, Lucas," she said, looking into his eyes. "I'll let you know after I move, okay?"

"Okay, Johnnie," he said, disappointed.

Johnnie watched him as he walked down the street. She was hoping he'd turn around so she could see his handsome face once more before she went into the house. He did, and she smiled. Then she thought about what her mother had done only moments ago. Her eyes narrowed when she thought about all that happened to her in the last year or so. She did everything her mother had asked her to do. *And what thanks did I get?* Johnnie entered the house with fury in her eyes.

Marguerite knew her daughter was upset with her, but she didn't care. The foremost thing on Marguerite's mind was keeping the money coming in from Earl. If that meant a strained relationship with her daughter, so be it. Marguerite had been where Johnnie was going. She knew it was a road leading to disappointment and bitterness. In her own way, Marguerite truly believed she was saving Johnnie from the same mistakes she'd made, but Johnnie was too young to understand. Marguerite could see contempt in Johnnie's eyes, and knew she had to say something to get her daughter to understand what she was trying to do. Marguerite wanted her to know how much she cared, and

61

that she knew the ultimate end with Lucas Matthews.

"Johnnie, I know you mad at me, but—"

"I don't wanna hear it, Mama!" Johnnie screamed.

"All I'm tryin' to do is keep you from making the same mistakes I made when I was yo' age. I know you don't understand now, but in time, you will."

"Do you have any idea how embarrassing that was for me? Do you? Lucas Matthews is the only somebody who truly cares for me."

"I care about you, honey," Marguerite said as compassionately as she could.

Johnnie laughed cruelly. "You care about me? You? That's a laugh. You're the one who turned me out! You're the one who pimped me! My own mother!"

Marguerite slapped Johnnie across the face with the back of her hand. Johnnie slapped her back and the two women engaged in an all-out brawl. Marguerite grabbed Johnnie, put her in a headlock, and shouted, "Who do you think you are, disrespectin' me and talkin' to me like some fool on the streets? Girl, don't you know I will kill you?"

Fueled by her fury, Johnnie was stronger than Marguerite, and was able to free herself of the headlock. She grabbed Marguerite by her thick hair, put her in a headlock and flipped her. Marguerite went down hard, making a loud thud when her body hit the floor. They rolled on the floor, grunting, trying to get in blows.

Marguerite yelled between grunts, "No face scratchin,' goddamn it. No face scratchin'!"

Suddenly, they were back on their feet, hitting each other on the head, but not the face. Glass shattered, keepsakes broke, but they kept fighting as if it were to the death. Both women remained careful not to cut up each other's face. Marguerite got tired and Johnnie tackled and climbed on top of her. She slapped her silly, yelling at her after each blow was delivered. *Smack! Smack! Smack!* The blows went against her head.

"Don't you ever—" *Smack! Smack! Smack!* "put your hands—" *Smack! Smack! Smack!* "on me again! You touch me again and I'll kill you! You hear me? I'll kill you!"

The stinging blows stunned Marguerite. As she shrank back from Johnnie, putting her hands up to ward off the blows, Marguerite realized her daughter was no longer a child in a woman's body. Johnnie was a full-grown woman with a mind of her own now.

Knowing she was now in charge of her life, Johnnie shouted, "You got a lot of nerve sayin' you love me! How, Mama? You love me how? A year ago, I was a church-going, good Christian girl! What am I now, Mama? I'm a whore! Your whore! That's what they call me at school! The white man's whore! Just like you, Mama! Do you know what happened to me on the way home today? Do you even care?"

Marguerite, on her feet now, tried to explain again, but Johnnie kept on giving her a piece of her mind.

"When I got out of school today, a crowd of kids followed me. They were sayin' all kind of cruel things about me. One boy kept talkin' about me. He kept sayin', 'Don't you suck his dick, whore?' Do you know how that makes me feel, havin' the whole neighborhood knowin' my shame? And for what? To put food on the table and clothes on yo' back? Well, I'm not gonna do it no more! Not for you! Not for anybody! From now on, I'm makin' the rules! And I will have Lucas Matthews. Lucas was the only somebody who stood up for me. He beat the boy up for sayin' what he said about me. Lucas likes me and I like him. And I'll tell you something else too, Mama. I'm gonna do it with him."

"What am I supposed to do, Johnnie?" Marguerite asked, full of sorrow and remorse. "How am I supposed to

63

live?"

"Don't worry, Mama. I'll keep takin' care of you. You showed me how. I'll say one thing for you, Mama. You were right about men. They all want me. Every last one of 'em. And now that I'm a woman, I'm gonna do exactly what you taught me. I'm gonna have whatever I want. Money, clothes, whatever! As a matter of fact, Earl is buyin' me a house. I'm moving out and there's nothing you can do about it!"

Johnnie left Marguerite standing there in the middle of the living room with her mouth open. She went upstairs to her room and packed her bags. A few minutes later, she heard Earl's Cadillac pull up. She picked up her suitcase, went downstairs and met him at the door.

"Where you goin'?" Marguerite asked.

"Anywhere but here," she said firmly.

Earl opened the door. He could see how enraged Johnnie was. "What's going on?" he asked. "Where are you going with that suitcase?"

"You takin' me to a hotel. I'm never comin' back here again."

"I am, huh?" Earl asked, still wondering what had happened between mother and daughter.

"Earl, I'm not in the mood. Take this suitcase and let's go before I change my mind."

"Johnnie, please don't leave," Marguerite begged. "I don't wanna be alone." Johnnie kept walking as if she didn't hear her mother's pleas. Marguerite turned to Earl. "Please don't take my baby from me."

Johnnie stopped in her tracks. She couldn't believe what she was hearing. Slowly, she turned around and angrily faced her mother. As she saw the pitiful look on her mother's face, she shook her head. "Take your baby, Mama? I don't even believe you. You sold your baby, Mama, on Christmas Eve, remember?"

Complete silence filled the room as mother and daughter looked at each other with tears in their eyes. Earl grabbed her suitcase and walked out of the house.

"I'm sorry, baby," Marguerite said, looking into her eyes. "I was only doing all I knew how. Please forgive me."

"I forgive you," Johnnie said, putting on her sunglasses. "I love you, Mama, but I gotta go."

Johnnie walked out of the house and got into the Cadillac. She could feel her mother's eyes on her the entire time, but refused to look at her. Earl started the car and pulled off.

Marguerite stood at the door, watching the Cadillac until it disappeared. Slowly, the anguish she felt found its way out and she cried loudly.

Chapter 18
"We'll see about that."

As they left the dilapidated neighborhood, Johnnie looked out the window and saw some of the girls in her neighborhood watching as she rode in the lap of luxury with her white paramour. In a way, she was proud to be seen in a Cadillac, but at the same time, it bothered her to know they could see the rumors they'd heard about her were now steeped in truth. She saw Billy Logan staring at her. His eyes and lips were still swollen from the pummeling Lucas had given him. At first, he couldn't tell if it was really her riding with a white man in broad daylight.

"Ya whore!" he shouted with conviction.

Johnnie pressed her middle finger against the window.

Earl was driving along quietly, wondering if he should ask her about the incident with her mother. He knew she was angry, but he didn't want to make the situation worse than it was. Instead of listening to his intuition, he decided to ask.

"So, what the hell is going on, Johnnie?"

"What do you think is going on, Earl?" she snapped.

Strangely, her acerbic attitude titillated him. Johnnie was beautiful, but she was sexy as hell when she was angry. He had never seen her angry before. Whenever he visited her, she was always dutiful and did as he asked. This was a new treat, and he wanted her right then. If it were dark out, he'd have pulled over to the nearest curb and had her slide down his pole. Just thinking about it gave him a serious erection. However, since she was upset, he knew there was no chance of her fulfilling him sexually. He decided to change the subject to something that would change her attitude. *But what could that be?* Then it came to him.

"Johnnie, would you like to see the house I bought for you?"

Almost like magic, Johnnie's attitude changed. She was smiling now. Earl knew he would have her later. Whenever she was happy, he got the best sex from her. She seemed to go all out to please him and he loved it. He couldn't get enough of her.

"You found me a place, Earl?" she asked, not a trace of anger in her voice.

"Uh-huh," he said, feeling like Santa Claus.

"Did you get me a nice place, in a nice neighborhood?"

"I said I would, didn't I?"

"When can I move in?"

"Well, the house needs some work. I have to have the place painted, put some carpeting down, and remodel the kitchen and bathrooms. I'd say in about a month. Probably a little while after school lets out for the summer."

"Well, what am I going to do until then?"

"I thought you were going to stay with your mother until then, but it looks like that's out of the question now. What happened?"

Johnnie knew she couldn't tell Earl the truth. If she told him how she felt about Lucas, he would certainly change his mind about buying her that house. She decided to deflect his question with one of her own.

"What difference does it make, Earl? You got what you

wanted."

"What's that supposed to mean?"

"You wanted me to have a place so you wouldn't have to come to the ghetto to see me. You don't like the way the black men in my neighborhood look at you when you show up to get your brown sugar. So, you decided to make it more convenient for you, didn't you, Earl?"

A little smile appeared on Earl's face. She was right, but what surprised him was how much she'd grown up in the last year. At that moment, he remembered the first time he had taken her on that Christmas Eve. It seemed like an eternity had passed. He thought about how good things were between them now and how much better it would be in the near future. *I'll have the best of both worlds.*

"The problem is," Johnnie began again, "you're still going to have to see black people, and they're still going to hate both of us no matter what neighborhood you put me in. You didn't think of that, did you, Earl?"

"We'll see about that," Earl said and patted her smooth thigh.

Chapter 19

"Ashland Estates"

As they drove to the new house, Johnnie was quiet. She thought about the fight with her mother and the whole neighborhood seeing the good little Christian girl ride off into the sunset with her white lover. Following that, Billy Logan's final words, "Ya whore," resonated in her mind over and over again. Although she had heard the constant whispers and subsequent laughter, she couldn't live with the idea of all of her classmates knowing her shame.

I can never go back to the neighborhood or the school again. By the time school opens tomorrow, it'll be all over the school. The kids will be talking about the fight between Lucas and Billy. Billy's face all puffy will spice up the stories being told. And with the kids seeing Lucas walking me home, they'll probably think I did it with him too. After all, I am a whore. What if Mama told Shirley about the fight we had? What if Shirley's kids overheard her? Shirley's kids will tell the other kids at school and further demoralize me.

In her mind's eye, she could see herself walking into the school and being accosted by her rivals; girls who she had once ridiculed about their lascivious ways. There was no way she could subject herself to that kind of humiliation. It was settled.

69

I'm dropping out and that's all there is to it. I'll find a job and invest my money. I'll learn how the stock market works from Martin then I'll be rich someday. I will not give away the best part of me for nothin'. I will not end up like my mother. Men want me. Fine. They'll pay for the privilege.

They turned onto Main Street, where a host of Baroque Parish's black businesses were located. Well dressed Negro men and women were everywhere, going in and out of stores and restaurants. The Sepia Theater, owned by local entrepreneur Walker Tresvant, was the first building Johnnie saw. Tresvant was a millionaire who held the mortgages on several buildings on Main Street, including an office building, which contained the offices of Attorney Ryan Robertson, Cambridge Books and Publishing, Bernard Coleman's architectural firm, and several other successful Negro owned and operated businesses.

Continuing down Main Street, Johnnie saw Philip Collins' barber shop, with its red and white stripes just outside the front door. Further down, she saw a sign that read: DENNIS EDWARDS' TAILOR AND CLOTHING STORE. Across the street from the clothing store was Nagel's Construction Company, which was right next to Michael and Beverly's Bakery and Sweets. At the end of the block near First Street was New Orleans' only Negro newspaper called *The Raven*. Across the street from *The Raven* was Mr. Big Stuff's World Famous Plantation Barbecued Ribs.

Just before Earl turned onto East Ashland Avenue, where the upper class Negroes lived, Johnnie saw a sign for Ashland Estates. Among its residents were many of New Orleans' educated colored professionals, the descendants of well-to-do slave owners. Among them were doctors, lawyers, an architect, and even a few published writers. The neighborhood was also full of maids who served as courtesans for their white employers. Many of these women were the mothers of illegitimate children spawned by these unholy unions.

As they rode down the street, Johnnie could see how pristine the neighborhood looked. *This must be a mistake. This must be where the white folks live.* The houses were huge and well-maintained, with manicured lawns. Seeing this impressive display of luxury, Johnnie couldn't help being roused from her dispirited thoughts. She was just about to ask Earl if they were in the right place when she saw a black man using a key to go into the front door of one of the homes.

She looked at Earl. He was smiling. He loved doing nice things for her. It made him feel necessary. But right now, he was smiling because of what she was going to do for him later.

Earl pulled into the driveway of a yellow two-story home with shrubs and daffodils near the entrance. He turned off the ignition and looked at her.

"Well, what do you think?"

"Is this my place, Earl?" Johnnie asked, unable to contain herself.

"Yes. It's all yours," Earl said, dangling the keys.

71

Chapter 20
"All you can handle, Earl."

Johnnie saw a black woman in the house next to hers peeking out of the window, watching them as they approached the front door. When the woman saw Johnnie looking at her, she closed the curtains for a moment or two, then resumed watching. *I wonder who she is. I hope we can be friends when I move in.*

Earl handed Johnnie the keys and asked, "Would you like to do the honors?"

"Yeah."

She walked into the foyer and gasped when she saw the cream-colored walls in the unbelievably spacious living room. To her surprise, the house wasn't in as bad a shape as she expected. There was a fireplace, a ceiling fan and well-maintained hardwood floors. As far as she was concerned, the house was ready for her to move in that day. Sure, it needed some furniture, some plants, some rugs and a few other trinkets to make it homey, but this was a palace—her palace.

"Earl, ain't nothin' wrong with this place. This is just fine. I can move in now."

"Well, let's look at the kitchen and bathrooms first."

"Bathrooms? You mean I got more than one?"

"Of course." He frowned. "What did you mean when you said you wanted a nice place? A place with a roof that doesn't leak or what?"

"Is your home this nice, Earl?"

"My house is a mansion compared to this. And I still say this place could use a little work. Come on. Let's look at the kitchen." Earl took Johnnie's hand and escorted her through the house, stopping at the dining room, which was next to the kitchen.

As she admired her new home, Johnnie knew she had made the right decision to move out and leave school. *What could schoolin' get me that my looks can't? I haven't even graduated yet and I have a house. Or do I?* "Earl, is this my house?"

"Yes. I told you it was. Why do you keep asking me about it?"

"Because I don't see no papers sayin' it's mine. And I know you gotta have papers to say you own anything in this world. Mama got papers on her house. I want papers on mine."

Earl reached inside his jacket pocket, pulled out a piece of paper and handed it to her. It was a deed with her name on it. "All you need to do is sign it and it's yours."

Johnnie took the paper and looked at it. Slowly, a smile began to emerge. It looked legal, but she wasn't sure. She would have to see her mother's to be certain.

But what if it is real? What if this is really my house? If it is truly my house, and it was this easy to get, what else can I get if I put my mind to it? Mama was right. Men will do anything to get sex.

They entered the kitchen hand in hand. Johnnie walked around the kitchen, thinking of what she could do with it, occasionally opening and closing cabinet doors. The kitchen needed some work, but all in all, it was in good condition.

She particularly liked the countertops and the breakfast nook, which had plenty of windows.

She looked at the stove and refrigerator, wondering if it would be pushing her luck to ask Earl for new ones. They were better than what she was accustomed to, but still she wanted them replaced. "Earl, honey," she said, looking at the stove, "I know you just spent a bunch of money on this house for me, but dear, I sure would like a new stove and refrigerator."

"I knew you would. I ordered them for you already."

"Really?"

"Yeah, really."

Johnnie kissed his thin pink lips. She could feel Earl's hardness pressing against her stomach. Johnnie pulled away, knowing that if she continued to let him get more excited, she would have to do it right there on the kitchen floor, and it would be messy without any means of cleaning herself up.

Earl pulled her back and wrapped his arms around her. He squeezed her firm rump, then her thick breasts. He wanted to take her right then and there, and Johnnie knew it.

"I'll take care of you later, dear," she promised, squeezing his hardness.

"How about a little right now?"

Johnnie knew he was all worked up. It didn't take much for Earl. Ever since she'd known him, whenever he was hard, he wanted to enter her immediately, whether she was ready to be entered or not.

"Think of how much better it's going to be once we get to the hotel, honey. I promise you it will be worth the wait, okay?"

"Okay." Earl beamed like he was walking on air.

"So, how much did you say this house cost you, Earl?"

"I didn't say," he teased as they walked into the first floor bathroom.

"You not gon' tell me, sweetie?"

"What do I get for the information?"

"All you can handle, Earl."

"All I can handle, huh?"

"Uh-huh."

Do I dare tell her how little I spent, especially since she thinks I paid a fortune? Not only that, but for the first time, she's calling me pet names and I like it. I want her to go on thinking I spent a lot, and I want her to continue the sweet talk.

"How much do you think I paid?" Earl asked, leaning against the counter.

"Gosh, Earl, I have no idea. Cain't you just tell me?"

"Well, I could, but that wouldn't be any fun now, would it?"

"Okay, fifty thousand dollars."

"Come on. It isn't any fun if you don't guess for real."

"Okay, thirty thousand."

"Close. It was twenty-five thousand."

The truth was fifteen thousand. The house was worth twenty-five thousand, one of the cheapest in the neighborhood, but he paid fifteen because the house had been repossessed and empty for over a year. The bank wanted to unload it in a hurry. They just wanted the payoff value.

Astonished, she said, "Twenty-five thousand dollars! You musta made a lot more than I made with those stocks you bought." *Hmmm, if you can make that kind of money in the stock market, I definitely have to learn how it's done.*

"I made enough for a few things. Now, let me show you the upstairs, and then we can get you a hotel."

Chapter 21

"The Savoy it is."

When she heard the car door slam, the woman next door quickly rushed to the window to watch her new neighbor leave. She wondered how soon she'd move in. She decided to bake the woman a sweet potato pie and welcome her to the neighborhood.

Johnnie looked at the window and saw the woman again. This time she waved to let the woman know she would be a friendly neighbor. The woman smiled and waved back enthusiastically. Both women thought they had made a friend even though they hadn't spoken to each other.

As they backed out of the driveway, Johnnie looked at the two-car garage and wondered if Earl would buy her a car. She decided to test the water. "Earl, how am I supposed to get to school livin' way out here?"

"The same way the other children get to school. On the bus."

Earl thought about what he had just said. *Children?* He forgot just how young she really was. In all the time he had known her, except for the first few times he slept with her, he never thought about how old she was. She looked like a woman. She acted like a woman. *She is a woman. After all, I made her a woman, didn't I?* But still he felt guilty for even being in the situation with her. He just wanted to fuck her a few times and be done with her, but she had grown on him like no other woman had in his life. There was no way he was going to give her up now—not ever.

Besides, everybody knows girls mature two years faster than boys. Her being sixteen is the same as her being eighteen or nineteen. What the hell difference does it make when you love someone? There used to be a time when girls had to be married by the time they were twelve or they were considered old maids. Shit, I did her a favor. I got her out of the ghetto and into a nice neighborhood. She wears nice clothes, shoes, and jewelry. She's got it made. How many other women would jump at this opportunity? On top of that, the pussy is out of this world.

Johnnie hoped her comment about school would make Earl think she was still attending so she could continue to have the freedom to do as she pleased. That way, during the day, she could sneak Lucas Matthews over, or maybe even Martin Winters. She wanted to work during school hours and invest her money. Plus, she could say she was going to the library to study, just in case she wanted to see them at night without suspicion.

"What hotel do you want to go to?"

"The Bel Glades. Isn't that where you used to work?"

"Now, you know they don't allow Negroes in there. But if you play your cards right, maybe one day I'll sneak you in."

"If I play my cards right, huh?" she said wryly. "In that case, take me to the Savoy. I shouldn't have any trouble gettin' in there, even with you. I hear tell that's where all the coloreds from the ghetto and the upper class whites go to fornicate."

"The Savoy it is."

"Earl, I want you to get those guys to hurry up with the house. I don't want to stay in the hotel for a month. I'm

77

going to need furniture and everything. Do you mind if I don't get carpeting? I like the floors as they are. I prefer rugs. Is that okay?"

"Anything you want."

***

Entering the Savoy, they were greeted by a short, stocky colored man with a balding head. He opened the glass door for them and smiled a professional smile like he'd done so many times that it was second nature. As they walked to the front desk to register, he shook his head. When he was sure they were far away, he shook his head again and said, "What a waste. Beautiful black girl like that givin' it up to the white man." It wasn't anything he hadn't seen a thousand times at the hotel, but each time he saw it, he would say the same thing. He turned his attention to the guests now entering the hotel.

The clerk was on the telephone when they reached the desk. He smiled and put his index finger in the air. A moment later, he hung up the phone and said, "May I help you?"

"Yes," Earl said. "We want the best room this hotel has to offer."

Chapter 22

"Freedom"

Johnnie opened her eyes the next morning, refreshed from a good night's sleep in the comfortable queen-sized bed. Earl, after dipping his pole in Johnnie, swaggered home to his wife and children in the middle of the night. Johnnie turned her head to the left, looking at the clock. It was 7:30. As she lay there, she thought of all the things she had to do that day. It was Friday. School would be starting in half an hour. It felt good to know she didn't have to go.

Let's see. What am I going to do first? I think I'll have breakfast downstairs in the café. Then I'll check out the hotel and what it has to offer. Oh, I know. I'll call Martin and see how my stocks are doing and give him my new address. I need to catch up with Lucas too. Maybe I can catch him on the way home from school. I'll tell him about my new place. I need to go downtown to Sears and pick out some things for the house. I might as well shop there. That way I'll be making money even though I'm spending it. I probably better call Mama. She's probably worried sick about me. I gotta go over there today anyway. I should probably get there before school lets out, but let me call Mama first.

"Hello."

"Hi, Mama."

"Are you okay?" Marguerite asked, relieved she finally called.

"Yes, Mama. I'm fine."

"Well, when are you comin' home? And how come you ain't in school?"

"Mama, I'm never comin' home again. At least not to live."

"What do you mean you're not comin' home?"

"I mean I'm not comin' home, period. But if you don't mind, I'd like to see your deed."

"See my deed for what?"

"Well, Earl is buyin' me a house and—"

"Girl, that man ain't gon' buy you no house. All men lie like that. Ain't you learn nothin' from me in all these years?"

"Mama, I'm not a child anymore. And yes, I've learned quite a bit from you; especially about men."

"If you have, why would you believe that shit about him buyin' you a house? They all talk that shit. I'm gon' buy you this. I'm gon' buy you that. They just a bunch of talk as long as you givin' it up. Then when they got enough, they gone.

"Well, Mama, Earl is different, he did—"

"Earl ain't no different. Do you know how long he begged me to have you? He been wantin' you since you was twelve years old. Now that he done had you, it's just a matter of time before his perverted ass gets tired of you and moves on to the next colored woman that makes his dick hard."

Well, if you thought he was so perverted, why would you even consider doing what you did?

"Mama, will you listen to me for a second?"

"Okay, go ahead."

"Okay, listen, he took me to the house yesterday and I—
"

"Girl, stop all that lyin'. That man ain't took you to no

80

house. And if he did, it was his or somebody he knows. Don't be so gullible."

"I'm not stupid, Mama."

"If you believe a white man like him is gon' buy you a house, you outta yo' mind."

"Mama, I'm sittin' here lookin' at the deed."

"You lookin' at it, huh? Is it real?"

"I don't know. That's why I want to come by and look at yours."

"Well, bring it on by. I wanna see this."

"Mama, I was in the house. He had the keys and everything."

"Where this house at?"

"Ashland Estates."

"Ashland Estates! That's where them stuck-up niggas live. They think they better than us. Maybe he knows somebody colored that owns the place. Maybe he owns it and gave you a phony deed. But anyway, those houses are expensive out there. You sure it was Ashland Estates?"

"Yes, Mama."

"And you say yo' name is on the deed?"

"Yeah."

"Hmmm, okay, bring it on by. I gotta see this."

"Okay, I'll be by after I do some shoppin' at Sears."

"At Sears? You got money to shop at Sears?"

"Mama, I have plenty of money. I even have a stockbroker who bought me some stock in the company, so it only makes sense to shop there."

Marguerite was quiet. She was thinking about what her sixteen-year-old daughter was telling her. *What if he did buy her a house? That man must sho' nuff be in love. Ain't no other explanation.*

"Mama? You still there?"

"Yeah, honey. I'm just thinkin' about what you said."

"Okay, well, I'll be by later on."

"Okay, now tell me why you didn't go to school today."

"I'll talk to you about that later, Mama. I'm about to take a shower.'"

"A shower, huh? Where you at, girl?"

"The Savoy Hotel. I have a nice room. Why don't you bring the deed down here and see the place? If you like, I can show you the house. I have the keys."

Marguerite wondered if she should tell her daughter that she plied her trade at the hotel regularly, then quickly dismissed it.

"Sure, I can come down there. What time?"

"Oh, you know what?" Johnnie said, remembering her plans to catch up with Lucas Matthews. "I have some stuff to do at the house anyway. How about I bring the deed, take care of some things, and then I can show you the house? You can see the hotel later, okay?"

"Okay. Talk to you then. Bye."

"Bye, Mama."

Chapter 23

"Is this chair taken?"

"Umm, umm, umm," Simmons muttered, shaking his head. "I'd like to break my dick off in that. Is she fine, or what?"

Johnnie entered the lobby of the Savoy, attracting attention from every direction. She was wearing a yellow outfit—sundress, hat, purse, shoes, and sunglasses.

"Yes, Lawd!" Myron, the daytime doorman, said.

Johnnie could feel all the attention. As usual, she felt a little self-conscious; especially when men stared at her ass. They stared at it so long that it felt like they were attempting to look into the crack. Nevertheless, she smiled politely.

"How you doin', you beautiful creature from heaven?" Myron asked, as cool as he could.

"I'm doing just fine. And you?" she said as she walked past him.

Myron took her politeness as an invitation to more conversation and followed her.

"Where you think you going, Myron?" Simmons asked. "You're on the clock."

Myron stopped in his tracks and went back to the desk, frowning at Simmons. "You can get mad all you want," Simmons said. "You're gettin' paid by the hour."

"That's bullshit," Myron said. "You just want to get the first crack of that sculptured ass."

"That's right," Simmons said and followed her. "I'ma have her climbin' the walls."

When Simmons got to Trudy's Café, he stood at the door and admired Johnnie's beauty from a distance, wondering what his chances were. He and many of his friends shared the notion that colored women who dated white men wouldn't date colored men. *What the hell? What have I got to lose? All she can do is say no.* He walked over to the table and asked courteously, "Is this chair taken?"

He didn't wait for an answer. He was sliding the chair back before he finished the question. Johnnie recognized him immediately. He was the man she had seen yesterday going into the house in Ashland Estates. Simmons was an average looking man, nothing at all like Lucas Matthews, Johnnie thought.

"Hi. I'm Robert Simmons, owner of this establishment. And you are?"

"Johnnie Wise," she said, extending her hand.

"Anyone tell you you're absolutely gorgeous?"

"All the time," she said without sounding arrogant.

Simmons was staring at her breasts. He could see her nipples through the sundress, and yearned to see more. Johnnie let him stare for a while; she was getting used to it. She noticed how when staring at her breasts, the expression on a man's face seemed to reveal his true nature.

"Something I can do for you, Mr. Simmons?" she asked, awakening him out of his deep gaze.

"You can call me Robert," he said, trying hard to keep looking her in the eye. "I just thought you might want some company now that your boyfriend is gone."

"You're rude, Mr. Simmons." Johnnie frowned.

"What do you mean, I'm rude?"

"For one, you invite yourself to my table and sit down without my sayin' it's okay."

The waitress came back with Johnnie's fruit salad and placed it on the table. "Is there anything else I can get for you?" she asked.

"No, thank you," Johnnie said.

"How 'bout you, Robert?"

"No thank you, Trudy."

"Enjoy your salad," Trudy said, placing the bill on the table.

"Now, as I was sayin'," Johnnie began again. "You invite yourself to my table, you stare at my breasts like you've never seen breasts before, then you ask me personal questions as if we're old friends or somethin'."

"Well, first, Ms. Wise, I invited myself because you were sitting here all by your lonesome and—"

Johnnie looked up from her fruit salad and said, "So, you think anybody who sits alone wants company?"

"Well no, but—"

"So, then it never occurred to you that I just might want to be alone, huh?"

Feeling like he was being cross-examined, he said, "If you didn't want me to sit down, why didn't you just say so?"

"You sat down before I even had the chance to answer your question, Mr. Simmons."

"Do you want me to leave?"

"If I do, will you?"

"I might."

"Then there's no point in answering your question, is there?"

"Not really."

Johnnie took deep breath and let it out like she was exasperated, then resumed eating her fruit salad.

"What do you want, Mr. Simmons?"

"For starters, I want you to call me Robert."

"The way Trudy does?"

"Yes. I'm just being friendly."

"Are you friendly with all your guests, Mr. Simmons?"

"Only the ones I find extremely attractive," he said, smiling again.

"So, are you having sex with Trudy?"

Simmons' guilt revealed itself on his face. He didn't like the idea of her asking about Trudy, especially since she was right. Johnnie knew she was on target and smiled. She shook her head in amazement then finished off her salad.

"What's that to you?"

"It's nothing to me, Mr. Simmons, but I would think one of us would be enough for one of you. What makes you think you can handle another woman?"

"Not to brag, but I'm insatiable."

Johnnie didn't know what insatiable meant, so she said, "Went to college, huh?"

Simmons laughed. Johnnie was amazed at the reaction she got from the comment and decided to use it whenever she didn't know what a word meant. That way, whoever used words she didn't understand wouldn't know the extent of her education.

I probably better get a small dictionary and carry it around in my purse if I'm going to pull this grown-up thing off.

Johnnie picked up the check and Simmons gently took it out of her hand, making sure his hand touched hers. He looked in her eyes hoping for some indication of how good his chances were.

"It's on the house."

"Thank you, Mr. Simmons," she said and started

86

walking toward the exit.

Simmons turned toward the cash register and shouted, "Trudy, put this on my tab."

Trudy waited until he turned around, then turned up her nose.

"What do I have to do to get you to call me Robert?" he asked, catching up with her.

"I don't know, Mr. Simmons, but I'm sure you'll think of something."

"How about lunch or dinner later?" he said as they walked through the lobby.

"I'll be busy later."

"With that white man?"

"With my mother, if you must know."

"So, the thing with the white man was just a one time thing, huh?"

Johnnie stopped walking. They were standing at the lobby exit. She put her hands on her hips, saying, "Is this how you plan to seduce me? By questionin' my relationship with a white man? How far do you think you'll get with that approach?"

"You're right, you're right. I'm sorry."

"Is it askin' too much for you to show me some respect? The same respect you would show any white woman that comes to this hotel with a colored man. Would you disrespect her even if she was with a colored man? I don't think so. If you won't disrespect her, don't disrespect me. Good day, Mr. Simmons."

Johnnie turned around and walked through the revolving door. Simmons stood there looking at her ass until she disappeared down the street. Then he turned around and saw Myron laughing.

"You can laugh if you want to, but I'ma get some of that."

Chapter 24
"Where did you get this?"

Johnnie walked into Sears, still angry about the inappropriate questions Simmons asked her. She thought the Savoy was the one place where she wouldn't have to be concerned about people knowing her business. She began wondering if everybody at the hotel felt the same way.

If he feels that way, why does he allow it at his hotel? Seems to me that if it was such a big deal, he would put a stop to it. Seems to me that since he let it go on at his hotel, he must approve. He probably got some white woman stashed away in one of them rooms someplace. As a matter of fact, I oughta ask him about white women when I see him again. I wonder if he stares at their breasts the way he stares at mine. I bet he don't. I bet he wouldn't even think about starin' at their breasts the way he stared at mine. Right out in public with no shame of what he was doin'. Humph, Mama just might be right about men. I wonder if Lucas is like that. Naw, Lucas would never do that to a woman. He would show a woman some respect.

"May I help you?" the store detective asked, flashing a

badge.

"I'm just doin' some shoppin', sir," she said, snapping out of it.

The detective was a tall man with wide, football shoulders. He was about six-five and intimidating. He wore a slight scowl on an otherwise friendly face.

"Shoppin'," he said, mocking her.

"Yes, sir."

"Let's see some ID."

Johnnie didn't have identification with her. It had never been necessary before now. She had to at least pretend she had identification. Rummaging through her purse, she acted surprised that it wasn't where she thought it would be.

"I'm sure I put my driver's license in my purse this morning, sir. I can't seem to find it."

"That's just what I thought," he said, grabbing her arm. "Come with me."

When Johnnie saw the other customers, most of whom were white, staring as she was being literally dragged through the store, the humiliation she felt overwhelmed her. She felt even more degraded when the few colored people in the store looked at her as though she was an embarrassment to them. She bowed her head and cried softly. The tears, one after another, rolled down her cheeks.

When they reached the detective's office, the degradation continued. He opened her purse and emptied the contents onto his maple-wood desk. A wad of money fell out of the purse. He picked it up and counted it. It was four hundred dollars in small bills.

"Where did you get this?" he asked, shaking the money in her face.

She just stood before the towering hulk of a man with her head bowed, tears still flowing. She knew she had to lie. *But what lie do I tell? I can't tell him my white lover pays me for sex, and I can't tell him I have a job. What if he asks me where I work then calls to see if I actually work there?*

"Well? Speak up!" he demanded.

"Sir, I don't want no trouble," she said, still looking at the floor. "I just came to do some shoppin'."

"Did you steal this money?"

"No, sir."

"Then where the hell did you get four hundred dollars? I think you stole it. Do you have any more?" He had made up his mind to take the money from her. Who could she tell? As far as he was concerned, the money, in all likelihood, was stolen.

"No, sir. That's all I have."

"I don't believe you. Up against the wall and spread 'em!"

"Sir?"

"You heard me. I said spread 'em."

When she just stood there frozen, he turned her around, pushed her up against the wall and began frisking her. As he patted her down, he squeezed her breasts and ass. Not finding anything, he said, "Where's the rest of the money?"

"I don't have no more, sir," she pleaded.

"I think you do. Take off the dress. I think the money's in your panties."

Johnnie couldn't believe what she was hearing. He wasn't looking for more money. He wanted sex. She could see it in his eyes.

"No, sir," she said, looking into his eyes. "I will not take off my dress. You can have the money, but no, I will not do it."

"Fine! You're going to jail then," he said and picked up the telephone.

"Okay, okay," she said and sniffed as the tears ran down her cheeks again.

When she pulled the dress up over her head, exposing

her naked breasts and panties, the door opened.

"Detective Little, what the hell is going on in here?" the store manager asked.

Johnnie pulled her dress down. Her humiliation was now complete.

"Sir, this woman looked suspicious, and when I asked her if she had identification, she told me no."

"Little, you know what I'm talking about." His voice was just a notch under shouting. "Why was she undressing?"

"I wanted to make sure she didn't have any stolen items on her, sir. You know how these people steal. It's the only thing they excel at. Left alone, they'll rob you blind."

Johnnie was enraged by what she was hearing. *He knows I didn't steal anything. I haven't been in the store long enough. It was all probably a trick to get my clothes off.*

"Look at this money, sir," Little said, showing him the four hundred dollars. "I found this on her."

"Is this your money?"

"Yes, sir."

"That's a lot of money for a colored woman. Where did you get it?"

"I saved it, sir," Johnnie said, finally figuring out what story to tell. She knew most men thought she was much older than what she really was. "I've been savin' for years— since I was fifteen. Decided to come and look for some new furniture. I just bought a house, sir." She walked over to the desk where all of her belongings were and picked up a folded piece of paper. She handed it to the manager. "Here's my deed, sir," she continued. "See, I wasn't gonna rob you, sir. Just doin' some shoppin', that's all."

The manager unfolded the deed then looked into her sad eyes and decided she was telling the truth. He handed the empty purse to her. Johnnie took the purse and collected her things. When she finished, she stood quietly, waiting to be officially released.

"Detective Little, what the hell did you think you were doing?" the manager yelled. "Did it ever occur to you that if she had four hundred dollars, she didn't need to steal from the store?"

"Sir, I, uh—"

"You're fired!"

"What kinda white man are you?" Little asked, shaking his head. "You're taking the word of a nigger over a white man? I've seen it all now. This country is going to hell in a hand basket because of you fuckin' nigger lovers."

"Get out before I have you thrown out!" the manager yelled.

"I'll be glad to leave. I feel sick to my stomach," Little said, slamming the door.

"Are you okay, Ms. Wise?" the manager asked, handing her a handkerchief.

"Yes, sir," she said, wiping her eyes. "Can I go now, sir?"

"Yes. I'm truly sorry for your inconvenience. I hope you'll continue to shop at Sears."

"Yes, sir," she said then walked out of the office.

Chapter 25
"Taking charge"

Johnnie calmed down considerably by the time she reached the offices of Glenn and Webster. However, she still had some residual anger from the way she was treated at Sears. As she rode the St. Charles streetcar to the central business district, she thought of her introduction to whoredom, the selling of her womanhood and self-respect, and the constant innuendoes from men. The problem with Robert Simmons this morning particularly came to mind. She knew she definitely had a way with men, but it wasn't until the streetcar passed through the Garden District, the city's uptown area with all of its fancy old mansions, that she made up her mind to take Martin Winters up on his offer of a "later date."

As usual, she could feel people staring at her, and the yellow sundress she was wearing didn't deter any of the men from gawking. With her head held high, she walked straight to Cynthia Lamar's desk. She was on the phone. Johnnie stood in front of her with an angry look on her face. Cynthia looked at her and rolled her eyes. Johnnie put her hands on her hips and patted her foot. She was in no mood to be subservient; not after what just happened to her, not after that kind of humiliation. A few seconds later, Cynthia hung up the phone.

"What can I do for you, Ms. Wise?"

I see you remembered my name. That's a good start, you little tramp. "I need to see Martin right now," Johnnie said gruffly.

"Do you have an appointment?"

"No."

"Have a seat and he'll get to you when he can."

"No," Johnnie said in the same brusque tone. "I will not have a seat. You tell him I'm here right now."

"Now, just a minute."

"Look, Cynthia," she said, raising her voice an octave. "I don't care nothin' about you screwin' a married man." She knew the comment would get a rise out of Cynthia. "As far as I'm concerned, that's y'all's business. I'm here to discuss my stock portfolio. Now, either you tell him I'm here or I will."

Stunned by Johnnie's brash manner and her knowledge of the ongoing affair with Martin, Cynthia went into his office. Johnnie followed her and closed the door. Martin sat at his desk, going over some papers when they entered.

Without looking up, Martin said, "Cindy, I thought I told you I didn't want to be disturbed."

"You did, but she started yelling about us having an affair and only God knows who heard her."

Martin looked up and saw Johnnie standing right behind Cynthia with her hands on her hips. She looked like she was enraged about something.

Confused, Cynthia asked, "Why would you tell her about us, Martin?"

"He didn't tell me anything," Johnnie said in a sharp tone. "Now, leave us alone, please."

"What the hell is going on, Johnnie?" Martin demanded.

"Johnnie, is it?" Cynthia asked, suspecting something

94

was going on between them.

"Cindy, why don't you wait outside," Martin said calmly.

"No! What the hell is going on between you two?"

"Nothing," Martin said, raising his voice.

Johnnie couldn't resist the urge to say, "Not yet, but trust me little girl, something is going to happen. Isn't that right, Martin?"

"Are you fucking her?" Cynthia asked. "Is that why she's being so bold?"

"Cindy, let's discuss this later," Martin said.

"No!" Cynthia said, full of rage. "We'll discuss it right fucking now!"

"No, we won't!" Martin said with equal force. "Now, get back to your desk!"

"Yeah, get back to your desk, Cynthia," Johnnie jabbed. "We business people have things to discuss."

Cynthia was about to say something but Martin cut her off. "Cindy, I mean it," he said, softening his tone. "I'll discuss this with you later. This is a client and you're behaving very unprofessionally. Please, return to your desk."

"Yeah, Cindy, he means it." Johnnie laughed.

Still frustrated, Cynthia turned around and looked at Johnnie, who was smiling from ear to ear. "Bitch," she said under her breath as she walked past.

"Ya mama!" Johnnie said loudly.

When Cynthia closed the door, Martin said, "What in the hell do you think you're doing barging into my office, making wild accusations? Just who in the hell do you think you are?"

"Oh, shut up and sit down, Martin," Johnnie said, full of confidence.

She had effectively gotten rid of Cynthia, and now she felt like she was in the driver's seat. After all, Martin propositioned her. As long as he wanted sex, she knew she was in charge. Martin stared at her for a couple of seconds and decided to play along, at least until he got a piece. He sat down and gestured for her to do the same. She did.

"Now, do you mind telling me why you're being so acrimonious?"

"Went to college, huh?"

Martin laughed a little. "Seriously though, Johnnie. What's happened? Did you and Earl have a fight?"

"No. This has nothing to do with Earl."

"Then what's this all about?"

Johnnie reached into her purse and took out the four hundred dollars. She threw it on the table. "I want you to buy me more stock in Sears."

After telling him about the incident at Sears and making plans to see Martin when she moved into her new home, she prepared to leave the office. She could feel his eyes on her ass, so she turned around to see if he was looking. He was. When she looked into his eyes, she saw the same look that Earl had that Christmas Eve when he took her for the first time. She knew then that Martin Winters would do whatever she wanted.

As she walked past Cynthia's desk, she said, "You can have him now."

Part 2
The Knowledge of Good & Evil

Chapter 26

"I didn't say that."

Johnnie was waiting in the school park for half an hour, watching the kids leave from a distance. She began to wonder if Lucas Matthews went to school that day. She was just about to leave when the door opened and he came out of the school, carrying his gym bag over his shoulder.

"Lucas!" she yelled.

He turned in the direction of the voice. When Lucas recognized her, he smiled and waved. He jogged in hurried excitement over to the park bench where she was sitting. "Where you been? I was wonderin' what happened to you today."

"I needed some time away from school, Lucas," she said, believing it would be best to tell him her decision to quit school later. "Guess what, though."

"What?"

"It looks like I'll be gettin' the house sooner than I thought."

"A house, huh? Where 'bout?"

"Ashland Estates."

"Uh-huh," he said skeptically.

"You don't believe me?"

"I believe you, Johnnie," he said with a heavy heart. "It's just that kids have been sayin' that you were goin' to be livin' with some white man. I didn't wanna believe it, but I guess it's true. Is it?"

It was like someone let the air out of her. Johnnie bowed her head. The look on her face said it all. Lucas was the last person she wanted knowing what was going on between her and Earl. She would have told him herself at the proper time.

"I suppose you don't want me now, huh?" Johnnie asked

Lucas felt sorry for her, but he still liked her. "No, I still do. Can you tell me somethin'?"

"Let me guess. You wanna know how I got into this situation, don't you?"

"Yes, but if you don't want to tell me, I understand. From what I hear tell, you ain't the first girl Shamus done did this to. But you seem to be the only one gettin' somethin' for your trouble."

"What do you mean, Lucas?"

"Johnnie, I'm not real smart, but any fool can figure out that a sixteen-year-old colored girl livin' in the ghetto cain't afford no house—let alone in Ashland Estates."

"So, it don't bother you that I'm with this white man?"

"I didn't say that. My mama had the same trouble. She told me womenfolk do what they gotta do to survive. I don't like the idea of you being with a white man in that way, but what could you do? I know you're still a good girl, and if you didn't have to do what you're doing, I know you wouldn't."

Lucas made her feel as if he was the only person in her life who truly cared about her. She looked in his eyes and saw sincerity in them. Taking his hand into hers, she kissed him on the cheek. A broad smile appeared on his face. He felt like royalty. He wanted to ask her to be his girl again, but thought it was too soon.

"Can I trust you, Lucas?"

"Yeah."

"No. I mean can I really trust you?"

"Johnnie, yes. You can trust me, okay?"

"Okay, listen. I have some obligations to fulfill, but I have plans that I cain't tell you about right now. All I can do is ask you to trust me. If you can trust me, I'll be your girl. If you can't, I guess I won't."

Lucas frowned.

"What's the matter, Lucas?"

"What plans do you have?"

"Lucas, you just said you trusted me."

"I do, but—"

"No. Either you trust me or you don't," she said, releasing his hand. "There are some things that you don't need to know right now. The last thing I wanna do is hurt you. I've been hurt and I know how it feels, especially when you've entrusted your entire being to a person. To have that trust betrayed is unbearable." She turned her back to him. "You wanted to know how I got into this situation? I'll tell you. My mother made a deal with Earl on Christmas Eve a year ago. On Christmas Eve! Do you know what that's like, to know you have to do something so offensive, something so disgusting, something so wretched that you want to heave every time you think about it?" She turned around and looked at him. "A year ago, do you think you would have heard the things you heard about me today?"

He shook his head.

"Don't you see? I have nothing left. Nothing." She laughed a little. "And get this. After I let Earl have his way with me, my mother walks into the room and tells me she did me a favor. She basically tells me my virginity was worthless and that I would have just ended up givin' it to some good for nothin' nigga. She tells me that all men want what a woman has between her legs and that I should learn to use it to get ahead. And you wanna know what's frightening? I'm startin' to believe she was right. You wouldn't believe the day I've had, Lucas. It all started at the Savoy."

"The Savoy Hotel?"

"Yeah."

"What were you doing there?"

"Me and my mother got into a fight after you left and I ended up moving out. It's just been one thing after another."

"And you rode with Shamus?"

"Yes."

"So, that's when Billy Logan saw you?"

"Yes."

"I'ma kick his ass again."

"No, Lucas. Leave it alone."

"Are you sure?"

"Yes."

"So, you stayin' at the Savoy, huh?"

"Yes, and that's where things went bad today. The owner got fresh. He wanted to have dinner with me. Then when I told him I had plans, he just totally disrespected me. So, I tell him a thing or two, then I go to Sears. I'm not in the store two minutes when the store detective started harassin' me. The next thing I know, he's haulin' me up to his office where he feels me up while he's supposedly looking for some money I was supposed to have stolen. Then he threatened to call the police if I didn't take my dress off. If it wasn't for the store manager, he would have forced me to have sex with him."

"Why cain't them crackers leave our women alone?"

"It ain't just the white men. It's the colored ones too."

"Don't they know you're only sixteen?"

"Earl does. But as you see, it hasn't stopped him. He's probably convinced himself that it's okay since I look older than girls my age are supposed to look."

"Probably, but I guess what makes me mad is if we did the same, they would castrate us—even if she wanted it."

"Not if you take her to the Savoy. For some reason, as quiet as it's kept, it's okay if you do it there."

"Yeah, I heard that too."

"You ever thought about it with a white girl, Lucas?"

"Huh? Uh, no."

She knew he was lying, but it didn't matter. This was who she had chosen to give herself to, fully and completely. If he wanted to see a woman, any woman, colored or white, she wouldn't object. "Lucas, I gotta be going. I'm supposed to go by my mother's and take her to the new house."

"Okay, I'm gonna trust you, but you're gonna stop doin' this as soon as you can, right?"

"I promise, Lucas. As soon as I can, I'll stop."

Lucas smiled. "Well, can I walk you home?"

"Sure, but not up to the door, okay? I don't want to start any mess with my mother. How about I call you when I get moved in and let you know where I'm stayin'."

Chapter 27

"You got a deal."

The 1947 powder blue Oldsmobile stopped in front of the house in Ashland Estates. There were a couple of Ford trucks parked in the driveway, owned by the men fixing the house. When Marguerite got out of the car, she was speechless. Johnnic's house dwarfed hers. She had seen the deed, but still some part of her refused to believe that her sixteen-year-old daughter was able to get a white man to not only purchase a house for her, but give her the deed to the place.

Marguerite wouldn't admit it, but she was just as jealous as she was happy. "Let me see that deed again, girl?" Marguerite said.

Johnnie handed her the deed and said, "Mama, how many times do you need to see it?"

"Yeah, it's the real McCoy alright," she said and handed it back to her. "Well, let me see the inside."

"Okay, Mama," Johnnie said, pulling the keys out of her purse.

As they started for the house, the neighbor she had

waved at the day before came out of her house. She was watching them the entire time, trying to decide if she should go out and introduce herself.

"Hi neighbor!" the woman said.

Johnnie instinctively knew who it was before she even turned around. The woman was wearing a pair of cut-off jeans and a white blouse tied in a knot around her waist. She was tall and well-built with black coffee skin, thick lips, and slightly slanted eyes.

"Hi!" Johnnie said with equal enthusiasm.

"I'm Sadie Lane," she said, extending her hand.

"I'm Johnnie Wise, and this is my mother, Marguerite."

"Welcome to the neighborhood," Sadie said.

"Thank you," Johnnie said. "You been livin' here long?"

"About ten years now."

"I suppose you know all the gossip on the block, huh?" Marguerite asked.

"Uh-huh."

"Then I can trust you to take care of my daughter."

"Daughter?" she said, forgetting that Johnnie had introduced Marguerite as her mother. "You look like sisters."

"Thank you, but no. She's my daughter."

"How old are you, girl?"

Johnnie wondered if she should tell her how old she was. She didn't know Sadie. *But what harm could it do?*

"I'm sixteen."

"Sixteen?" Sadie said, astonished. "Girl, you look like you could easily be twenty-nine or thirty. I bet you have all kinds of trouble with the men folk, huh?"

"Yeah, they always compliment me."

"Well, I better let you all see your new place. I just wanted to introduce myself and let you know I'm a friendly person. If you ever need anything, let me know, okay?"

"I sure will, Sadie."

"You promise?"

"Yes, I promise."

"Have you forgotten your manners, Johnnie?" Marguerite asked. "Invite her over to see the place."

"I've already been inside, but I'd like to see it when you move in, though. Is that all right?"

"Yes," Johnnie answered.

"When are you moving in?" Sadie asked.

"Hopefully, in a couple of weeks. But as soon as possible."

"Okay, well, I'm sure we'll be seeing a lot of each other."

"I hope so, Sadie."

"If you like, when you're finished looking around, you can stop by and have some coffee or something. I'll tell you all the latest gossip in the neighborhood."

"You got a deal," Marguerite said.

"Okay, great. I'll see you all then," Sadie said then walked back to her house.

"She talks to us like she's talkin' to white folks, don't she, Mama?"

"Yeah, she probably works for white people or somethin'. You could probably learn a lot from her."

"You think so?"

"Yeah."

Chapter 28

"I'm a businesswoman."

Wearing a white bathing suit that showed off her tight body, Marguerite was lying on a cushioned lawn chair by the pool at the Savoy, thinking about Johnnie's beautiful home. Johnnie's house was located in an affluent colored neighborhood, replete with professionals of every genre. Their money notwithstanding, they were just like the poor coloreds where she lived. According to Sadie, the husbands were hardworking men who provided for their families, and their wives were church-going hypocrites who gave them hell every night then wondered why they ran around on them. Yet, somehow they thought they were superior to the coloreds who weren't professionals. Some of the marriages were healthy, but none were without problems.

In spite of how she felt about the arrogant Negroes who lived in Ashland Estates, Marguerite would much rather live there than her Sable Parish neighborhood.

Why didn't I demand more from my lovers? I was just as pretty as she was when I was her age, yet I have nothing to show for it except an old broken down house in a neighborhood where I'm not accepted. I should be doing much better than what I'm doing. I mean that house is a mansion compared to mine. And that yard. All that room.

She got a two-car garage and she cain't even drive one car, let alone two. It just ain't right. That should be my goddamn house, not hers. Hell, I introduced her to Earl. I got her started and she gets a house outta the deal? What do I get? Nothing!

"Mama, what are you thinkin' about?" Johnnie asked and took a sip of her iced tea.

"You really wanna know?" Marguerite frowned.

"Of course."

"I'm jealous as hell, Johnnie. I cain't believe this shit. You ain't even seventeen years old yet, and you got a big-ass house in a rich neighborhood and your whole life ahead of you. And what do I have? Not a goddamned thing! Don't get me wrong, honey, but shit, that's fucked up! You know what I mean?"

"Yeah, I know what you mean, Mama."

"And to top that shit off, you layin' around the pool drinkin' iced tea in the best colored-owned hotel in New Orleans. Somehow the shit don't seem right."

"Mama, you gotta demand more. That's what I did. If men are going to use us, we gotta be smart about it. We gotta start doin' some usin' of our own. That's why I have stocks now."

"For real?"

"Uh-huh."

"Stock in what?"

"Buchanan Mutual is where I started. Now I have stock in Ford, General Motors, Coca Cola, Sears, and I have a plan to branch out from there. Martin calls it a diversified portfolio."

"Who in the hell is Martin?"

"My stockbroker."

"What?"

"That's right. I have a stockbroker now, Mama. Every woman ought to have one as far as I'm concerned."

"Are you and Martin together too?"

"Not yet. But he wants me, and I basically told him he would have to teach me how the stock market worked if he expected to be with me."

"And he went for it?"

"They all go for it, Mama. You sho' was right about that. Well, not Lucas. He's not like that."

"You still call yo'self seein' that boy."

"I told you I was gon' see him, Mama. I meant that."

"Does he know about Martin?"

"No! And ain't no reason to tell him."

Marguerite shook her head and said, "Girl, you got the skills of my Mama already in you. She could do the same thing with men. She had 'em all wrapped around her finger, but you done took whorin' to a new level."

Johnnie pulled her sunglasses down far enough for Marguerite to see her eyes and said, "I'm not a whore. I'm a businesswoman."

"A businesswoman, huh?"

"Uh-huh."

"So, tell me about this plan of yours."

"Well, first I'm droppin' outta school and—"

"Oh yeah, we was supposed to talk about that."

"There's nothin' to talk about. The decision's made."

"Well, can you at least tell me why?" Marguerite asked.

"The straight truth is I'm embarrassed, Mama. I can never go back to that school again. The thought of everybody knowing what I'm doing, knowing the details of my life really bothers me. And what they don't know, they'll simply make up. I just can't bring myself to look into the face of the girls that I belittled. I guess what's worse is I'm so good at it. I'm so good at it, it scares me. It's like the sky's the limit. It's like nothing's beyond my reach. And yet, I'm afraid to reach out and grab it because if I do, if I do grab all that I'm offered, what does that make me? But if I don't take all that I can, I become the classical fool. The court jester for all to witness. No, school is out—forever."

For the first time, Marguerite understood what she had done to Johnnie. Sure, her daughter had gotten over it as she predicted, but Johnnie hadn't accepted her fate the way she had. In the pit of her stomach, she felt uneasiness. It wasn't nausea. It was a nervousness of great expectations. It was hope. Hope that her daughter would one day fulfill all of the dreams that she once had for herself. Marguerite was torn. She wanted Johnnie to do better than she did, but at the same time, she didn't want her to do too much better. Johnnie's success would magnify her abysmal failure as a parent and a whore. But still, she couldn't wait to hear how Johnnie planned to do something with her life.

"I see you've put a lot of thought into this," Marguerite said.

"That's all I've been thinkin' about—mornin', noon, and night."

"Tell me the plan then."

"No, Mama. First, I wanna hear about my daddy. You promised to tell me about him and what happened between you two over a year ago, remember?"

"Yes, I remember. You sure you wanna know about him and us?"

"Uh-huh."

Just then, Johnnie spotted Robert Simmons coming in their direction.

"I see you didn't learn anything from our conversation this mornin', Mr. Simmons," Johnnie said.

"Of course I did," Simmons replied.

"Then why are you here?"

"I like the abuse," he said, looking at Marguerite.

Marguerite looked surprised. She wondered if that

comment was meant for her. And if it was, how would he know? She dismissed the whole idea. *There's no way he'd know.*

"You like the abuse, huh?" Johnnie said.

"To a point." Simmons grinned. "You two sisters?"

"No, this is my mother, Marguerite. This fool is Robert Simmons."

"This is your mother?" Simmons said, surprised and also ignoring the insult. "We've met, though. She's a guest of the Savoy from time to time."

Surprised by the revelation, Johnnie looked at her mother. She wondered what was going on. *Who was she bringing to the Savoy? It certainly wasn't a colored man. It had to be a white man. But who?*

"I'll tell you about it later, honey," Marguerite said, scowling at Simmons.

Chapter 29

"Papa was a rollin' stone."

"Excuse me, Mr. Simmons, but is it your policy to intrude on your guest's privacy?" Johnnie asked.

"Am I intruding? I thought I'd say hello, that's all."

"Well, hello and goodbye, Mr. Simmons," Johnnie said gruffly.

Without a word, Simmons left. As he walked back to the hotel, he thought about them.

This is so typical. Like mother, like daughter. Two tramps. And both of them screw white men for a living. What's this world coming to?

Looking at Marguerite, Johnnie said, "So, what's he talkin' about, you bein' a guest here from time to time?"

Feeling the pressure of the question, Marguerite decided to change the subject. The best way to do that without too much suspicion would be to tell her about her father. *Hopefully, by the time I'm finished, she'll forget about what he was talking about. If I told her my client was the Grand Wizard of the Klan, and she tells someone, white folk will kill us all.*

"I thought you wanted to know about your father."

"I do."

"Well, it started when I was fifteen. Just like you, I was

given to a white man. I met Michael, Benny's father, in school, much like your friend Luke."

"His name is Lucas, Mama."

"Whatever. Anyway, my mother told me he was no good, but of course I didn't listen to her and ran away with him to Chicago. We weren't together two months before I was pregnant with your brother Benny. The next thing I knew, he was gone. Ain't seen him since. So, there I am in a big city, all by myself. I didn't know anybody and I didn't have a dime to my name. So, what did I do?"

"What?"

"I turned to the only thing I knew, whoring. I made enough money to get a bus ticket back to New Orleans. When I walked in the house, my mother just shook her head. She couldn't wait to tell me, 'I told you so.' I just went to my room and cried myself to sleep. When I woke up, we talked about the baby I was carrying. She told me she would help me out if I helped myself. To her, helping myself meant I had to whore. This was all after I had the baby, of course. At first, it was the most humbling thing I ever had to do. Then before I realized it, I was being sought quite a bit. It was then that I knew I was good at this, much like you mentioned earlier. Unfortunately, I didn't have the mind my mother had with money. The mind you apparently inherited from her along with her good looks and charm. I just got the good looks and charm. That's why I don't have nothin' to show for it after all this time."

Johnnie's eyes welled with water. It was so sad, and she hadn't heard the worst of it yet, she thought.

"So anyway, I go to Congo Square one night to dance and have a good time. And guess who happened to be playing there that night?"

"Who?"

"Louis Armstrong and the Hot Five."

112

"Mama, is it true that Congo Square was set aside in the early 1800s for free and enslaved Coloreds to sing and dance and play their drums?"

"Yes, it sure was."

"And you met Louis Armstrong there?"

"Well, first I met yo' daddy. He was the saxophonist in his band. You should have seen him up there on stage with that charcoal-gray zoot suit on; playin' that saxophone like it would be his last time." She had a smile on her face but didn't realize it. "I was standing at the edge of the stage screamin' like a crazy woman. He saw me, came over, and played to me. He was so handsome. He was a little short, but man, could he play. His name was John Wise."

"So, y'all named me after him?"

"Yes, he insisted on it. He wanted a boy, but he loved you just the same when we found out I had carried a girl for nine months."

"So, y'all got married, huh?"

"Yeah, and it was the worst decision I ever made."

"Worse than runnin' away with Michael?"

"Oh God, yes. John was a ladies' man to no end. Sometimes I think he couldn't help himself. Women was always throwin' themselves at him. I know you know by now, if there's one thing a man cain't do, he cain't turn down some free pussy. If a woman, any woman, blind, cripple, or crazy open her legs, he gon' get a piece. That's why I don't even bother with love no more. Girl, that thing hurt me so when I found out he was seeing other women on the road. I thought if I traveled with him, he would stop. I was there to give it to him whenever he wanted it. And do you know that nigga was still fuckin' everything that moved? Then when I did it with Satchmo, all hell broke loose."

"You did it with Louis Armstrong?" Johnnie asked, totally shocked.

"Yes, Satchmo was always pressin' up against me. Told me I was finer than sunshine and sweeter than the mornin' dew. Told me only Dorothy Dandridge was prettier."

"So, what happened?"

"John found out about it and beat the hell outta me. That's what happened."

"Now, wait a minute. That ain't right. He was doin' it first, wasn't he?"

"That don't matter to a man, Johnnie. A man don't know how to handle his emotions because of the way they was brought up. A man keeps his emotions deep inside him. It usually takes the death of a loved one for a man to cry. The damn fools. They haven't figured out that God gave them tear ducts for more than funerals. But anyway, when a man is deeply hurt by a woman, you can count on him beatin' or even killin' her for doing the very thing he did to her. And it don't matter to him how many times he did it. The fact that you did it once is enough to shatter him emotionally. Since he doesn't know what to do with his pain, he allows his pain to turn to anger. And when that happens, Johnnie, you better get outta there as quick as you can. 'Cause if you don't, he's liable to kill you."

"So, then what happened?" Johnnie asked, completely fascinated by the story she was hearing.

"What happened is him and Satchmo got into it."

"What?"

"Sho' did. Busted Satchmo's lips and loosened some teeth. Satchmo had to cancel a few gigs behind that. He ended up firing yo' daddy. John told me he was going to start a band of his own. Told me he'd be back in a couple of months. He ain't been back to New Orleans since."

Johnnie took a deep breath and let it out slowly, deliberately. She had often wondered what became of her mother and father. Now she knew, and it wasn't any better

114

than not knowing.

"I would have liked to have met him, Mama," she said, taking off her shades and wiping her eyes.

Marguerite could see the tearstains on her daughter's face.

"You cryin', honey?"

"Yeah. It's so sad."

"You understand now why I did what I did with you and Shamus?"

"I understand, Mama, but you're still wrong for doing it."

"That may be true, but my heart was in the right place. I just didn't want you to have to learn life's hard lessons the way I did. You're a woman now. The choice is still up to you. Remember me tellin' you that way back then?"

"Yes, I remember. But how do you expect me to stop now? My reputation is ruined. Besides, I'm deep into my plan now."

"Yeah, that's right. You were supposed to tell me about that."

"You think you slick, Mama."

"What do you mean?" Marguerite laughed.

"You're changing the subject again."

"You don't need to know everything I do."

"So, you not gon' tell me?"

"No. I agreed to tell you about your father, not about the men I see."

"Fair enough," Johnnie said, thinking, *I'll just get it outta Mr. Simmons.*

Chapter 30

"Girl, you somethin' else."

"Do you remember me sayin' we gotta be smart about this usin' thing?" Johnnie asked.

"Yeah."

"I've been thinkin' about this for a while, ever since Earl mentioned investing my money. If we're smart, we can be rich one day. If we can just be smart about it."

"What are you talkin' about, girl? You're talkin' in riddles." Marguerite frowned.

"It's like you said earlier, Mama. Men will do just about anything for sex, but if you do to them what they do to you, they cain't handle it. For all of their brawn and brute strength, they're emotional weaklings. I'm learning to use and control them without them knowing it. I'm learning to make them do things I want them to do. And get this. I make them think it was their idea."

"Girl, women have been doin' that to men for centuries. That ain't nothin' new. What are you going to do that hasn't been done?"

"Well, women may have been doing it for centuries, but I'm just startin' to understand this thing. So, the first thing I'm gonna do is be picky. I'll make the choice, not them. I'll only deal with men who have something to offer."

"Details?"

"I mean I'll choose men who have something I need, no matter what that something is. Take Martin. He wants me, but he knows he has to teach me what he knows first. That's what I mean. I cain't afford to just take their money and be satisfied. What good is money if you don't know what to do with it? That's why you were upset earlier, right?"

"Right. That and that big-ass house you have." Marguerite nodded her head. "But what if all they have is money? What then?"

"If all they have is money, we charge 'em more. If they cain't afford us, too bad. This is business, and we gotta think of ourselves as businesswomen, not whores."

Marguerite listened to her daughter. *She certainly is smart. Why couldn't I think like that when I was her age? Ain't no tellin' where I'd be now if I had.*

"The second thing I'll do is be fickle. When they've served their purpose, I'll cut 'em loose and move on."

"Yeah, but what if he doesn't want to let you go?"

"Then I'll use whatever methods I need, up to and including callin' his wife, his mother, or his priest if I have to."

Marguerite laughed. "Girl, you somethin' else."

Johnnie looked her mother in the eyes and said, "Mama, this is serious. I've made up my mind. There's a better world out there for people with the know-how and the guts to live good. Look around you. Here we are relaxing by the pool, being waited on hand and foot. And how much is this costin' you?"

"Nothin'," Marguerite said.

"Me neither. But it's costin' Earl something. And that's what we have to do. We make them pay for everything. In return, we give them whatever they cain't get at home. I don't see myself livin' the way we lived ever again."

Marguerite nodded her head slowly. She had already formulated a plan to get more money out of Richard Goode. *It's not like he can get what I give him from anybody. I know what he likes and how to give it to him.*

"The third thing I've got to do is learn to talk the way my new neighbor does. I notice you have a little *savoir faire* around white people too."

"That's because I don't want white people to think I'm just some ol' uneducated nigga, so I make sure I speak real good around them."

"Well, we gotta learn to do it regularly. We gotta remember this is a business. As businesswomen, we gotta do the things that business people do. We gotta talk the way business people talk. That means we gotta keep our eyes and ears open and learn all we can from people who know things we don't. And—"

"Johnnie, do you really think this'll work?" Marguerite asked.

"Do you want to keep livin' where you livin', wishin' you was livin' in Ashland Estates?"

"No."

"Then you better do something to make a better life for yourself."

"Telephone call for Johnnie Wise," the bellhop repeated a few times.

"Over here," Johnnie said, raising her hand.

The bellhop brought the telephone to her and plugged it in.

"Hello."

"Where have you been?" Earl demanded. "I've been calling your room for hours. Then it occurred to me that you might be enjoying the amenities of the hotel."

Johnnie looked at her mother and rolled her eyes.

"Who is it?" Marguerite mouthed.

118

"Earl, honey," she said and rolled her eyes again, "I'm just relaxin' a little. You comin' by?"

"No, I just wanted you to know that I talked with the men fixing the house and they're going to put a rush on the job. You should be able to move in next weekend."

"Really?"

"Really," he said. "Did you get a chance to look for some furniture and things like that?"

"I went to Sears this morning and the store detective harassed me. If it wasn't for the store manager, he might have raped me in his office."

"I'm sorry. I'll speak to the manager before I leave tonight."

"Leave? Where you goin'?"

"Didn't I tell you? I have to go to Chicago tonight. West is having some big meeting and he wants me to go with him."

"When will you be back?"

"In a couple of weeks."

"A couple of weeks," she repeated, attempting to sound disappointed.

"You sound disappointed."

"I am, Earl," she said, trying to keep from smiling. "But what am I going to do for money? I don't have any furniture or food or nothin'. By the time you get back, I want you to be able to come home to a good meal and a place to lay your head."

"How about I stop by the hotel before we go to the airport and give you some money to take care of everything?"

"That would be great, Earl," Johnnie said, looking at her mother. "You think you'll have enough time to give me a little tonight, just to tide me over 'til you get back in a couple of weeks?"

"I'll try, okay?"

119

"What about the hotel bill? Will you be able to take care of that too?"

"Yeah, no problem."

"I hate to be pushy, honey, but you know I want some nice furniture, right?"

"I know, Johnnie," he said, speaking in hushed tones. "I gotta go now."

"You know it takes a lot of time to get around this city on public transportation."

"No way. I'm not buying you a car," Earl said through clenched teeth. "Now, I gotta go."

He hung up. Johnnie heard a second click, then put the receiver back on the telephone. She ignored the extra click and said to her mother, "See, that's how it's done."

"Girl, you somethin' else." Marguerite laughed. "You remind me so much of my mother. So, is he goin' to get you a car?"

"Not yet, but he will."

Chapter 31

"There had to be a better way."

"So, Earl's goin' to Chicago, huh?" Marguerite asked.

"Yeah. Said he's got some business meetin' to go to with his father-in-law."

"You sound like you don't believe him."

"I don't. Earl is a liar, Mama. He's always been a liar, and he'll always be a liar. He may be tellin' the truth now, but chances are he's lyin'. Probably got some black woman in Chicago to see. Who knows?"

"What are you goin' to do while he's gone?"

"Enjoy myself for a change. It'll be good to know he's gone for a couple of weeks while I get my house together. I'm going to Sears tomorrow and buy me some furniture."

"The way they treated you, why would you go back to Sears?"

"Because I have stock in the company, remember? If I buy from the companies I've invested in, it'll be like shoppin' on a permanent discount."

"How can I get some of them investments?" Marguerite asked.

"Just give me your money and I'll get you the stocks. I'll even show you everything I learn from Martin. That way you can do it yourself. Some day, I might just become a stockbroker and open my own brokerage firm. Just think! If

I did that, I'll have access to my own little market."

"What do you mean?"

"How many colored folks do you know that invest their money?"

"None."

"Me neither. There's the market right there. If I can learn this stock market thing, get some colored folks to invest, I could make a fortune."

"Okay, so when can we invest what I have now?"

"How much do you have?"

"About six or seven thousand dollars."

"What?"

"Yeah, about that much."

Johnnie took her shades off again and stared at her mother. She knew Earl had paid her mother to have her, but she had no idea how much money Marguerite was being paid.

Sensing her daughter's wrath, Marguerite innocently asked, "What's wrong with you?"

"What the fuck do you think is wrong with me?" Johnnie said so spontaneously that she didn't realize she had sworn for the first time in her young life. The words just came out of her like a powerful, unpredictable hurricane.

"Don't you curse me, girl," Marguerite growled.

"Curse you? Is that all you can say? Pray that I don't drown yo' good for nothin' ass in this pool."

Marguerite was amazingly cool, calm, and collected. She took a sip of her iced tea and said, "Ahhhh. This tea sho' hits the spot on a blisterin' hot day like today, don't it?"

"Mama, if you don't tell me somethin' and I mean tell me somethin' quick, I won't be responsible for my actions."

"Tell you what, girl?"

"Don't play dumb, Mama," Johnnie said, unable to contain the contempt she felt. "You told me Earl paid for everything that day."

"He did."

"How much did Earl pay for me, Mama?"

"A lot."

"Mama, if you don't start givin' me some answers, and I mean right now, cursin' you will be the least of your worries."

"You threatenin' me, girl?"

"If you don't tell me what I wanna know, so help me God, I'll choke the livin' shit outta you! And I mean it!"

"You serious, huh?"

Johnnie stood to her feet and calmly said, "I won't ask you again."

"Okay, okay," Marguerite said nervously. "Sit down. People are starin'.'"

Johnnie eased back into her lawn chair and put her shades back on. "Now, how much did he pay you that first time?"

"Hear me out, okay? Just hear me out is all I ask."

"Will you get on with it?"

"Earl offered me five hundred, but I got him up to a thousand because you were a virgin."

"Is that supposed to make me feel better?"

"No, but I just wanted you to know I didn't let you go cheap."

Johnnie just shook her head in disbelief and said, "So, where did all the money come from?"

"I've been savin' for years. Ever since the depression."

"So, what you're tellin' me is you didn't have to sell me at all, right?"

"Yeah, I did," she said sincerely. "The money was an excuse, but you needed to learn how men operate. You needed to learn what they think of women and how to handle yourself."

"And it never occurred to you to let me learn some things on my own?"

"You have learned some things on your own, Johnnie," she said, almost proud. "Look at you now. You're a beautiful young woman with a beautiful home, some money in your purse, and the knowledge of how to get more. You're doing better than I did when I was sixteen. You oughta be grateful."

"Grateful?"

"You goddamn right," Marguerite said with conviction. "Where would you be right now if it wasn't for me? You wouldn't be in this nice hotel. You wouldn't know Martin Winters. You wouldn't have all these stocks and shit. And you certainly wouldn't have all these grandiose plans, would you?"

"So, let me get this straight. I'm supposed to be grateful for bein' introduced to a life of whoredom?"

"A life of business, remember?"

Johnnie laughed sardonically and said, "Do you have any idea what my plans were before you did this to me?"

"I suppose you're going to tell me you were a visionary before I helped you see the light."

"So, no matter what I say, you're going to justify what you did and pat yourself on the back for doin' it. This is unbelievable."

"Believe it," Marguerite said, feeling sure of herself. "I did what I thought was best for you. And if I could make a few nickels for doin' it, why not? Now you won't ever have to fall in love with the first man who fucks you like so many foolish women do."

"You mean like you, Mama?"

"I mean exactly like me. You don't have to like it, but you need to quit lookin' backward and start lookin' forward. Life is full of ups and downs, Johnnie. Remember that. And stop all this cryin' you do all the time. You're going to have to learn to be stronger than that. You've got your whole life in front of you. If you don't like what I taught you, then stop. If you do, then follow your plan. You've got something my own mother didn't have."

"What's that?"

"Vision. You've got vision, Johnnie, and a brain to go along with it. Besides, whatever you wanted to do before is still available to you. But whatever you do from this point forward is your own doin'. Don't blame me for the rest of your life. Instead, do what you will. Make the best of what you've learned."

"I wanted to be an evangelist, Mama. How am I gonna do that now?"

"Some of the best saints were the worst sinners. If you want to be an evangelist, be one. Don't let whatever mistakes you think I made stop you from being who you wanna be."

Johnnie was silent for a few moments, considering Marguerite's ideology.

There's a lot of truth in what she's saying, but there had to be a better way than this. There had to be. On the other hand, if I stop now, I'm back in the ghetto, back in the same high school, facing the same ridicule. How can I go back to being a good girl now, after all I've been through? How can God accept me now? He can't, can he? I'll do this a little while longer. Just 'til I get on my feet. Maybe I do have vision. Maybe I can become a stockbroker someday.

"Mama, are you ever going to tell me who this guy is that brings you to the Savoy?"

"No. A woman always has secrets, Johnnie. Remember that."

I'll remember that all right. You don't have to tell me. I'll find out, though. Believe me, I'll find out.

125

Chapter 32

"Keep your motor runnin'."

Johnnie went back and forth between Sears, the new house, and the hotel just before she moved out of the Savoy. With the money Earl had given her, she bought several bedroom sets, bathroom ornaments, towels, rugs, drapes, and other decorative furnishings. By the time she finished, the house looked like the palace she envisioned. She was especially proud of the king-sized, hand carved cherry-wood bed she picked out. The head and footboards had winged angels playing trumpets carved into it, and the four bedposts almost reached the ceiling. She also purchased a mirrored bureau that stretched from one end of the wall to the other, with ten-foot armoires at each end. One armoire would be used for clothes and the other housed the portable RCA television.

Johnnie was walking to the front desk of the Savoy to check out. A week passed and Robert Simmons hadn't had any contact with her. Johnnie stayed out of sight until the day she was ready to check out. This, of course, was all a part of Johnnie's plan to get him to tell her about her mother and her dealings at the Savoy. She believed if Simmons didn't see her for a while, he would become even more infatuated with her. She knew Simmons would be more desperate to have her, fearing it would be his last opportunity. When she reached the desk, Simmons was reading the morning mail.

"Robert," she said softly, "I'll be checking out this afternoon. I have some errands to run this morning. When I return, I'll be ready to check out."

"I see you've decided to call me Robert." He grinned.

"I thought it was the least I could do. You have a wonderful hotel and a great staff. I felt as if I was at home. Thank you."

Noticing the change in attitude, Simmons fell right into her trap.

"Well, since this is your last day with us, perhaps you'll have that dinner with me?"

"I cain't do dinner, but I can do lunch if you like."

"How about Trudy's Café?"

"Sounds good, but can we eat on the terrace? It's such a beautiful day out."

"Cool. What time should I expect you?"

"One-thirty okay with you, Robert?"

"Fine. I'll see you then."

"Until then," Johnnie said, walking toward the exit.

Myron smiled and opened the door for her. Simmons watched her as she went through the door. He shook his head wantonly and said to himself, "Yeah, I gotta get me some of that."

***

Johnnie walked into Glenn and Webster's amidst the usual stares, wearing a navy skirt, a white blouse and a pair of navy-and-white pumps. She saw Cynthia Lamar sitting at her desk, filing her painted red nails.

"Do you have an appointment, Ms. Wise?" she asked, looking for a fight.

"Are we going to have to do this every time I come to see

Martin, Cynthia?"

"Let me tell you something. Martin is mine, and no colored wench is going to change that. No matter how much money you have, you'll always be a nigger to him."

"And you'll always wonder what we have that you don't that makes your men chase after us with little regard for their own cracker women. Now, are you going to announce me or do I have to barge in like I did last time?"

With a stoic look on her face, she picked up the phone and said, "Your voodoo princess is here." Then she hung up.

Johnnie was about to say something when Cynthia beat her to the punch.

"I know, my mama, right?"

"That's right," Johnnie said and walked into the office grinning.

"How are you today, Johnnie?" Martin asked, extending his hand.

"Wonderful, Martin," she said, shaking his hand and taking a seat. "I'm moving into my house later this afternoon."

"Great. You must be elated."

"Quite elated, actually."

She didn't know what elated meant, but went with it anyway. She figured it must mean excited or something.

"So, what can I do for you today?"

"A couple of things, actually, Martin," Johnnie said, crossing her legs. "I want to diversify my portfolio a little more."

"What companies are you looking at?"

"Well, I was at Sears quite a bit this week, and I noticed how many people were buying televisions."

"So, you're interested in one of the television makers?"

"Not exactly. It's my opinion that the market for the makers of televisions will be up and down. Some will even go out of business. So, I'm thinking of going to the source."

"What do you have in mind?"

"I'm thinking of investing in the networks. I think they will last regardless of what television is on the market. What do you think?"

"I think you're on to something," he said, thinking, *I better get some of this before she figures out how easy this shit really is. If I wait too long, she won't need my advice.*

"You really think so?" Johnnie asked, feeling good about herself.

"Yes, but I think you should also go with AT&T Corporation."

"Why, should I do that?"

"I'll be glad to explain it to you over dinner at your place. You name the date and time, and I'll be there, portfolio in hand, ready to chat about the market, among other things."

"First things first, Martin," Johnnie said and tossed a wad of money on the table.

"How much is this?"

"Five thousand dollars."

Martin counted the money and began making out the receipt, thinking, *You must be every bit as good as Earl says. I can't wait to get you in the sack.*

"How do you want to spread this out?"

"I'd like to put some in AT&T, but since you won't explain it to me, I guess I'll have my dinners with a man who can appreciate my natural talents."

"If I explain everything now, I won't have a card left to play later. That is, if I'm going to get the opportunity to appreciate your natural talents up close and personal."

"The card you hold is your knowledge of the market, Martin. That alone will be your calling card."

Johnnie watched him to see if her flirtatious words would be enough to get him to divulge his rationale for investing in AT&T. If it worked, she knew she would have no trouble getting the rest of the information out of him.

"So then, if I tell you why you should invest in AT&T, I still get to come to dinner?"

"No. You get to come to dinner because I want you to. You get to explain why I should invest in AT&T because it's your job."

"Okay, you got me." Martin laughed. "AT&T is an innovative company."

Innovative. That's another word I don't understand. "Innovative, huh?" Johnnie repeated, trying not to let on that she didn't have a clue what he was talking about.

"Just three short years ago, AT&T invented a technological marvel called the transistor. They're currently working on the first transatlantic telephone cable, and they're looking into launching the first earth-orbit commercial communication satellite."

"That's good enough for me," Johnnie said. "I'm sold." *I've got a lot to learn about this investment business.* "Well, Martin, I'm kinda in a hurry. Let me give you my new address so that you can send my dividend check there from now on."

"Okay, sure. Where do you live?"

"In Ashland Estates."

"Ashland Estates? It's pretty expensive out there, isn't it?"

"For colored folks? Yeah, probably so."

"What's the street address?'

"Number 3415 Imagination Drive," Johnnie said and picked up her purse. "Okay, just so we're clear, we're investing in NBC, ABC, CBS, and AT&T, right?"

"Right."

"I'll be calling you Martin," she said with a quick wink of the eye. "Keep your motor runnin'."

Chapter 33

"For real, Robert?"

After buying a dictionary at Cambridge Bookstore on Main Street, Johnnie waited for Simmons in Trudy's Café while looking up words. The word "transistor" led her to the word "semiconductor"; which led her to the word conductor; which helped her to understand that a transistor was a semiconductor that manages or controls electricity. The word "innovative" was already added to her repertoire of words. She couldn't wait to use it.

Maybe I can work my new words into my conversation with Robert.

Robert slid into his seat without making a sound. He was wearing a navy blue suit, a white shirt with a blue-and-white tie and expensive cologne.

He's obviously trying to make a favorable impression.

Johnnie closed her dictionary and put it back into her purse. She decided to play to his ego before springing the trap she knew he'd fall into.

"My, my, my, don't we look and smell like the rich and famous," Johnnie said with a wide smile, showing her perfect teeth. "I see you've decided to wear the same colors I'm wearing."

"Yeah, I wanted you to see how good we looked together," Simmons said, feeling like a hunter about to capture his prey.

Trudy came over to their table frowning, and practically threw the menus at them. Her blood seemed to boil even more when she realized Robert was so enamored with Johnnie that he didn't notice she was furious with him. They'd had sex together right after breakfast that very morning.

Johnnie could feel the thick tension in the air, but pretended not to notice Trudy's rage. *She doesn't like the idea of Robert having lunch with me in her restaurant. I can use her attitude to set up the trap.*

"What would you like?" he asked, still oblivious to Trudy's indignation.

"I'll have a chef salad and an iced tea, please."

Trudy was so upset by the sight of the two of them all dressed up like they were going to a ball sponsored by one of the local social clubs, her face looked like she had been sucking lemons.

Still looking at Johnnie, he said, "I'll have the ribs and fries."

"Anything to drink?" Trudy asked, hoping he would look her in the face, so he could see how badly she wanted to slap him.

"I'll have an iced tea too," he said, completely ignoring her.

Fed up, Trudy snatched the menu out of his hand and stormed off. Finally realizing something was wrong with Trudy, he glanced at her as she stomped off to the kitchen.

"I wonder what's wrong with her," Simmons said.

"Perhaps it's your innovative style, Robert," Johnnie

said, feeling good that she was able to work her new word into the conversation so quickly.

"What do you mean, innovative?" he asked.

"Certainly an educated man like you knows what innovative means."

"I know what the word means," he said, feeling a little insulted. "I'm just unsure what you mean by it."

Trudy returned and placed Johnnie's chef salad and their drinks on the table.

"I'll bring your ribs and fries out in a couple of minutes, Robert."

"Thank you, Trudy," he said. "Is there anything wrong?"

As far as she was concerned, he had a lot of nerve asking her if there was anything wrong. She folded her arms and tapped her foot on the carpeted floor then she walked away in disgust.

"I wonder what's wrong with her," Simmons said, shaking his head.

"You're much too modest, Robert," Johnnie said. "You know what's bothering her. You're still screwing her and yet you have the nerve to have lunch with me in her restaurant."

"I'm innovative how?" he asked, avoiding the insinuation.

Johnnie shook her head, nearly frowning as disgust overcame her. "You can be creative when you want sex, but your selection of women is way beyond the normal bounds of decency."

Before he could respond, Trudy came back with his meal and practically threw it on the table. She stormed off again. Ignoring the way she threw his food at him, Robert picked up a bone and took a bite.

"Now, what do you mean when you say the normal bounds of decency?" he asked and took another bite.

133

"You're good, Mr. Simmons," Johnnie said, calculating his responses every step of the way.

"Mr. Simmons again, huh?"

"That's right," she said with a straight face. "You wanna play games? Fine. We'll play games."

"I have absolutely no idea what you're talking about."

With a quizzical look on her face, Johnnie said, "So, you're not screwing my mother? It's bad enough that you're screwing Trudy at the same time, but my mother, Robert? And you're trying to screw me too." She paused briefly. "Oh, I get it. You're keeping it in the family, right?"

Confused, he said, "Where did that come from?"

"So, you're not screwing my mother?"

"Hell, naw."

"I suppose you're going to tell me you're not screwing Trudy either."

"That's none of your business," he said with a polite smile.

"You're right, but screwing me and my mother at the same time is my business."

"Did your mother tell you that?"

"No, she wouldn't tell me it was you, but I know it's you. Who else would it be, Myron? You're the ladies' man. Am I wrong?"

"I am a ladies' man. That part is true," he said with conceit oozing from his pores. "But your mother and I have no dealings whatsoever. And I can prove it."

Johnnie sat there quietly, hoping that his vanity would compel him to tell all. She curled her lips and said, "A real man would take responsibility for his own doing."

"I am a real man," Simmons said, feeling somewhat humbled by her attack on his manhood.

"A real man would tell the woman he's interested in the truth. If you had a relationship with her and it's over, that's one thing. But to flat out lie about it is quite another. I don't want you to think that I'm a totally unsympathetic woman. I understand. If you've had the mother and you want the daughter, you cain't tell the daughter that you've had the mother because you know I wouldn't want to have anything to do with you."

"Listen, Johnnie," Simmons said, hoping that if he told her the truth, all would be well between them. "Can you keep a secret?"

"Yeah," she said, barely able to contain herself.

"I'm not seeing your mother, but I know who is."

"Who?"

"You gotta keep this to yourself," he said in hushed tones. "If this got out, there would be a scandal of epic proportions. Not only would there be a scandal, but there's likely to be a full-scale race riot, church burnings, lynching, and only God knows what else."

Skeptical, Johnnie laughed. "Who is it, Richard Goode?"

"Uh-huh. Been goin' on for a while too."

"Mr. Simmons," she said, straight-faced, "you sure can tell some real whoppers. Ain't no way. My mother wouldn't screw a Hitler wannabe like Richard Goode for any amount of money."

"That ain't all she doin'."

"What do you mean?"

"They're doin' some perverted shit too."

"What do you mean?" Johnnie frowned.

Simmons finished cleaning a bone and took several swallows of his iced tea. "I shouldn't be tellin' you this, but since you won't believe me, I'll tell you. After they finish with the sexual part of their interlude, she ties him to the bedpost and beats his naked ass with a riding crop. Then he tells her he's ready and she sticks a dildo in his ass."

She didn't know what a dildo was, but acted as if she

135

did. "A dildo, huh?"

"Uh-huh."

"And you saw this?"

"Yeah, I've seen them about a hundred times," he said, not realizing that he would now have to explain how he could see something like that.

"Were you in the room?"

"No," he said.

"Then how do you know?"

"Trust me. I know."

"So, you spy on your guests?" Johnnie frowned. She got what she wanted. Now it was time to dismiss him and be on her way. "You are a truly pitiful human being. You wanna screw both mother and daughter while you're already screwin' Trudy. First you make up this ridiculous story about a well known Klansman and my mother. Then to make matters worse, you bring dildos and homosexuality into it. Like I said, you're very innovative."

"But I'm telling the truth."

Johnnie stood to her feet and said, "I don't know which is worse; you attempting to screw me and my mother at the same time or you telling me this unbelievable story and expecting me to fall for it. Let me give you a tip, Mr. Simmons. The one thing a woman treasures above all else is honesty. You, sir, have made a mockery out of the truth. Shame on you." She walked out.

Robert began eating his ribs again, unaware of the game that was just played on him. *Ain't this some shit. You tell the bitches the truth and they don't believe you. Fuck it. From now on, I'll lie my ass off. Here I am sitting here all dressed up with no place to go, nobody to screw and a stiff dick in my pants.*

He looked up and saw Trudy staring at him. She was still angry with him for ignoring her. He raised his hand and called her over to the table.

"What, Robert?" Trudy said with her arms folded.

"Sit down, baby," he said, thinking, *I can always get some from Trudy.*

"Why should I?"

"Because you know how I feel about you."

"Uh-huh. I suppose that's why she left."

"That's exactly why, baby," Simmons said. "She's been after me since she got here. She told me she was checking out this morning and asked me to have lunch with her. I thought it was the least I could do."

"For real, Robert?"

Simmons, looking as sincere as he could, said, "For real, baby."

Chapter 34

"Welcome to the neighborhood."

Johnnie was sitting in the breakfast nook of her kitchen, finishing an article about AT&T in the *Wall Street Journal*. The article chronicled AT&T's past technological achievements. It went on to discuss the coming transatlantic telephone cable and the launching of an earth-orbit commercial communication satellite. When she finished reading, she thought about what Martin Winters told her about AT&T and how innovative the company was. Sipping a hot cup of New Orleans blend, the corners of her mouth turned up when she thought about the money she was going to make. Her smile became even broader when she thought about being in her own kitchen, in her own home. For some odd reason, her thoughts shifted to what Robert Simmons told her about her mother and Richard Goode.

Is she really that hard up for money? Or does she like the idea of beating the Grand Wizard of the Ku Klux Klan into submission? Is that what this is all about? Or maybe it's some insane combination of the two. Maybe she's hard up for money and she likes the idea of beating him. No, that can't be true. She's got about seven thousand dollars. It can't be the money. Maybe she's just greedy and cold-hearted. She had the money and still sold me to Earl. If she could do that, it could be plain ol' greed. But what about the beatings? Why would she agree to that? Does beating him somehow excite her? I wonder. What am I racking my brain for? I could be thinking of a way to get Lucas over instead of dwelling on her and the weird things she does. I'll never understand her.

Johnnie heard some light tapping on the glass of her back door. When she looked up, she saw Sadie Lane looking at her through the glass. Sadie lifted a sweet potato pie so Johnnie could see it. Johnnie took another swallow of her coffee and went to the door.

"Hi, Sadie. Come on in."

"I hope I wasn't disturbing you."

"No, I was just doin' some thinkin'."

"I hope you like sweet potato pie," she said, placing it on the table. "I promised myself to bring you one and welcome you to the neighborhood when you moved in. You sure it's okay?"

"Yes. I could use some company, Sadie. Have a seat."

Sadie sat down at the table. Johnnie went over to the sink and pulled a butter knife and plates from the dish rack.

"So, what do you do for a living, Johnnie?" Sadie asked when she returned with the knife.

Sadie suspected that the white man she'd seen her with that first day was her sugar daddy. Since Johnnie was only sixteen, Sadie also guessed that he was the one who purchased the house. She just wanted her suspicions confirmed.

"Nothing yet, but I plan to get a job as soon as I can," Johnnie said, slicing the pie and placing a piece on each plate.

"Do you plan to work part-time after school, or what?" Sadie asked, attempting to ask personal questions as delicately as possible.

"I quit school, Sadie."

"May I ask why?"

Do I tell her the real reason why I quit? She'll probably think less of me if I do. "What good is it going to do me? When I graduate, what will I do then? Go to college? Even if I do that, what will I do afterwards?"

"There's plenty you could do. The neighborhood is full of professionals, Johnnie."

"Professional men, not women, Sadie."

"Well, we do have some women teachers in the neighborhood. There's also Lisa Cambridge, the owner of Cambridge Books and Publishing. And then there's Beverly and Michael Addison, who own the bakery on Main Street."

"I don't mean to be rude, Sadie, but didn't you say you were a maid the other day?"

Using her fork, Sadie took another piece of the pie and put it in her mouth. She was trying not to react negatively to Johnnie's obvious antagonism to her suggestion of doing something with her life.

"Yes, I'm a maid, but you don't have to be," she said softly. "I guess I was hoping that you wouldn't make the same mistakes that most black women make."

"What mistakes?"

"Settling for second best. Or deeper still, taking what we can get instead of becoming who we really want to be. I wanted to be a choreographer, but I ended up working for the Mancinis in the Garden District, and here I am. Look at me, I'm twenty-nine years old and I've got three children by Santino Mancini."

As Johnnie listened to her, she immediately felt a sort of kinship with Sadie. She wondered if this was something that happened to all black women. *Are we all destined to become whores for the white man? What is it about us that makes him want us so bad?*

"So, does Mr. Mancini pay for your home?"

"Yes. I assumed you were in the same boat with that white man I saw you with that day."

"I am," Johnnie said, suddenly ashamed.

"Well, I hope you're using protection."

"What do you mean, protection?"

"Johnnie, the last thing you want is to end up with that man's children. If you do, you can forget about any of those lofty dreams you have. And don't tell me you don't have them. I know you do."

"Lately I've been thinkin' about becoming a stockbroker."

"A stockbroker, huh?"

"Yes. Do you have any stocks in any of the major companies like Coke or Ford or General Motors?"

"No. Do you?"

"Yes, and I think there's a lot of money to be made doing it."

Sadie shook her head in amazement, unable to believe how much further ahead Johnnie was in her thinking than she was at that age or even now. She laughed a little and said, "I came over here to give you some advice, but it seems as though you should be giving me advice."

"Maybe we can advise each other, Sadie. I know a few things you don't, and you obviously know some things I don't."

"Like what, Johnnie?"

"Like how to talk like white folks, for one. And two, what is this protection business?"

"You mean your mother never told you how not to get pregnant?"

Johnnie shook her head. She considered telling her how she and Earl came to know one another, but thought better of it.

"So, Marguerite never discussed the birds and the bees with you?"

141

"No, but I know some stuff that girls in school told me."

"Did they tell you what prophylactics are?"

Johnnie shook her head. She felt stupid for not knowing what was obvious to Sadie. She wanted to ask her a thousand questions. *Mama was right. Sadie is a woman I can learn a lot from. How can she be so right about people and at the same time be so wrong about everything else?*

"Listen, Johnnie, anything you want to know, I'll be glad to tell you. If you don't mind being a maid until you become a stockbroker, I can probably get you a job with the Beauregards. They live next door to the Mancinis."

Beauregards? Hmmm, I wonder if they're related to the same Beauregard that my grandmother used to see. If so, I would love to meet the white side of the family and get to know them too. I could work for them and learn all about them, and they would never know who I am.

"I don't mean to be rude, Sadie, but if you knew about protection, why didn't you protect yourself from pregnancy?"

"I knew you were going to ask me that," Sadie said, shaking her head slowly. "The first one was an accident. But after that, he wanted more children with me. Santino said he loved me and that he would take care of us for the rest of our lives. In other words, I took the easy way out. I just hope you do something different with your life. I haven't had a real relationship in so long that I've practically given up on the idea. So, I just try to make the best of what I have with Santino until something better comes along. But then I think . . . who's going to want me when I've got three kids to take care of? Besides, Santino would never let me go. He really does love me."

"What is with these white men that they have to come to colored women for happiness?"

"It isn't just the white men, Johnnie. The colored men are doin' the same thing right here in Ashland Estates.

When a man falls for a woman, I mean truly falls for a woman, he loves her for life, just like a woman. The trouble with men is most don't truly fall in love with the women they marry."

"Then why do they marry them, Sadie?"

"I don't know, but I have a theory. You wanna hear it?"

"Yeah," Johnnie said, feeling closer to her as the conversation progressed.

"I think men look for a woman they think is chaste and kind and a good homemaker, ignoring her sexual propensities. And when—"

"What does propensities mean?"

"Interests, or inclinations."

"Oh, okay," said Johnnie, looking at her with admiring eyes.

"What?" Sadie asked, wondering why she was looking at her like that.

"You're so much smarter than I am. I mean, you know all these big words and stuff. I wish I could talk like you do. You know, talk white."

"First of all, it isn't talking white. It's being able to speak the King's English with proper diction."

"You mean diction, as in dictionary?"

"No, I mean to use precise pronunciation. As for big words, all you need do is read. And when you come to words you don't understand, don't just keep reading in a futile attempt to understand them in the sentence. Take the time to develop a vocabulary of your own."

"Okay, Sadie," Johnnie said, feeling like a pupil with a new teacher who has taken a personal interest in her.

"Now, back to my theory. When a man marries a woman, he thinks very little about his sex life with her because she's going to be the mother of his children. For that reason, he puts her on some pseudo throne that she

143

doesn't belong on. She wants sex just like he does but she can't tell him that because the moment she does, he'll look at her differently. Husbands often think their wives are simply giving into sex because he wants it. In many cases it's true, but that's only because she's given up on ever being a liberated sexual being."

"Sadie, you sho' got a way with words."

"Well, thank you. But if you ever start reading books, you'll have a way with them too."

"You think so?"

"Sure. Now, is there anything you want to know about sex, Johnnie?"

"Yes, but first I want you to help me get the job with the Beauregards. And could you . . . this is really kind of embarrassing, but can you tell me what a dildo is?"

Chapter 35
"The Pay-Off"

Marguerite, overcome by deep-seated jealousy, was sitting in her Oldsmobile waiting for Richard Goode in the parking lot of a Cajun restaurant on the outskirts of town. All she could think about was how her sixteen-year-old daughter had bettered her. Johnnie had a nice house and Marguerite thought she deserved one too. After all, she had earned it, she told herself. If she was going to get a nice house like that, she was going to have to take some drastic steps. Marguerite threatened to tell the *Sentinel*, a liberal New Orleans newspaper, of Richard Goode's double life as the Grand Wizard preacher who regularly sleeps with a known black whore, if he didn't fork over twenty-five thousand dollars.

Goode quickly agreed to pay her off. He couldn't afford to have the Klan know of his flagrant hypocrisy. He had led them to believe that race mixing was not only evil, but no self-respecting white man would ever do such a thing. When he was asked why so many well-to-do white men did it during slavery, he explained it was necessary to create more mud people to increase profits. Since slavery was over, there was no need to create more mud people who would only end up dependent on good white Christians for their survival.

Goode told her he would pay her, but their relationship was over. Marguerite suggested meeting at their usual corner, but Goode refused that or the Savoy. He told her that not only didn't he trust her, he didn't trust Simmons or any other nigger anymore. Goode went on to tell her that if she could blackmail him, so could Simmons for the same reasons.

Marguerite smoked a cigarette while she waited and daydreamed about the kind of house she would buy in Ashland Estates. Johnnie told her that Earl paid twenty-five thousand for her house, and she hoped she could get one similar to hers for the same amount. Marguerite could see Goode's dark blue Chevrolet in her rearview mirror. Goode slowed down enough for her to see that it was him. She started the car and followed him. They drove about twenty minutes south of the restaurant on a dark road. Finally, Goode pulled over and got out of the car. He was holding a duffel bag. Anxious to get the money he promised, Marguerite got out of the Oldsmobile and walked over to Goode with a bright smile.

"Hi, Richard, honey." Marguerite laughed. "Just to show you there's no hard feelin's, I'll give you one last spanking on the house."

"Get in the car, bitch!"

Marguerite laughed a little more. She thought he was just playing his role as the dominant white man like they had done a hundred times before. She blinked twice when he pulled out the German Luger. She stared at the gun as though seeing a mirage.

"Get in, bitch!" he snarled and hit her in the head with the gun.

The blunt blow sent her reeling as a wave of blackness washed over her. She staggered like an old boxer fighting to maintain balance, and lost when her knees buckled. Marguerite heard another thump then she felt the pain just before crumbling to the ground. She could feel blood running down the side of her face. Desperate and weakened by the abrupt blows, she tried to crawl away from her brutal attacker.

"You black bitch!" Goode shouted and kicked her in the side as she crawled. "Did you really think you could blackmail me?"

"I didn't mean it! I didn't mean it!" Marguerite shouted, her mouth full of salty blood.

Goode kicked her again and she fell onto her back.

"Please don't kill me, Mr. Goode," Marguerite pleaded. "Please don't kill me! I'll do whatever you want! I won't tell nobody! I swear I won't! Just don't kill me!"

Goode walked over to her and kicked her in the face. Marguerite could feel the side of her face swell like a helium-filled balloon. Somehow, she was able to get back on all fours. Her heart was pounding from intense fear. She crawled over to where he was standing and grabbed his boot, holding on for dear life.

"Beat me, Mr. Goode! But don't kill me!"

Goode reached down and grabbed her blouse, pulling her limp body forward with each blow he delivered with the Luger. The beating was so severe that blood began to spurt from her broken nose. Lying on the ground, unable to move and barely conscious, Marguerite realized he would kill her no matter what. Her only chance was to try to get the gun from him, but she was too debilitated.

"Get up, you black nigger bitch!"

Marguerite tried to lift her head, but couldn't. She knew she only had one chance to get the gun. She hoped he would come closer so she could try.

Goode stooped to see if she was conscious. When he

tried to pick her up to continue the beating, Marguerite reached for the gun. She was so weak, all she could do was get her hand on it. He snatched the gun away with ease and backhanded her with it. She fell backward to the ground again. This time she was out cold. He went over to her car and let the air out of the driver's side front tire. He wanted it to look like she had gotten a flat. That way, people would think someone came along and killed her.

But Sheriff Tate was sitting in his squad car watching it all. Tate had followed Marguerite to the Cajun restaurant without being spotted. He felt powerless to do anything now. The Klan was powerful. Tate was afraid that if he did anything, it would give the Klan a reason to go on a rampage, maybe even kill him and his family. He sat in his squad car, hoping Goode wouldn't kill Margurite.

By the time Goode got back to Marguerite, she was conscious again, trying to crawl away. He kicked her in the side and she fell onto her back again. He put the Luger to her forehead and looked into her eyes. The terror he saw in them gave him a rush.

"Please, Mr. Goode," she pleaded through bloody lips that had swollen to twice their original size. "Don't kill me. Please don't —"

Without mercy, Goode squeezed the trigger while she was still pleading, and ended her life. Pow! Then he got into his car and slowly drove away.

Sheriff Tate's body jerked violently when he heard the shot and saw a quick flash of light. He knew Marguerite was dead and he wept.

Chapter 36

"I don't believe what I'm hearin'."

Johnnie was in bed when the pounding on her front door rudely ripped her out of a deep, peaceful sleep. Startled, she opened her eyes and saw swirling red lights through the sheer curtains in her bedroom. She turned the lamp on and looked at the clock. It was 4:30. The pounding began again. *What's going on?* Johnnie walked over to the window and looked out. There was a police car in front of her house and a horde of people gathering on her lawn. The pounding continued. After putting on a robe and slippers, she went downstairs, fearing she was about to be put out of her house or something.

Maybe the deed is a fake. What has Earl gotten me into? This is probably somebody's house or something.

As she approached the door, the pounding began again, but it sounded much louder than it had upstairs. When she opened the door, she saw Sheriff Tate and Shirley, Marguerite's neighbor. Without being told, she knew something had happened to her mother.

In a nervous panic, Johnnie asked, "What's wrong? What's happened? Did something happen to my mother? Is she all right?" Her words were rushed and filled with fear. No one said anything. They all just looked at her, hoping they

149

wouldn't have to say aloud what they knew. Johnnie's lips quivered. "Is she dead?"

Johnnie's late night visitors bowed their heads when they heard the question. No one wanted to be the bearer of such tragic news. They all felt genuine sorrow; especially Sheriff Tate. He had known and loved Marguerite for more than two decades.

"No, God. Not Mama. No," Johnnie kept saying between sobs. Feeling a sudden emptiness in the pit of her stomach, she fell to her knees. Shirley helped her to her feet and held her tightly in her bosom, rocking her as the two women cried together. "What happened?" Johnnie asked, confused and overwhelmed with emotion.

"I know this is a difficult time, Johnnie," Sheriff Tate said, but you have to identify the body."

"Sheriff Tate," Johnnie began. "You know my mother. Didn't you see her?"

"Yes, but we need a member of the family to make a positive ID."

"How did it happen, Sheriff?" Johnnie asked.

"She had a flat tire and it looks like somebody came along and killed her."

"But why, Sheriff?" Johnnie asked. "Who would want to hurt her?" After the words found their way out of her mouth, it came to her. She knew who killed Marguerite. Robert Simmons told her about the affair with Richard Goode. He also warned her of the consequences if it ever became public. "It was Richard Goode!" Johnnie shouted, unable to contain her sudden anger. "I know it was him. He was the only one it could have been."

"Uh, uh, we better go inside, Johnnie," Sheriff Tate said, surprised by her knowledge of the relationship.

Sadie, who was a part of the gathering crowd, and Shirley helped Johnnie to the couch. Her legs weak from the news, Johnnie felt as if she would faint with each step.

"Johnnie," Sheriff Tate continued, "you have to be careful what you say in front of people."

"Why, Sheriff?" Johnnie shouted. "You know I'm right, don't you? You know he did it, don't you?"

Sheriff Tate bowed his head again and wept. "I knew your mother. I knew her before you were even born. I know your brother Benny too. I loved that woman. I did," he said. "But we have to keep our heads about this. What's done is done. We can't bring her back."

Sadie and Shirley looked at each other, stunned by what they were hearing. Shirley knew Marguerite still entertained men at night, but she didn't know who they were.

"So, what the hell are you going to do about it, Sheriff?" Sadie demanded.

"There's nothing we can do."

"What do you mean there's nothing we can do?" Shirley asked.

"Listen to me," Sheriff Tate said, almost pleading. "What do you think'll happen if I accuse, or anyone else accuses the preacher of murder? What do you think the Coloreds are gonna do? I'll tell you what they'll do. They'll demand Goode be arrested. And if I do that, you know what's next, don't you? That's right. It'll be a race riot like you've never seen. Hell, even decent white folks won't stand for it. They won't allow a white man to be arrested for killing a colored woman without eyewitnesses. If I told what I know, everything is going to come out; her prostituting herself, my relationship with her, them meeting at the Savoy hotel, everything. And even if I arrested him on suspicion, do you really think any jury is going to convict him? The district attorney will get an all-white jury and set him free. In the meantime, colored men, women and children will be dragged out of their homes and beaten, maybe even killed. My family

151

could be killed too. We have to be practical about this. We can pursue justice if you want to, but the truth is, Goode will have to answer to God for his crime, as do we all."

"I think you should arrest him, Sheriff," Sadie said. "At least the people will know what kind of man their so-called preacher is. And he'll know everyone knows he killed a colored woman that he was sleeping with. Maybe the Klan will denounce him. If they do, we can get him then."

"No. He's right," Johnnie said, much more composed and calculating.

"What?" Shirley and Sadie shouted in unison.

"Don't you see?" Johnnie continued. "We haven't had a Klan uprisin' in years, since I was four or five."

"I don't believe what I'm hearin'," Shirley said.

"Shirley, what will the Klan do if they find out their leader was seeing a black woman regularly at the Savoy Hotel? I know y'all know what goes on there."

"How can you be so nonchalant?" Sadie asked. "Your mother is dead. Killed by the Grand Wizard of the Ku Klux Klan. You don't want to do anything about it?"

"Of course I wanna do something about it, Sadie, but we gotta look at the big picture," Johnnie said, no longer crying. Her eyes were full of cold, calculating rage now. "You know what's going to happen if Sheriff Tate arrests him? Don't you realize none of us'll be safe? They'll come in our neighborhood and kill and burn everything and everybody. No, we gotta handle this quietly. Goode will get his."

Johnnie would never admit it, but she was actually relieved now that her mother was dead. Although she had her own place, she still felt her mother's powerful influence. Now that was over. Johnnie was finally free of her. Nevertheless, anger and guilt consumed her. She knew it was wrong for a daughter to be glad that her own mother was dead, but that was exactly how she felt. Still she was angry that a white man could kill her mother or any other black woman for that matter, and nothing would be done about it. Worse yet, she knew the sheriff was right. What he was saying made a lot of sense.

Why endanger the lives of all the black men, women, and children of New Orleans when nothing can bring my mother back? Why provoke a race riot that would not only cost innocent lives, but would no doubt destroy businesses and quite possibly the entire black community? I may have to pretend like I don't know who murdered my mother now, but as God is my witness, one way or another, I'm gonna see to it that Richard Goode gets his.

Chapter 37
"I'm ready now."

Back home in her childhood house, Johnnie searched Marguerite's bedroom for a Buchanan Mutual insurance policy. While she searched, she couldn't shake the sight of Marguerite on a slab in the cold, poorly lit basement of the city morgue. As she opened each drawer, she continued to see flashes of her mother's battered and bruised body. The coroner read off a litany of contusions and lacerations found on her face and body.

Marguerite had a broken nose, a broken jaw, missing teeth, broken ribs, and a punctured lung. According to the coroner, Marguerite would have probably died from the head injuries alone. Her head looked as if it had been beaten with a baseball bat. The bullet in her brain saved her from an agonizing death.

The coroner's comments made Marguerite's quick death sound like it was some sort of consolation prize. The only thing that made Johnnie feel better was the knowledge of her brother's imminent return to New Orleans. She hadn't seen Benny and Brenda in years and longed to see her nephew, Jericho. Nevertheless, Johnnie wondered how she would explain what had been going on since Benny moved to San Francisco. Her brother wouldn't understand how she could be living in Ashland Estates while their mother still lived in the ghetto. Johnnie had a lot to explain.

Maybe I can just move back home until the funeral is over. That way, I don't have to explain anything. But what if he asks me to move to San Francisco with him? What do I do then? He could try to make me leave.

Am I becoming my mother? Have I become greedy just like her? Why not move out West? I could leave this life and start all over. No one knows me out there. Yeah, and that's the problem. I can learn the stock market business if I stay. I don't know any stockbrokers out there. I'm just starting to make my mark here. I'll leave when I have enough money and a career to go out West; not before.

I'll just have to convince him I can handle things on my own here. What if he asks me how I'm going to live? What will I say? I better think of something. Oh, I know. The insurance money. It should be worth about ten or fifteen thousand dollars. Sadie said she could get me a job as a maid. I'll tell him I'm going to wait until I graduate, then move to San Francisco. I'll tell him I'm going to work after school to help support myself. He'll think I'm very mature for my age and let me stay. He'll have to.

"Ah, here it is," Johnnie said aloud. "I wonder what it's worth."

She pulled the papers from the faded yellow envelope and unfolded them. She skimmed the policy, looking for the amount.

"Fifteen thousand," she said, feeling good. "This'll take care of the funeral and whatever bills need to be paid."

The screen door, badly in need of oil, screeched when it opened. Johnnie could hear it from her mother's bedroom. She was suddenly reminded of her first encounter with Earl in that very room. Someone knocked. Johnnie went to the door and moved the curtain to see who it was. She smiled

155

when she saw Lucas standing there with a red rose.

"Hi, Lucas," she said, surprised and excited. "You're a sight for sore eyes. Where have you been?"

"I've been around, Johnnie," Lucas said solemnly. "It's just hard to find you since you moved out. I don't have your address or anything."

"Well, come on in and have a seat. I'll write down the address and phone number for you."

Lucas hesitated. Although he knew Marguerite was dead, he remembered the tongue-lashing her mother gave him the last time he came to her house. After realizing how silly it was to keep standing there, he entered the room and sat down on the couch. A few moments later, Johnnie came back with a piece of paper and handed it to him.

"Is that for me?" Johnnie asked, referring to the rose.

"Yes," he said, offering it to her. "I forgot I had it in my hand."

She took the rose and smelled it.

"Ummm. Where did you get it?"

"In the Quarter at Charlie's flower shop."

Johnnie kissed him on the cheek and thanked him.

"I'm sorry about what happened to your mother, Johnnie. Does the sheriff have any idea who did it?"

"No," Johnnie said, fearing that if she told him the truth, he would do something foolish and get himself killed. She hugged Lucas and said, "I'm glad you're here. Lucas, do you know how to drive?"

"Yep."

"Can you teach me? I had my mother's car towed here, but I don't know how to drive. I need to go to Fletcher's funeral home. Will you drive me?"

"I'll be glad to, Johnnie," Lucas said and held her tight. "Whenever you're ready, okay?"

"I'm ready now. Let's go."

Chapter 38

"But thanks anyway"

Johnnie and Lucas were greeted at the door by a ghastly-looking colored man wearing a black suit and tie. When he smiled, his false teeth gave him the appearance of a meek Garden District butler. He led them to Mason Fletcher's office, where they waited for arrival of the funeral director. The office walls were strewn with artwork of Eli Whitney, Harriet Tubman, Sojourner Truth, Marcus Garvey, and Dr. Charles Drew. Fletcher's desk was made of solid oak and glistened. There was a small plaque on his desk with a quote from Frederick Douglass that read: *Learn trades or starve.* Hand carved onyx figurines of Booker T. Washington and Nat Turner sat on both sides of the plaque. The wall to wall burgundy carpet was so thick that walking on it left temporary footprints.

After the ghastly-looking colored man with the false teeth left them, they casually walked around the room, reading each caption under the pictures.

It wasn't long before Mason Fletcher walked into his office and greeted them with an undertaker's smile and a firm handshake. He was wearing a light gray double-breasted suit with a gray tie and shoes. Mason Fletcher was of average height, thin, with graying temples. He wore a well-

157

groomed salt-and-pepper beard. He eased into his leather chair and gestured for them to sit down. They did.

"Ms. Wise, I'm sorry for your loss, and I assure you we here at Fletcher Funeral Home will do our utmost to see to it that your mother is laid to rest in the manner you deem appropriate."

"Thank you, Mr. Fletcher," Johnnie said with tear-filled eyes.

Mason reached into his pocket and handed her his white handkerchief. Johnnie took it from him and wiped her eyes.

"I'm sorry. I just can't seem to stop crying when I think of her."

"We understand, don't we, mister—"

"Matthews, and yes, we do," Lucas said, holding Johnnie firmly.

"Well, what do you have to offer, Mr. Fletcher?" Johnnie asked.

"Why don't I show you some of our caskets and then we can talk about a price."

They went into the parlor, where he kept twenty or so caskets. As they looked at each casket, Fletcher described its features, offering more details about the more expensive caskets.

"Mr. Fletcher, have you seen my mother?"

"Yes, I have."

"Will you be able to make her look like she did . . . before?"

"Yes, but it will be expensive."

He's going to try to get as much money out of me as he can. "I have to tell you that I don't have much money."

"I'm sure we can work something out, Ms. Wise."

After looking at all the caskets and hearing his sales pitch on each, Fletcher recommended one of the more expensive caskets, just as Johnnie knew he would. She decided to go with a less expensive one that was the same powder blue color as Marguerite's car.

"So, how much is this going to cost me, Mr. Fletcher?" Johnnie asked.

"Depends on what you want," Fletcher said.

"How much does the average funeral cost?" Lucas asked, feeling like he had to say something, although he was impressed by Johnnie's command of the situation.

"Anywhere from two thousand to ten thousand," Fletcher said in such a way that it didn't sound like a lot of money. "You know your mother. What would she want?"

"Well, she always told me it was a waste of money to spend anything more than a thousand dollars on a funeral. I'm sure we can't afford your prices, Mr. Fletcher. Sorry to waste your time."

"Don't be so hasty," Fletcher said. "I told you we can work something out. Can you afford eighteen hundred?"

"I can afford twelve."

"What about fifteen?"

"Throw the tomb in and you've got a deal."

"Deal," Fletcher said and extended his hand to shake Johnnie's.

Johnnie shook on the deal, but Fletcher held on to her hand a little longer than he should have, nodding slightly and smiling lecherously. Johnnie got the feeling that if she offered herself to him, the price would be considerably less, perhaps nothing at all.

"I'll check on you in a couple of days to see how you're holding up, Ms. Wise."

"No need, Mr. Fletcher," Johnnie said, picking up on the hint. "I have Lucas to lean on when I feel weak. But thanks anyway."

159

Chapter 39
"A Streetcar Named . . ."

The couple spent the entire day together, going from store to store, looking for a dress to wear to the funeral. Johnnie found a black dress, a hat with a veil, black shoes, a black pearl necklace, and a black purse. Lucas, like most men who shopped with women, was bored and frustrated by the endless shopping, and the New Orleans heat made him even more impatient. Johnnie, however, had no idea how frustrated he was because Lucas never let her see it. He was her friend and she needed him.

When they finished shopping, they ate lunch and drank ice cold lemonade in Jackson Square. Johnnie and Lucas were eating Poboys sandwiches they had purchased from Mr. Big Stuff's restaurant. Johnnie told Lucas her plan to get her brother to let her stay in New Orleans.

Lucas didn't want her to leave any more than she did. Although he thought her plan would work, the possibility of it not working and losing her terrified him. He had fallen hard for Johnnie, and believed she had sincere feelings for him too.

It was dark now. The muggy heat felt like a ball and chain they had to carry from place to place. Having been scorched all day, they decided to go to an air-conditioned theater to get out of the sweltering heat. They didn't care what movie was playing. They just wanted to enjoy the cool air, if only for a couple of hours. *A Street Car Named Desire* was being shown at a local theatre.

While the movie played, Lucas found himself thinking intensely about Johnnie's success, which troubled him. *I don't even have a job and Johnnie already has her own house. She even has stocks and shit. And she's got plenty of money. She even bought me a new suit. She paid for the movie tickets, the popcorn, and the soda. How am I going to keep her happy without any money? Earl buys her everything. What can I buy her that she doesn't already have? Nothing! Instead, I'm stealing roses from the Quarter to give to her. I've got to do something to impress her. I gotta get a job or she'll never leave that cracker!*

Johnnie was deeply engrossed in the film version of the Tennessee Williams play. The Blanche Dubois character, brilliantly brought to life by Vivien Leigh, mesmerized her. It was like watching her future being portrayed for all to see. She understood Blanche Dubois because in many ways, their lives were mirror images of each other. Both women started their lives one way and ended up another. Both women possessed haughty ideas about themselves and were brought down to a baseness that was uncharacteristic of how they saw themselves. Both women had to lie to themselves to keep at least a measure of respectability.

Johnnie wondered if she too would end up like Blanche Dubois, a used-up woman whose beauty was fading to black, after opening many doors that were now closed; a woman who had it all and lost it; a woman who was desperate to find somebody, anybody to accept and take care of her despite her depraved past. Blanche's tragic end was a malignant insanity, brought about by a self-righteousness that turned her world of base sexual activity into a magical

161

kingdom, complete with a straight-jacket and a rubber room. As the credits rolled, a river of tears ran down Johnnie's face. She wiped her eyes with the napkins she picked up at the popcorn and soda stand.

They walked to the car quietly, both of them in deep thought. Johnnie was still comparing her life to that of Blanche Dubois and even her mother's, wondering if she, too, would end up dead in this dog eat dog world. She felt insecure for the first time in a while. With her mother gone, all she had left was Earl, the man who started her on the path she was on, and Lucas, who was so smitten with her he accepted her as she was. Johnnie decided she would hold on to Lucas for as long as he wanted her.

Chapter 40

"What happened?"

"Johnnie, you wanna drive?" Lucas asked.

"Now?" Johnnie asked, snapping out of her thoughts.

"No time like the present, as they say."

"You sure?"

"Yeah," Lucas said, reassuring her. "I learned to drive at night too. It's easier. Less traffic."

"Okay," Johnnie said, suddenly invigorated.

When Lucas got out of the car and walked around to the other side, Johnnie slid over behind the wheel. She had carefully watched him drive all day. Even though she was nervous, she believed she could do it.

"I gotta push the pedal here every time I shift, right?"

"Yeah. It's called the clutch," Lucas said. "The hardest part to learn is how to take off. Put your foot on the clutch and the brake at the same time." She did. "Now shift into first."

"Where's first at?" Johnnie asked, grabbing the stick.

"Look at the knob on the stick."

She did.

"See the drawing?"

"Uh-huh."

"That tells you where all the gears are."

"So, first is straight up?"

"Yeah."

"You want me to put it in first now?"

"Yeah."

She tried to move the stick up, but it wouldn't move. Confused, Johnnie said, "It won't move, Lucas."

"That's because you in neutral," he said, finally feeling like he had something to contribute to their wonderful day together. "First is over, then up."

"Okay." She moved the stick over, then up. She felt the car ease forward just a bit. A broad smile flashed across her face. "Now what?"

"Take your foot off the pedal and the brake."

She did, and the car jerked forward a couple of times then stalled.

"What happened?" she asked, confused.

"I just wanted you to see what happens if you don't have your foot on either the clutch or the brake. To keep that from happening again, you have to take your foot off the brake and put it on the gas pedal."

"Okay," Johnnie said nervously. "You want me to do it now?"

"Yeah.

She did.

"Now press on the gas and ease off the clutch at the same time."

She tried, but the engine revved loudly.

"That's okay," Lucas said. "Everybody does that. That's why I wanted you to see what happens when you do it wrong. Try again."

She did. This time Johnnie lifted her foot off the clutch too fast. The car jerked forward and stalled again.

"Don't worry about it," Lucas said. "You'll get it. Just keep trying."

Johnnie started the car for the third time, determined to get it right this time. She eased off the clutch, pressing the gas just enough to go forward without stalling. She was elated.

Lucas had her stop the car and start it about twenty times in the parking lot before he was sure she could do it consistently.

Johnnie felt confident now too.

"Well, you ready to get on the road?" Lucas asked.

"Yeah," Johnnie said, exhilarated.

"Just remember to clutch and shift. Clutch and shift, okay?"

"Okay."

Chapter 41
"You all right?"

After an hour or so of almost flawless driving, Johnnie asked Lucas if he wanted see her house. Johnnie only stalled once on the way to Ashland Estates, but she was getting better as they drove, clutching and shifting all the way, feeling for the first time in a while like the teenager she was. She turned onto Imagination Drive then into her driveway. She stopped the car and kept the engine running while Lucas opened the garage door.

He twisted the handle and heard the metal on the inside slide over and lock into place. Then he raised the door and got out of the way. Lucas closed the garage door after Johnnie drove the car in, and they went into the house.

"Would you like something to drink?" Johnnie asked as they walked into the kitchen.

"Yeah, what do you have?"

She opened the refrigerator and looked inside. "I've got Coke, water, and orange juice. You know what? I think I should invest in one of the Florida orange companies. I think I will."

"I'll have a Coke," he said ruefully.

Sensing something was bothering him, Johnnie said, "What's wrong, Lucas? Didn't you have fun today?"

"Yeah, Johnnie," he said, still somber. "But it bothers me that you paid for everything. You've got this big house in this rich neighborhood. You got all these stocks and money. I ain't even got two nickels to rub together."

Seeing the dissappoinment in his eyes and wanting to reassure him, she took his hand into hers and kissed it. "Lucas, when you put your trust in me that day at the school park, I told you then I would be your girl, didn't I?"

"Yes, you did, but it don't make me feel like a man when you got money and I don't."

"You wanna buy me things like the rose you gave me today. I understand. But if it bothers you that much, maybe you should get a job after school. You graduate in June anyway. You gotta get a job sometime."

Lucas bowed his head when she mentioned the stolen rose. He thought since they were on the subject, he might as well 'fess up. "Listen, Johnnie. You know that rose I gave you?"

"Yes."

"I stole it."

"What?" she said, a little shocked. "Lucas, you didn't have to do that."

"That's just it, Johnnie. I feel like I do. Here you are livin' high on the hog in this big beautiful house. You got money, a house, and a car—everything. What do I have to offer you? Nothin', that's what. I'm thinkin' if I don't do something, you ain't gon' wanna be with me."

"Lucas, don't you realize you're the only person in my life that cares for me—the real me? I need you, Lucas. Please don't be ashamed. I've decided that you're who I want and no one else. As far as I'm concerned, I'm yours as long as you want me."

"For real?"

"For real," Johnnie assured him and stretched her neck

up to kiss him.

They embraced each other as their desire increased. Little by little, the kiss became deeper until finally, their sexual urges took over. Out of control, they pulled and tugged at each other's clothes. Lucas opened her blouse and unhooked her black bra. He lifted the cups and took her silver dollar-sized nipples into his hungry mouth. A sigh found its way out of her open mouth as her neck relaxed and fell backward. The taste of her nipple made him bite down ever so gently, yet with ravenous yearning.

Johnnie's sighs were coming at regular intervals. She had never felt anything like what she was feeling now, not even in her lust-filled fantasies about him. Johnnie took his face into her soft hands and licked his lips. She could feel his powerful erection against her pelvis. He pulled her even closer with a crushing, passionate embrace that made her feel safe. Suddenly, she pulled away.

"What's wrong?" Lucas said desperately.

"Let's go upstairs."

Lucas wanted her right there, but he agreed and they left the kitchen. Before they could get upstairs, he turned her around and kissed her deeply again.

Johnnie knew he would take her soon, but she wanted to get in the bed. She pulled away and ran upstairs, knowing he'd come after her. She laughed when she heard him run behind her.

They rushed up the stairs, their lust ever growing. Johnnie ducked into the bedroom and let him catch her. She pulled off Lucas' T-shirt then finished removing her blouse and bra. When he saw her breasts, the blood flow to his member increased.

Lucas was powerfully built with thick, muscled biceps, a deep chest and a rippling abdomen. When he took off his pants, his hard rod bulged outward. They watched each other pull off their underwear, admiring each other's bodies.

Johnnie's eyes dropped to his throbbing rod. It was long and thick. Just looking at it made her want him inside her even more. She was extremely wet now. "I have something for you," Johnnie said, breaking the silence.

"What?"

"A prophylactic."

"A what?"

"You know. A condom. A rubber."

"Oh, okay."

She went over to the nightstand and pulled one out. After handing it to him, she slid into bed and waited for him.

Lucas opened the condom, slid it down as far as he could, and got in bed, climbing on top of her. He looked at the headboard and saw the winged angels blowing their trumpets. He moved his thick member around until he found her opening and pushed himself in. She was still tight to him, even being as wet as she was. He pushed forward. Her moan was soft but sounded a little pained.

"You all right?" he asked, concerned about her comfort.

"Yes," she said.

He gently pushed forward a little more, not wanting to cause any more pain.

Johnnie clenched her teeth as he went further and deeper inside. Right away, she began to compare the only two men she had ever known. Lucas was much bigger, she thought.

Finally, he was in as far as he could go, and with each stroke, the pain subsided more and more until she felt pleasure. She began to moan, softly at first, then louder and much more uncontrolled. The exquisite pleasure overwhelmed her. She wrapped her legs around his waist and met each of his thrusts with her own. Her hips were so strong that when she pumped, she was almost lifting them both off the bed.

Johnnie felt herself reaching an orgasm and kept the same furious pace until she exploded violently. She could feel Lucas' heart pounding through his chest. His thrusts continued at a feverish pace. Johnnie kept pace with him until finally, he too exploded violently. As his breathing returned to normal, she urged him to get up and take the rubber off.

Lucas went into the adjacent bathroom and flushed the condom down the toilet. He looked at himself in the mirror and smiled triumphantly. He had made love with Johnnie and it was great. But his sexual thirst hadn't been quenched, so he went back into the bedroom and grabbed another condom.

Chapter 42

"I have some terrible news."

Having extinguished the fire that burned in them, Johnnie and Lucas lay in bed exhausted, looking up at the ceiling. Johnnie contemplated the differences between Earl and Lucas, wondering if it was the size that made the difference. Then it came to her. It wasn't the size at all. It was how she felt about the two men. Sex with Earl was an obligation. Sex with Lucas was even more pleasurable than masturbation because it wasn't just the climax that made the experience mind-blowing. It was the taste of his kiss, the warmth of his body, the intoxicating scent of him, and the flavor he emitted. She cared for Lucas, but she didn't feel the same way for Earl, so quite naturally, she deduced it would be better with a man she cared about.

I wonder if I'm in love with Lucas. Is this what love feels like? Is sex supposed to feel this way? I hope Lucas enjoyed it. I want to be a good lover to him. I want us to be together forever. I guess I do love him if I—

"You thinkin' about your mom, Johnnie?"

"No. I was thinking about you," she said and faced him. "Am I a good lover, Lucas?"

"Yes."

"You mean it?" Johnnie asked, desperately wanting to

171

please him.

"Yes, the best ever."

Johnnie resisted the urge to ask him how many women he'd had. She feared that if she asked him, he could ask her. Even though she had only been with Earl, Martin Winters would be coming by for a date one day soon.

"Lucas, do you think I'll end up like Blanche Dubois?"

"I was hoping that movie didn't bother you, Johnnie."

"You were?"

"Yes. I watched that story and I was thinkin', boy, we picked the wrong day to go to the movies."

"Well, to tell you the truth, I did feel like that was me up there on the screen. I felt so sorry for that woman."

"I didn't."

"You didn't?"

"Hell naw."

"Why?"

"As long as colored folks have to fear white folks, I don't give a damn what happens to 'em. You think they care about us? Everywhere we go we gotta wait until they're finished then take whatever they don't want. Like tonight. We have to sit in the balcony if we wanna see a movie. Why? Because they don't wanna sit up there."

"Next time, let's just go to the Sepia Theater on Main Street. Then we can sit wherever you want."

"Okay, but the shit just pisses me off, ya know. Like if we want something as simple as a drink of water, we have to drink from a rusted fountain. And where's the fountain? Right next to a clean, sparkling white fountain. If they don't want us to drink the same water from the same fountain, fine. But why does our fountain have to be rusted and theirs in perfect workin' condition? When we get books at our school, how come the white folks had it first? How come we gotta bow our heads and worry about shit that don't even cross their minds? And how come they can have sex with our women but we cain't have sex with theirs?"

Lucas realized he shouldn't have said that, but it was too late. It had already slipped out. He quickly changed the subject, hoping he didn't hurt her feelings.

"I'll tell you something else too, Johnnie. Wasn't no colored man that killed your mother either."

"Who do you think did it?" Johnnie asked, wondering what his suspicions were.

"Everybody knows it was a white man that did it. Who else would do something like that? What is the sheriff doin' about it, huh? Nothin', I'll bet. All them crackers are alike. Killin' colored folk when it suits they fancy. Stringin' up colored men for lookin' at they precious white women. I'll tell you somethin' else too. If the white woman is so precious, why cain't he leave our women alone? How come he don't sow his seeds in her? Make her pregnant. Did you know Ashland Estates is full of colored maids that the white man keeps? It's like his own little harem out here."

The telephone rang.

"Hello."

"Johnnie," Earl whispered, "I've got some terrible news."

Johnnie looked at Lucas and put her forefinger to her lips. Lucas looked at her and curled his lips, then sucked his teeth.

"What's wrong, Earl?"

"I can't talk right now. I'm back in town and I'll be by tomorrow night to tell you all about it."

"Okay, Earl," Johnnie said. Just before she hung up the phone, she heard a second click, which puzzled her.

"See what I mean," Lucas said then got out of bed and went into the bathroom.

Chapter 43

"A woman does what she's gotta do."

After a couple of hours of vigorous lovemaking, Lucas and Johnnie held each other and lay quietly in bed. A cool wind found its way into the bedroom and dried the sweat on their naked bodies. They were quite comfortable, lying there, basking in the glow of physical love. So relaxed were they that they were on the edge of sleep. Suddenly, they were aroused from the stupor-like slumber when they heard the neighbors across the street yelling at the top of their lungs.

They got out of bed and went over to the window. Dennis Edwards, the local tailor, and Denise, his wife, were having a knock-down, drag-out argument about Dennis' whereabouts earlier that night. Denise accused him of sleeping with a maid, Lee Shepard, who lived two blocks away on Freedom Boulevard.

According to Sadie, everybody knew about the affair, but Dennis didn't care. Lee Shepard treated him the way he thought his Christian wife should. Whenever he went over to her house, she had a hot meal ready. She bathed and massaged him without having to be asked. Denise, on the other hand, was a pistol, finding something to complain about nearly every day. She gave him hell about the least little thing, constantly comparing him to her daddy, who had spoiled her to the point that few men would have been able to satisfy her.

"Ya been with that whore again, haven't you?" Denise said, pointing her finger in his face.

"Don't point your finger in my face!"

"I'll point my finger wherever I fuckin' please," Denise continued, her finger almost touching his nose.

"I said don't point your finger in my face!"

"What are you gonna do about it?"

"Denise, take your finger outta my face!"

"I can smell that bitch's scent on you, Dennis!" she yelled, still pointing her finger at the tip of his nose. "Yeah, I know you was with the bitch!"

Lucas and Johnnie were on their knees with their heads resting on their crossed arms, watching the fireworks in amazement. They could see everything through the open bedroom window. Dennis tried to grab his wife's finger but Denise moved it and pointed the other one in his face. When he tried to grab that one, she pointed the other. They went back and forth like this for several minutes, with Denise yelling, "She's a trampy-ass bitch!" over and over each time he grabbed at her finger. Frustrated, Dennis turned to leave. Denise grabbed his shoulders from behind and screamed, "Where you think you goin'?"

"I don't know, but I'm gettin' the fuck outta here!" Dennis said, shrugging his shoulders in a vain attempt to get her off.

"You ain't goin' no goddamned where!" Denise yelled, jumping on his back and wrapping her arms around his throat. "You stayin' here."

Dennis stumbled and took a few steps backward.

"You think I'ma let you leave so you can go back and fuck her some more? You gon' keep yo' black ass here and fuck me! That's what you gon' do!"

175

Denise wrapped her legs around Dennis' waist. As he struggled to break free, she tightened her grip. Dennis began spinning around in circles like a human top, hoping to make Denise dizzy, but she held on. The spinning made Dennis dizzy instead, and he stumbled backward again, falling onto the bed. Exhausted, he quit struggling. Denise loosened her grip and he rolled over. She stood up and looked down at her subdued husband, feeling like the queen of the Amazons. She undressed Dennis without opposition then she took off her robe and straddled him.

"Your mother was right, Lucas," Johnnie said with a laugh. "A woman does what she's gotta do."

Chapter 44

"Whatever you make is good."

Johnnie opened her eyes slowly, wondering if the previous night was another satisfying but empty fantasy. She smiled when she saw Lucas' massive arm wrapped around her waist. His embrace made her feel safe, and for the first time she felt wanted for who she was. Most men only saw a beautiful peach that was ready to be plucked; they didn't know she had the capacity to make them feel the kind of love that comes along once in a lifetime. The warmth of Lucas' naked body against hers made her want the moment to go on forever. She knew it wouldn't, but she wanted it to last as long as possible.

I wonder if Lucas will be able to handle this relationship and the things I have to do. I hope he can, because I really like him. I like the way he did it to me last night. It felt so good, so real. I wonder if it will be like that every time. I can't believe how many times I came. Earl doesn't make me come unless I think about Lucas. But with Lucas, I'm free to be myself. I can relax and enjoy our lovemaking. I know what I'll do. I'll make it hard for him to leave me. I know he likes me a lot. I just have to keep him wanting me somehow.

Lucas moved a little and Johnnie wondered if he was awake. She turned over and looked in his face. His eyes were open.

"So, you're awake," Johnnie said and put her head on his bare chest.

"Yeah, I've been up for a while," Lucas said and kissed her forehead. "I'm sorry, Johnnie."

"For what?"

"For adding to your burden last night. For shootin' my mouth off about the way white men use colored women. I'm just jealous, ya know."

"It's okay. I can understand you feeling that way."

"It just kinda reminds me of being a slave."

"How do you mean?"

"Well, basically, the white man still owns us in a way. He determines what we can do, how much money we make, what kind of schools we go to and what kind of neighborhood we live in."

"But Lucas, there's a lot of well-to-do Negroes living out here."

"Yeah, because most of them are the kind of people that think they're better than the ones where I live. The white man loves it when we try to act white. Tryin' to be like him, hatin' our own people. House niggas. Most of 'em anyway."

"You think I'm a house nigga too, Lucas?"

"No. You're smarter than him. My mother says a colored woman has to be smarter than the white man is. She makes him think he's usin' her, when all the time she's usin' him."

"Well, I won't have to do it forever, Lucas. I need you to hang in there with me."

"And I need to feel like a man. I decided to get a job, like you suggested. That way, I can at least pay my own way and occasionally pay yours. But from now on, I think we better find out what the movie's about, no matter how hot it is, okay?"

"Okay." Johnnie laughed. "And we'll go to the Sepia,

178

okay?"

"All right, baby," he said, kissing her cheek.

"You want me to make you some breakfast, Lucas?"

"Yeah, I'm starvin'."

"What do you want to eat?"

"Whatever you make is good."

Chapter 45

"Then there's no need to worry."

Lucas smelled the bacon and eggs all the way upstairs, and hoped the food tasted as good as its delicious aroma. He came downstairs and walked into the kitchen wearing the same clothes he'd worn the day before. Sweat stains were under the armpits of his shirt. Lucas showered and sprayed on some of Johnnie's perfume to camouflage the musty smell. Johnnie smelled the stench of his sweat but pretended not to notice. He tried to conceal the odor, and that was enough for her. She would feed him then take Lucas home so he could change his clothes.

"Have a seat," Johnnie said. "The grits are almost ready."

Lucas slid a chair across the linoleum floor, sat down and waited for her to sit with him. Johnnie came over to the table with the pot of grits and poured some into their bowls. She put the pot back on top of the stove and came back to the table. Lucas started filling his plate with bacon and eggs.

Johnnie cleared her throat. "Let's say our grace before we eat, okay?"

"I'm sorry, Johnnie. My mother taught me better table manners than that."

"Will you say it, Lucas?"

"Huh? Uh, I'm not into church and stuff."

"Don't you believe in God, Lucas?"

"I guess so."

"Okay."

Then she closed her eyes and bowed her head. Lucas did the same. Listening to her give thanks, he admired her belief in God despite everything that happened to her. When she finished, they said, "Amen."

"I been meanin' to ask you about them angels you got carved into your headboard," Lucas said.

"What about them?"

"What made you pick that headboard?"

"Lucas, you know my life. I gotta believe that God is watchin' me and balancin' out my own sins against the sins committed against me. Otherwise, I would feel like a little girl lost in a world that doesn't obey its own rules. You know what I mean?"

Lucas' mouth was full of food, so he nodded his head a couple of times. Johnnie watched him devour her food like he hadn't eaten in a week. She was going to ask him when he had last eaten, but she didn't want to put him on the spot.

"It's going to be strange when we go to the funeral."

"Why is that?" Lucas asked then took several gulps of his orange juice.

"It's been a year or so since I went to church. I'm wondering how I'll be received. I used to sing in the choir and play the piano there. I led worship service and things like that. When I go to the funeral Friday, I'm wondering how it's going to go."

"I won't let 'em bother you, Johnnie."

"I'm not worried about them bothering me, Lucas. I'm concerned about what Reverend Staples is going to say."

"Why you worried about him?"

"Because he's the reverend."

"Is he a good reverend?"

"Yes, I think so."

"Then there's no need to worry, is there?"

Chapter 46

"We sure did."

Sadie tapped on the back door. She had a tray of fresh beignets. The two women were having coffee and neighborhood gossip every morning since Johnnie moved in. They were quickly becoming the best of friends.

"It's probably Sadie," Johnnie said when she heard the tapping. She went to the door and moved the curtain a little. "Come on in, Sadie. I want you to meet my man."

When Lucas heard her acknowledge him as her man, he stopped eating and looked up, blushing and grinning from ear to ear. He stood to his feet and extended his hand.

Sadie sat the tray of beignets on the table. She took his hand, looking him up and down, ignoring the musk of the sweat-stained shirt and the accompanying smell of perfume.

"How old are you, boy?" Sadie asked, sounding like his mother.

"Seventeen," he said, as proud as could be. "How old are you?"

"He's handsome, but he doesn't have any manners," Sadie said, looking at Johnnie, who was just as surprised by the question as she was.

Lucas wondered what was going on. Sadie and Johnnie seemed to be on the same wavelength. That much he understood.

Sadie asked, "Didn't your mother ever teach you not to remind a woman of how much older she's gotten since the last time some untrained whipper-snapper like you asked the same question?"

"What's wrong with askin' your age? You asked me how old I was. I only asked you the same."

"Lucas, is it?" Sadie asked.

He nodded.

Sadie said, "Suffice it to say that women think it's uncouth for a man to ask a woman her age. However, we reserve the right to ask men their age. It's our prerogative."

"Well, I don't know what prerogative means, but it sounds like women wanna draw a line in the sand and tell men not to cross, then they wanna cross that same line whenever they feel like it."

Sadie thought about asking Lucas if he knew what suffice and uncouth meant, but instead, she laughed and said, "That's right. Now, let's see what you've learned. How old are you?"

"Seventeen," he said, then sat down and continued eating.

The two women laughed uproariously.

"Don't take it so hard, Lucas," Sadie said, still laughing a little. "This is one of the few rights women have."

"Would you like to join us for breakfast, Sadie?" Johnnie asked.

"Don't mind if I do," Sadie said, pulling out a chair. "Did y'all see that comedy act across the street last night?"

The telephone rang.

"We sure did." Johnnie laughed as she walked to the phone. "Hello."

"Hey, little sister. It's ya big brother, Benny!"

Chapter 47

"We'll be waiting."

"Hi Benny!" Johnnie said with false excitement. *How did you get this number?* "What state are you in now?"

"I'm here," Benny said firmly. "How do I get to your place?"

"Huh? My place?"

"Yeah, Mama told me all about you and Earl, the house, and some boy you like—the whole nine. I believe his name is Lucius or something like that."

"Well, uh, uh, uh," Johnnie continued stammering, unable to find the words she felt obligated to say. Feeling Sadie's and Lucas' eyes burning a hole in her back, she turned around and saw them staring at her, bewildered by what was happening. "Benny, I've gotta come home anyway. I can show you how to get here."

"Okay, when you leavin'?"

"About an hour. Is that too long?"

"No, we'll be waiting," he said. "Brenda and my first-born son are here."

"Okay, bye," Johnnie said quickly and hung up the phone.

"So, your brother Benny is home, huh?" Sadie said. "Isn't he the boxer?"

"A boxer?" Lucas repeated, feeling a little intimidated.

"Yeah, he's a boxer," Johnnie said mechanically. "Sadie, I don't know what I'm gonna do. My mother told Benny about Earl and the house—everything."

"Weren't you going to have him stay here anyway?" Sadie asked.

"No. I had decided not to tell him anything. I was gonna talk him into letting me stay here until I graduate, but now I gotta come up with something else."

"Why don't you just tell him the truth?" Lucas asked. "Maybe he'll kick Earl's ass. That's what he deserves."

"Lucas, please," Johnnie said. "You're not helping."

"I know you don't expect me to help you and Earl stay together, do you?" Lucas asked.

"You're upset right now. Can we talk about this later, baby?"

The telephone rang again. Reluctantly, Johnnie answered it. "Hello," she said tentatively.

"Hi, sweetheart," Earl crooned. "I told you I have some news I need to tell you. I'll be by tonight, okay?"

"Earl, that's not such a good idea," Johnnie said, putting her index finger over her lips.

Annoyed by what he had just heard and seen, Lucas curled his lips and sucked his teeth. Sadie watched him stare at Johnnie with increasing anger, and knew it was time for her to make a quick exit. Otherwise, she might have to witness the same sort of shouting match they had all watched the previous night at the Edwards' house.

"What do you mean it's not a good idea, Johnnie? I told you I have something very important to tell you. Why can't I come by tonight?"

"Apparently you haven't heard, but my mother was murdered."

"Murdered? Why didn't you tell me this last night?"

"I would have but you had to go, remember?" Johnnie asked, watching Lucas simmer as he listened to her conversation.

"All the more reason to get together. You need to be with someone. You shouldn't be alone at a time like this."

"I'm not alone," Johnnie said unintentionally, closing her eyes immediately after she spoke the words. "Sadie's here and my brother's in town. He just called."

"Who is Sadie?"

"You know, the lady next door that waved at us that day before you had to leave town. How was Chicago?"

"That's what I wanted to talk to you about," Earl said, lowering his voice as if someone was coming.

"You wanted to talk to me about Chicago? Why? What happened?"

Lucas was fuming. It looked as if smoke was about to come out of his ears. Sadie picked up her plate of food and mouthed, "I'll catch up with you later," then she tiptoed out of the kitchen and quietly closed the door.

"Any chance you'd be able to meet me tonight at the Savoy?" Earl asked.

"I can try. What time?"

"About nine-thirty."

"No promises."

"Okay," he said and hung up.

Johnnie waited for a second click, but didn't hear one. Slowly, she hung up the phone.

Chapter 48
"No, but hurry up."

"Lucas, I know you're mad, but please don't be," Johnnie said, leaning against the counter, watching for any reaction that would tell her where they stood and what approach to take next.

Lucas sat quietly, thinking about the situation he was in. He loved her—that much he knew. He also knew he couldn't put up with her and Earl's relationship.

Johnnie could see the resignation in his eyes. She could tell he wanted out, but he was reluctant to say the words.

"Johnnie, I can't deal with this," Lucas said in a voice saturated with remorse. "After the funeral, we gon' part company."

"Don't leave me, Lucas," Johnnie said desperately.

"I have to. I can't take this."

When Johnnie burst into tears and covered her face with her hands, Lucas felt like someone had ripped his heart out. He wanted to be hard and walk out, but love made him go to her and put his arms around her. He kissed her forehead.

"Its gon' be all right," he said softly.

"Lucas, I don't know what I'd do without you. Please don't leave me."

"What self-respectin' man would put up with this?"

"One that loved a woman with everything within him," Johnnie said, crying into his sweat-stained shirt. "One that loved a woman enough to sacrifice his pride. A real man, Lucas. I thought you were a real man, my real man. I love you, Lucas. Do you love me?"

"Yes," he said, looking into her brown eyes, seeing the sincere love in them.

Johnnie immediately turned to the one thing she was good at; the one thing that men always wanted from her; the one aspect of her life that gave her power over men—sex. "I want you inside me," Johnnie said.

"Right now?" he asked, surprised that she wanted to do it suddenly. He knew what she was doing, but he wasn't about to turn down great sex just because he was upset with her.

"Yes," she panted.

Johnnie felt his hard penis pressing against her when she kissed him. Unzipping his pants, she reached inside and massaged him through his underwear. Lucas quickly unbuttoned her blouse, unsnapped her bra and took her nipple into his mouth. The warm sensation caused her to moan. Johnnie, who was still leaning against the counter, relaxed her neck and let her head fall backward until it rested against a cabinet door.

Lucas continued sucking and nibbling on her sensitive, erect nipples. His hand found its way up her dress and into her panties. He heard an erotic sigh escaped her open mouth. While his finger massaged her, he grabbed the back of her head and kissed her, pressing hard with both lips.

"You wanna go upstairs?" he asked.

"No, let's go into the living room."

Lucas practically dragged Johnnie into the living room, consumed by an unbridled fire that needed to be extinguished immediately. He quickly kicked off his pants

189

and finished removing his underwear, which was almost off. He climbed over her, positioning his long, thick, throbbing rod to enter the inferno that could only be doused with orgasmic release. Finding the entrance, he began the long slide upward until she had all of him.

Lucas pulled out of her and whispered, "Turn around."

"What?" Johnnie asked, looking into his face.

"Turn around; I want to go in backward."

"You mean you want me to sit on you?"

"Yeah, let's try that."

Obediently, she stood up, turned around, and eased down gingerly. The penetration felt even deeper and it hurt. She tried to take the pain for his sake, but she felt like he was going to blast through her uterus.

"Lucas, I can't take it like this. We gotta stop."

"Okay," he said. "How about if we stand and do it like this? It might be easier."

"Okay," she said, standing up again. "Now how do you want me?"

"On your knees."

"On my knees?"

Believing it would please him, she did as he asked.

He entered her like that. "It don't hurt, do it?" Lucas asked.

"No, but hurry up. I gotta pick up my brother and sister-in-law."

As he moved in and out of her, Johnnie wondered where he learned this position and if there would be more positions like this in the future. Soon, she felt herself on the verge of an orgasm again.

Part 3
A Snake in the Garden

Chapter 49

"What are you doing here, Matthews?"

Johnnie dropped Lucas off at Napoleon's Bayou, a supper club in the French Quarter, where jazz and blues groups played nightly. He didn't tell Johnnie that Napoleon, who had mob connections in Chicago, ran the local policy racket and had asked him to become a runner. As far as Lucas was concerned, he had to do something to get her away from Earl. Since money was what it was going to take, Lucas was determined to do whatever he could to make as much as he could, as quickly as he could.

Napoleon Bentley was a third-generation Spaniard whose familial roots traced back to a noble family from Madrid. He loved jazz and the blues and got along with Negroes so well that he was dubbed the blackest white man that ever lived in New Orleans. He also had a penchant for Negro women, but nobody minded since he treated colored folk so well. Devilishly handsome and wealthy, Negro women found him extremely attractive. He was six-three, well built, with a granite chin and a reputation with women that rivaled Don Juan. To look at him, one would never suspect that he'd killed over a dozen men for reasons ranging from petty theft to contract hits for the syndicate. Still there was a ruthlessness about him that gave him an aura of power

Napoleon spotted Lucas the moment he entered the scantly lit supper club and signaled him to come over to the bar. He smelled Lucas' stench of sweat covered by perfume, but ignored it. Napoleon asked Lucas to be a numbers runner when he was a freshman, but even then, he looked like a man. At that time, judging by his football player physique, Napoleon thought he was at least twenty-four, and was stunned when the youngster told him he was just a fourteen-year-old high school freshman. In Lucas, Napoleon saw an opportunity to train a leg breaker who could collect debts, and eventually, an apprentice to perhaps run operations while he visited Chicago and Harlem.

"Lucas, my man, did you get any of those football scholarships you were looking for?"

"No. Not even from Grambling," he said, sounding frustrated.

"What's wrong? You seem agitated about something."

"I'm having trouble with my girl, Mr. Bentley."

"Woman trouble. Yeah, I know what you mean. You can't live with them and you can't live without them. What's the problem?"

"Money, Mr. Bentley. I don't have any. I need a job. Do you still have the numbers running job?"

"Yeah, I got it, Lucas," Napoleon said, putting his arm around him. "But from now on, I want you to call me Napoleon."

Just then, Sheriff Tate walked into the Bayou and signaled Napoleon to come over to where he was standing.

Napoleon turned Lucas toward the mirror so that he could see himself. "Look, for the last time, at poverty," Napoleon said. "Come . . . let me show you the secret to success in any endeavor."

They walked over to Sheriff Tate. Napoleon pulled a yellow envelope from his breast pocket and handed it to the sheriff. Tate took the envelope and opened it. He pulled out the money and Lucas' eyes lit up.

Lucas had never seen that much money at one time. The envelope contained one hundred dollars; chicken feed to Napoleon, but a fortune to Lucas, enough to take to Johnnie so she wouldn't have to stay with Earl, he thought.

"What are you doing here, Matthews?" Tate asked gruffly.

"He works here now, Tate," Napoleon said. "I've got big plans for him. In a few months, you'll be getting your payoffs from him."

"Fine. I don't care who pays me, as long as I get paid. You understand me, boy?"

"Sheriff Tate, his name is Lucas Matthews, and I would consider it a personal favor if you called him by his name. Do you understand?"

"You just make sure he delivers on time," Tate said then turned to Lucas. "And don't even try to cheat me."

"He won't. Will you, Lucas?"

"No, Mr. Bentley."

"Napoleon, Lucas, Napoleon."

Chapter 50

"Lucas, this is my wife, Marla."

After Sheriff Tate's bribe was paid, Napoleon took Lucas to his home in Rivera Heights. He lived on Long Island Boulevard, just two blocks away from Earl, who lived on Superior Lane. As they rode through the neighborhood in the 1951 Chevrolet Styleline convertible, Lucas was astonished by all the luxury. The mansions were huge and the grass was so green. In the shack he lived in, all they had was dirt. Nothing grew in his front yard, not even dandelions. Rivera Heights was even more impressive than Ashland Estates.

Lucas began to understand Johnnie's reluctance to give up her home and all the trappings of a kept woman. He decided right then that he too would live well. When he got himself together financially, he and Johnnie would marry and start a family. And Ashland Estates was the perfect place to start.

"Napoleon, how much you gon' pay me to run numbers for you?" Lucas asked when they pulled into the driveway.

"How does twenty-five a week sound?"

"I was thinkin' more like fifty."

"Fifty?" Napoleon repeated. "I've never started any runner off with that kind of dough. Then again, none of them were smart enough to ask, Lucas. I can see I was right about you. You're a smart kid who can handle himself on the streets. Stick with me and you'll make a lot more than fifty a week."

"Yeah?" Lucas said, raising an eyebrow.

"Yeah," Napoleon said. "Now, let's get you cleaned up. When that gal of yours sees you, she won't even recognize you."

Lucas was dazzled by an elegance he was unprepared for. The size of the living room was staggering. There was thick carpeting, expensive furniture, a cobblestone fireplace, plants in large orange pots, all sorts of ceramic trinkets, and a grandfather clock that was chiming.

"Wow!" Lucas couldn't help saying. "This is really nice, Napoleon."

"Thanks, my man," Napoleon said, then called out for his wife. "Marla!"

Marla walked into the room wearing an apron around a pair of cream-colored pants and a sleeveless cream-colored blouse with zigzag patterns. Marla was a 38-year-old, five-six blonde bombshell. To look at her, you couldn't tell she had two children in college. Marla was flattered when she saw how Lucas was staring at her, like he wanted to rip her clothes off and thrust himself inside her with no regard for her. She found Lucas attractive too and smiled.

"Lucas, this is my wife, Marla," Napoleon said gruffly, unaware of the thick cauldron of lust that was brewing. "Lucas is going to be working for me at the club. Get him some of my clothes, and burn the ones he's wearing. I'm going to take him shopping."

Lucas was taken aback a little by the way Napoleon talked to his wife. There was no way he'd talk to Johnnie like that. *But hey, it ain't none of my business.*

"Lucas, why don't you take a shower?" Napoleon asked.

"When you're done, take a dip in the pool. Marla will find you some clothes while I make a run. I'll be back in a couple of hours. Make yourself at home."

"Are you hungry, Lucas?" Marla asked, sounding like a dutiful wife and mother. "I just baked an apple pie. Would you like a slice with some vanilla ice cream?"

"Yes, ma'am," Lucas said. "But can I take a shower first?"

"Sure," Marla said. "Right this way."

"Don't worry, Lucas," Napoleon said, opening the front door. "Marla will take good care of you."

Marla could smell the funk through the perfume like everyone else, but she too said nothing. She took him to the nearest bathroom. "Hand me your clothes when you take them off, and I'll get you something to wear when you go shopping with Napoleon."

"Thank you," he said, entering the bathroom.

When he took off his clothes, he realized he didn't have a fresh pair of underwear to put on. He took off everything anyway and handed the bundle to her through the door.

Chapter 51

"I'm pretty sure he never stopped loving our mother."

"Hi, Benny. Hi, Brenda!" Johnnie said, excited to see her brother and sister-in-law. "Where's little Jericho?"

"Hi, sis," Benny said and stood to his feet.

Johnnie ran over to him, hugging him with all her might.

"Let me look at you, girl," Benny said, taking a step back, his hand on her shoulders. "You sure filled out since I saw you last. How long has it been?"

"About five years," Johnnie said. "I was eleven then."

"Five years," Benny said, shaking his head. "Has it been that long?"

"Uh-huh. Five years," Johnnie repeated. "Y'all must be tired. Y'all ready to go?"

"Naw, what we ready for is an explanation for what happened to Marguerite," Brenda said firmly. "What that good for nothin' sheriff got to say?"

"Yeah," Benny said, "I know it was Richard Goode. Mama told me she was seeing him. Said she had a plan to get some money outta him. She told me that right after she told me about the house Earl bought you out there in Ashland Estates."

"Apparently Mama told you a lot of things, Benny,"

Johnnie said, lowering her head.

"Look, Johnnie, I know it ain't yo' fault you got involved with that child molester," Benny said, hugging her. "But you don't have to stay here. You can come out to the coast with us. Start all over. You're a good-looking girl. You can find a decent man out in San Francisco to take care of you."

"What if I don't want to be taken care of, Benny?"

"What?"

"You heard me. What if I don't want to be taken care of? What if I want to take care of myself? What if I want to be on my own? I have a house in my name. I'm getting a job and I have some stocks, plus I have the insurance money Mama left me. I can take care of myself."

"What about school, Johnnie?" Brenda asked.

"What about it?"

"Don't you wanna better yourself?"

"I have, Brenda. And it didn't have nothin' to do with formal schoolin'."

"You think this is what your daddy would've wanted for you, Johnnie?" Benny asked.

"Who cares what he thinks? Any man that would leave his wife and daughter, promising to send for them, and never comes back, doesn't even matter to me."

"Is that what Mama told you?" Benny asked. "She told you that he left to find a job and didn't come back?"

"Yes, she told me the whole thing. About her and Louis Armstrong, the fight between him and my daddy over her—everything. She even told me about his running around on her then getting mad because she did the same thing."

Dumbfounded, Benny shook his head. He looked at Brenda, wondering if he should tell Johnnie the whole truth.

"You might as well tell her, Benny," Brenda suggested. "She needs to find out sooner or later."

"Sit down, Johnnie," Benny demanded.

"What's going on?" Johnnie asked, uneasy with what was happening.

"These are the wrong circumstances to hear this, but Mama lied to you about your daddy and my stepfather. Johnny Wise was a good man. He was good to me and he was good to our mother. I even took his last name when I left New Orleans. What happened between our mother and Johnny was her fault. She told you he was running around on her. Well, the truth is she was running around on him."

"That's not true," Johnnie firmly disagreed.

"Yes it is, Johnnie. I saw her with a lot of different men. She just couldn't stop prostituting herself. For all I know, she ran my father off too."

"Well, what really happened?" Johnnie asked.

"Mama had Sheriff Tate run him outta town. That's what happened."

"What?"

"That's right. Sheriff Tate and our mother had been seein' each other for years. Tate wanted to keep seeing her, and Johnny was in the way. So, he trumped up some phony charges against him. He told him if he didn't leave town, he would see to it that he went to Angola Prison for a long time."

"How do you know this?"

"I heard Tate say it. I was right upstairs in the bedroom."

"So, my daddy didn't abandon us?"

"No, Johnnie, he didn't," Benny said. "She wanted to keep whorin', and he wouldn't stand for it. That's why he beat her. Frankly, I don't know many men that would put up with that kinda shit."

"Where is he now, Benny?"

"He lives in East St. Louis. He's got a wife and four kids. He's happy now," Benny said and laughed a little. "I guess the sheriff will let him come back for the funeral now that she's dead."

"You talked to him?"

"Yeah, we've kept in touch the whole time. He's bringing his family in. They should be here in a couple of days. You wanna know what's strange?"

"What?"

"I'm pretty sure he never stopped loving our mother."

Chapter 52
"Would you like some peach cobbler?"

Sadie saw a two-door 1952 two-toned Mercury Monterey coupe pull into Johnnie's driveway and park next to Marguerite's Oldsmobile. She came out of the house with some peach cobbler to meet her new friend's family. Sadie found Benny exceptionally attractive. His bone-colored pullover shirt fit him like a glove, showing off his boxer muscles. He had a well-muscled chest, powerful looking arms, and a thick, muscular back. She wanted him. Then she saw his wife getting out of the car, carrying a baby swaddled in a blanket. She heard a faint cry from the infant.

Brenda said, "Johnnie, he needs changing."

"Hi, Johnnie!" Sadie said, a little excited.

"Hi, Sadie," Johnnie said with equal enthusiasm. "I want you to meet my big brother, Benny and his wife, Brenda."

Brenda turned around just in time to see the lustful looks Sadie was giving her husband. She looked at Benny to see how he was responding to the wanton looks. As she suspected, he was already thinking of a way to leave her and baby Jericho so he could slip his rod into Sadie. While she hated the idea of Benny sleeping with other women, Brenda put up with it because she loved him. She prayed every night that God would deliver him from the spirit of lust, but so far, she hadn't seen any results from her nightly supplications. Brenda spoke cordially to Sadie and even forced a smile, but inwardly, the heart that was broken by the man she loved ached a little.

"Can you show me where the bathroom is, Johnnie?" Brenda asked.

"Yeah, come on in, y'all," Johnnie said, pretending not to notice what had just happened between Benny, Brenda, and Sadie. "You too, Sadie."

As they walked in the house, Benny said, looking Sadie's sensuous body over, "Yeah . . . that peach cobbler sho' do look good to me. I bet it's sweet too."

"It's very good," Sadie said, acknowledging his not so subtle flirtation.

Benny and Brenda were far more impressed with Johnnie's house than they anticipated. While they were both proud of how well she'd done for herself, they were also angry that a sixteen year old girl had been bought and sold like chattel.

"Let me show you where the bathroom is, Brenda," Johnnie said.

"Where's the kitchen?" Benny asked. "I wanna get me a piece of that good-lookin' cobbler."

"Sadie, you mind showing Benny the kitchen while I show Brenda where the bathroom is?" Johnnie said.

Sadie went over to the stained glass cabinet and took out a small plate decorated with an assortment of colored roses, and placed it on the table. Benny watched her every move. He especially liked the way Sadie's hips swayed from side to side. The shorts she was wearing were tight, showing off her shapely butt. Benny shook his head and bit down on his bottom lip, thinking it would be nice to bed her.

Whispering, Benny said, "Sadie, what you gon' be doin' later tonight?"

"Whatever you want me to do for as long as you want me to do it," Sadie replied, looking into his brown eyes. She went over to the counter, picked up one of Johnnie's pens, wrote her telephone number on a piece of paper and handed it to Benny. "Put this someplace where you won't lose it. I'm looking forward to tonight."

On their way to the kitchen, Brenda purposefully talked to Johnnie loudly enough for Benny and Sadie to know they were on their way to the kitchen. That way she could at least have the pretense of ignorant bliss.

"So, your sister tells me you're a professional boxer," Sadie said, attempting to give the appearance of innocent conversation as Brenda and Johnnie entered the kitchen. "Would you like some peach cobbler, Brenda?"

Chapter 53
"You're just a baby."

Peering around the bathroom door, completely nude, Lucas shouted, "Mrs. Bentley, I'm outta the shower."

"Okay," Marla said. "I'm coming." Moments later, she knocked. Lucas cracked the door just wide enough for her to hand him a pair of black swimming trunks. "When you're decent, come out to the patio. You can have your pie and ice cream out there."

"Okay, ma'am."

"Call me Marla, Lucas," she said. "We're down to earth. Having lots of money and white skin isn't necessarily synonymous with bigotry."

"Yes, ma'am," Lucas said, unsure of what she'd said.

"Don't take too long, okay? The ice cream will melt."

Lucas slid his long, muscular legs through each opening of the trunks, then tied the string tightly. Looking in the mirror, he made an Atlas pose and smiled at himself. A few moments later, he pulled back the curtains and looked at the pool. He saw Marla wearing a two-piece bathing suit and got an immediate erection.

When Marla heard the patio doors open, she turned around and looked at his bronzed body. Her eyes dropped to his bulging crotch. She took a deep drag of her cigarette and blew out smoke rings.

Lucas couldn't help staring at her in that hot pink bathing suit, which showed off her vivacious curves. When he saw her staring at his stiff shaft, he sat down quickly, picked up his fork and dug into the pie and ice cream. To his surprise, the pie was still warm. He could feel Marla staring at him behind those dark shades he'd seen Marilyn Monroe wearing.

"Aren't you going to have some, Marla?"

"No, Lucas. When a woman reaches my age, she has to be careful what she eats."

Lucas opened his mouth to ask her how old she was, then quickly changed his mind, remembering the lesson Sadie had taught him earlier that morning. Marla recognized his desire to ask a question and invited it.

"Don't be afraid to ask me whatever's on your mind," she said, feeling in control.

"That's okay, Marla," Lucas said shyly.

"Don't be coy," she said, sure of herself. "If you want something from a woman, you have to be courageous. What's the worst thing that could happen?"

Lucas shrugged his shoulders and continued eating without looking at her.

"Look at me, Lucas."

He stopped eating and looked Marla in the face. He couldn't see her eyes and it made him a little nervous. She took off her sunglasses and watched how his boyish face revealed his desire to have her.

"Do you think I'm pretty, Lucas?"

Embarrassed, Lucas lowered his eyes. He felt like she could see right through him.

"Well, do you?" Marla repeated.

"Yes," he said reluctantly.

"And I bet you wanna know how old I am, don't you?"

He nodded.

"I'm thirty-eight."

Lucas opened his mouth to say something again, then quickly closed it.

"Don't worry about it, Lucas," Marla said. "You're probably thinking I'm old. You should know that women are like fine wine. We get better with age."

He nodded his head and finished off the rest of his pie and ice cream. He couldn't help looking at her, wondering what it would be like to recklessly thrust himself inside.

"Would you like some more pie and ice cream?"

"No, thank you," he said, lying.

"So, how old are you, Lucas? Twenty-two, twenty-three?"

"Seventeen."

"You're just a baby," she said, grinning. "Tell me, are you a virgin?"

Feeling like he had to prove that he was a man, he said, "No. I've had plenty of girls."

"Plenty, huh?"

"Yeah, plenty."

"Any of them women? Or were they all little girls who have yet to understand their own sexuality?"

"What do you mean?"

"I mean have they all been teenagers? Have you had a woman my age yet? I can teach you the art of making love and make you a strong yet sensitive lover. Would you be interested in learning how to make love to a real woman?"

"Marla, I already have a girl," he said, doing his best to resist the temptation to accept her offer. "Besides, Napoleon is my friend. He gave me a job and everything."

"Napoleon is your friend? That's a laugh. Napoleon doesn't have any friends. He uses people to get whatever he wants. One day it's going to catch up with him."

Stunned and confused, Lucas wondered about their relationship. Napoleon was rude to her right in front of him, and Marla obviously had no respect for him. Yet, they were man and wife. It made no sense.

"I know you want me, Lucas," Marla said, interrupting his thoughts. "When you change your mind—and believe me, you will—I'll be available."

Having no idea how to respond to such an offer, he asked, "Is it okay if I take a swim now?"

Chapter 54

"The Yankees are on the radio."

"Dammit, Marla!" Napoleon shouted after seeing her and Lucas frolicking in the pool. "Didn't I tell you I'd be back in a couple of hours?"

Marla and Lucas stopped suddenly and stared at Napoleon with childlike fright in their eyes, fearing they had been caught red-handed. But Napoleon wasn't upset about seeing them together; he was upset because she didn't have Lucas dressed and ready to go shopping.

"Didn't I tell you to have him ready by the time I returned? What didn't you understand, Marla? Was it the part about having him ready? Or did you forget what time I said I'd be back? I said I'd be back in two hours. Have him ready. Was that too complicated? You've got a fucking college degree and can't even follow simple instructions."

Marla felt about two inches tall. It wasn't so much what he was saying. It wasn't even his shouting; he belittled her all the time. What bothered Marla most was that he verbally abused her in front of others, depreciating her worth as a woman and as a human being. She begged him thousands of times not to degrade her in front of their guests. Marla felt even worse when she looked at Lucas and saw how out of place he felt while Napoleon ripped her to shreds.

"Lucas!" Napoleon shouted suddenly. "Don't you think my instructions were clear?"

"Napoleon, it was my fault," Lucas said, attempting to take the heat off Marla. "I shoulda paid more attention to the time."

"It's not your fault, Lucas," Napoleon said, finally calming down. "But I admire your gallantry. Marla, get him some clothes. I'll be waiting in the car. The Yankees are on the radio."

Marla and Lucas got out of the pool and went into the house. She led him to their bedroom, where she had already laid out an outfit for him.

"These should fit you nicely," Marla said, admiring the way the water still glistened on him. Lucas dried off and held the button-down shirt up to his neck, saying, as he looked in the mirror, "This should fit me pretty good."

Marla decided to get revenge for the way Napoleon treated her on the patio. She walked up behind Lucas and placed her small hands on his sizable pectorals.

"What are you doing?" Lucas asked, scared to death they might get caught. "Napoleon could come back any second."

"I know," she said, turning him around. "Isn't the very notion of being caught delicious?"

Marla pulled his head down and kissed his thick lips. Lucas tried to pull away, but she had a firm grip. As he backed away, Marla came forward, still kissing him. Suddenly, she pushed him onto the bed. Climbing on top of him, she could feel his massive erection pressing against her stomach. Lucas continued struggling. His heart raced.

"Let it happen," Marla whispered.

Lucas was torn. He wanted Marla, but he loved Johnnie. He knew he should get out of that room, and with his powerful physique there was no way she could keep him against his will. Nevertheless, he let it happen. Marla had his thick rod in her hand, stroking it gently at first. She gave him a blowjob. Lucas moaned and gave in to the sensual pleasure, but was still uneasy. He lifted his head. The bedroom was door open.

"Marla, the door is open."

"I know," Marla said, unusually calm. "The idea of being caught excites the hell outta me."

Chapter 55

"*So, nothing can be done?*"

"Have you heard a word I've said?" Napoleon asked.

"Huh?" Lucas said, feeling nervous and guilty at the same time. He had betrayed Johnnie and Napoleon. He felt bad about what he did, but he wanted to see Marla again. He enjoyed the sexual excursion a little too much.

"Still thinking about that gal of yours?" Napoleon asked.

"Huh? Uh, yeah, yeah," Lucas said, wondering why Napoleon hadn't questioned him about what he'd seen at the pool. He wanted to ask him about it, but thought, why bring it up? *If he doesn't say anything, why should I?*

"Don't worry, Lucas, my man. When we get you all dressed up, she won't be able to resist you; especially after you get a few bucks in your pocket."

"You really think so?"

"I know so. Here," Napoleon said, handing him a brand new, crisp one hundred dollar bill. "Show her this and she'll be putty in you hands. Money is the one thing a woman can't get enough of."

"She's got her own money, Napoleon. She doesn't need

mine. I need my own so that when we go out, I can pay like a real man should. I just want her to respect me as a man that doesn't have to depend on her to pay for everything."

"I understand. I wish Marla had her own money. That way she could get the hell outta my life." He paused for a second. "She's got her own money, huh?"

"Yeah. She's even got a stockbroker."

"A stockbroker?" Napoleon repeated.

"Uh-huh."

"This must be some widow who inherited a small fortune from the insurance, huh?"

"Naw, she's only sixteen," Lucas said, proud to be her boyfriend at that moment. "She's real smart, and she's the prettiest, the sweetest, and the most giving girl in the world."

"Really," Napoleon said skeptically. "Bring her by the club tonight. I'd like to meet her."

Remembering her rendezvous with Earl, Lucas said, "Well, her mother was killed a few days ago. And she's got family in town. Maybe another time."

"Her mother isn't Marguerite Wise, is she?"

"Yeah. How did you know?"

"Read it in the *Sentinel*. The papers say whoever did it must have been pissed as hell. If they catch him, he'll be black. If they don't, you know a white man did it. If a white man did it, and if he's rich, he'll be untouchable by the authorities. If he's Joe Blow, the police can do something, but you won't find a jury to convict him."

"So, nothing can be done?" Lucas asked.

"I didn't say that. Something can be done. We just have to be careful. We have to plan our strategies. But first we gotta find out who did it, then we determine what the fallout will be if we kill him."

"Fallout?"

"Yeah, you know . . . the consequences. There are

213

consequences to everything, Lucas."

Lucas nodded his head in agreement. Then he remembered what Marla said. *'Napoleon doesn't have any friends.' It doesn't make sense. He's being a friend to me. He's given me a job, put money in my pocket. He's taking me shopping. And how do I repay him? By having unnatural sex with his wife. What the hell did I do? Damn, that's fucked up. But what can I do about it? I can't apologize for it. And she wants to see me again too. Fuck it! I'm never seeing Marla again.*

"Let me check with Johnnie, Napoleon. Maybe you can meet her tonight."

Chapter 56
"Pray for me."

The invitation from Lucas was a godsend. Johnnie had spent the day trying to figure out how she was going to get out of the house. It hadn't occurred to her to use Lucas as an excuse, but when he called and asked Johnnie to meet him at Napoleon's Bayou, she felt a sense of relief. She told Benny and Brenda about a date with Lucas, and that they were meeting at the Scpia to see a movie. The couple didn't believe her. They knew she was going to see Earl. If Johnnie saw Lucas at all, it would be after she saw Earl.

Benny saw the opportunity to get away from Brenda for awhile to see Sadie, but told Brenda he was going to follow Johnnie to see where she was really going. He also told Brenda that if Johnnie saw Earl, he would have a talk with him after Johnnie left. Brenda knew Benny was mainly interested in spending some time with Sadie. She wanted him to know that she knew. She was getting tired of his philandering. Just as he opened the front door to leave, Brenda decided to speak her mind.

"Benny?"

"Yeah, Brenda, baby. What is it?"

"Just so you know, you and Sadie ain't foolin' nobody. I guess what I don't understand is why you're disrespecting me by making it so obvious."

"What are you talkin' about?"

"You know what I'm talkin' about, Benny! Are you going to stand there and tell me you're not going to see Sadie tonight? Your foolishness gon' end up being a curse on our children."

"What do you mean?"

"Your runnin' around, Benny. You think you just out there havin' the time of your life, but have you considered the fact that your waywardness could be manifested in one or all of our children? What if the next one is a girl, Benny? You know what they say; the apple don't fall far from the tree. How you gon' live with yourself if our daughter end up being a whore like you and the women in your family? What if she ends up dead, killed by her white lover? How you gon' live with yourself?"

"That won't happen, Brenda."

"Oh? And why not?"

"'Cause you a good Christian woman. God won't let that happen for your sake. Me? You knew how I was when you married me. I cain't help the way I am. And you right. It's in my family. I come from a family of whores. In fact, a whore, who's dead now because of it, raised me. But that ain't gon' stop me from talkin' to Earl tonight. Now, I gotta go before Johnnie gets too far away."

"Benny, if you just accept Christ as your Lord and Savior, he can change you, if that's what you want."

"Well, pray for me, Brenda," Benny said then gently closed the door behind him.

Chapter 57

"Now, what was so urgent?"

Johnnie pulled into the lot behind the Savoy Hotel and parked Marguerite's Oldsmobile. It was 9:30. She knew she'd see Earl open the back door like clockwork. Seconds later, Earl opened the door and looked out. He saw Johnnie and waved at her. She got out of the car, walking hurriedly to the door.

Benny pulled into the parking lot in time to see her enter the building. He drove around until he spotted Marguerite's Oldsmobile then he parked a couple of rows away. He didn't realize it, but he was parked right next to Earl's Cadillac. He knew it wouldn't be a long wait. If she really liked Lucas, she would be in and out as quickly as she could, he thought. He decided that now would be a good time to call Sadie to decide where they would meet, and walked to the front entrance of the Savoy to use the pay phone in the lobby.

Before Johnnie could get in the room, Earl started fondling her breasts. A couple of seconds later, his hand was up her skirt and inside her panties. She was about to protest when he planted a sloppy, wet kiss on her lips.

217

I don't know how much more of this I can take.

Pulling away and leaning back a bit, with her hands firmly on his chest, Johnnie said, "I thought you had urgent news, Earl."

"I do, honey," he said, almost desperate. "I just need a little first, that's all. Just a little to help me relax. It's been awhile since we did it."

"It's only been a week." Johnnie frowned. "Have you forgotten that my mother was murdered?"

"No, honey. I haven't forgotten, but . . ."

"But you still expect me to put out regardless of what I'm going through, right?"

"I wouldn't put it that way."

"What way would you put it, Earl?" Johnnie asked, putting her hands on her hips. "Tell me, Earl. I'm curious as hell."

Earl bowed his head. He felt ashamed of himself, but he still had a stiff erection in his pants.

"The truth is," Johnnie continued, "you don't even care, do you? As long as you get yours, you couldn't give a damn about me and how I'm feeling."

"Johnnie, I do care. It's just that it's been a long time and—"

"Since when is a week a long time? I can wait a week or much longer. How come you cain't?"

Earl just looked at her, hoping that she would feel sorry for him and please him like she'd done so many times before.

"Fine, Earl. I'll do it, but I wonder what it'll take for you to care about someone other than yourself."

Moments later, Earl was inside her, making his animalistic groans of ecstasy. He was so into the moment that he was unaware of her complete detachment. Johnnie was just lying there, hoping he would hurry up and finish so

218

she could find out whatever it was he had to say. Then she'd be on her way to meet Lucas. Unfortunately, Earl was uncharacteristically slow, savoring every stroke. Johnnie decided to hurry him along. She arched her back and pumped a few times. Just as she knew he would, Earl lost control. He was now moving with the urgency of a rabbit in heat. Finally, it was over.

Earl was still inside her. His breathing was slowing down, but she could still hear him panting in her ear.

"Earl, could you roll over, please? You're heavy."

"I'm sorry, honey," Earl said and rolled off her.

Johnnie went into the adjacent bathroom and washed herself. She looked into the mirror, saying, "You can do it. Just a little while longer. Then you'll be free of him forever."

"What did you say, honey?" Earl shouted. "I can't hear you through the door."

"Why do you think I have it closed?"

"What?"

"Oh, nothing," she said, opening the door. "Now, what was so urgent?"

Chapter 58
"That's my son!"

Taking Johnnie by the hand, Earl led her over to the table and they both sat down. She could tell by the dejected look on his face that whatever he had to say disturbed him deeply. His eyes welled with tears which fell when he began to speak.

"West is planning to move me out of the company."

"What? Why?" Johnnie asked.

"After all I've done for him," Earl said, almost shouting. "I've done everything he asked me to. I even gave him the grandson he's always wanted. Now I have no further use."

"What are you talking about? What happened in Chicago? Did he catch you with another woman or something?"

"No. Nothing like that."

"Then what happened?"

"We were staying at the Drake Hotel. We were supposed to meet in the lounge for dinner and drinks. I was late because I was in a meeting that ran over by about forty-five minutes, so by the time I got there, they were already drinking."

"Who?"

"West and Phil Seymour, the head of the Chicago office."

"Oh."

"West was telling Phil how I trapped Meredith into marriage and how he had to step in because we were only two notches above the poverty line."

"How did you trap her?" Johnnie asked, curious about how a white woman could be trapped into marriage.

"I didn't trap her," Earl said angrily.

"You didn't, huh?"

"No, I could never do that!"

"Earl, please," Johnnie said, looking at him disdainfully. "Isn't that what you did to me?"

"That was different."

"Different, huh? Different how?"

"Uh, uh, let's just stick to the subject." Earl frowned. "West was telling Phil that he was just allowing me to be in a position of power and authority for little Buck's sake. When Buck was of age, he would get rid of me."

"Well, why does he have to get rid of you? I thought he had you start at the bottom so you could work your way up."

"He did. That was his fatal mistake. I know everything about Buchanan Mutual. I will be compensated for my years of dedicated service."

With an uneasy tone in her voice, Johnnie said, "What are you going to do, Earl?"

"West won't give me what I've earned. Fine! I'll take it! I've got about fifteen years to steal as much money as I want. I'll take ten thousand here and ten thousand there. They'll never miss it."

"Don't the banks keep a record of the checks they cash?"

"Yes. But I won't be using checks. I'll be taking the money from the cash he uses to pay off the politicians in Washington. They call it campaign contributions."

"What?"

"Yeah, that's right! All the insurance companies do it.

221

They all have their political lobbyist. But you know what hurts the most?"

"What?"

"He had the nerve to tell Phil that little Buck was blood and I wasn't. Whose blood does he think is in his veins? His? That's my son! Mine!"

Johnnie truly felt sorry for him. She wished she had made love to him the way he wanted. Looking at his anguished face, she stood and walked over to where Earl was sitting. She took his head into her arms and listened to him cry for the first time. She rocked him gently in her arms, shushing him like a mother with an infant. Johnnie lifted his head and wiped the tears from his eyes, then she led him back to the bed and made love to him just the way he liked it. When she finished, Earl gave her ten thousand dollars in large bills.

"What's this for, Earl?"

"It's for you, and there's more where that came from. See, I haven't forgotten about your mother being killed. If I can do anything to help find out who did it, let me know."

What are you going to do? It was a white man that killed her. "Okay. I gotta be going. Thanks for the money. See you sometime after the funeral when my brother leaves town."

"Okay," Earl said, sounding like the weight of the world was lifted from his shoulders.

"Bye," Johnnie said sweetly. She blew him a kiss as she backed out of the room.

Chapter 59

"Then lead the way."

It was about 10:20 when Johnnie came out of the Savoy. Benny spotted her and ducked, hoping she wouldn't look in his direction. She would certainly recognize his car. In her haste, Johnnie didn't see him, even though she looked right at him. She got into the Oldsmobile and pulled off. Benny took a swallow from the bottle of beer he purchased in Trudy's and patiently waited for Earl to exit the building.

Ten minutes later, he saw a white man coming out of the same door Johnnie had just exited. Assuming it was Earl, Benny got out of the two-toned Monterey and approached the man walking in his direction. Benny leaned against the car and waited until the man was close enough to see his face. After seeing him at his mother's house many times, he recognized Earl immediately. He was a little older and a little heavier, but it was still the Earl Shamus he knew years earlier.

"Hi, Mr. Shamus," Benny said, remembering that was what he liked to be called.

Earl stopped in his tracks. His eyes narrowed as they strained to see the man's dark face in the moonlight. The man looked very familiar for some reason, but he couldn't quite put the face and the name together. As he got closer,

Keith Lee Johnson

Earl slowly began to recognize the man.

"Benny?" he said hesitantly.

"That's right. It's me, Mr. Shamus. Benny."

Suddenly, hundreds of images flooded Earl's mind. He remembered Marguerite sending the young man outside with his little sister on many occasions. He also recalled the profound loathing he'd seen in his eyes as he left their home. He didn't think much of it at the time, but now, in a quiet, dark parking lot with no Whites around, Earl was terrified. He could see the same unabated hatred in the young man's eyes.

The glare on Benny's face caused Earl's stomach to churn as fear overwhelmed him. Benny continued looking into Earl's eyes, waiting for just the right moment to begin the assault, waiting for that moment when a man knows he's overmatched and there's nothing he can do about it. He wanted Earl to know before the actual beating began that he was going to beat him senseless. Then it came, the moment of inescapable truth; the moment of impending doom; the moment when a man's life flashes before his eyes. Suddenly, without warning, Benny threw a vicious left hook to Earl's flabby body that dropped him to one knee.

"Did that hurt, Mr. Shamus?" Benny asked, taunting him. "That musta hurt. That's the kinda body shot that'll break a muthafucka's ribs."

Still on one knee, gasping for air, Earl tried to talk, but couldn't say anything because the wind was knocked out of him.

"Oh, you need some air, huh?" Benny asked, pulling him up. "Didn't you know I would find out what you did to my sister?"

Benny hit him in the stomach again. Surprisingly, Earl didn't go down this time. Instead, he doubled over and grabbed his stomach. He turned to try to run away but he

224

didn't have the energy. Benny lifted his right leg and shoved him head first into his Cadillac. There was a loud thud when his head hit the passenger door. Disoriented, Earl crumbled to the ground like a house of cards. Benny went over to finish the beating, but Earl started whimpering like a wounded animal.

"What's wrong, Mr. Shamus? Lost your nerve? It's different dealing with a man, ain't it?"

"What do you want, Benny?" Earl finally asked, gasping.

"When you say your prayers tonight, be sure and thank God you're white. That's the only reason I don't kill yo' good for nothin' ass. I got a wife and son now that need me. But if I find out you hurt my sister in any way, I'll be back. And being white ain't gon' save yo' ass. You understand?"

Earl, nodded. Benny stood Earl up, brushed the dirt off his suit and straightened his lapels. "There you are, Mr. Shamus. All nice and pretty again," Benny said in a butler's tone. "Which one of these cars is yours?"

"This Cadillac."

Benny laughed a little and said, "So, I was parked right next to you, huh?" He grabbed Shamus by the arm, escorted him to the driver's side of the car and opened the door. He waited for him to get in, then he closed the door.

Benny looked into the car. "You have a good evening now, Mr. Shamus. And don't forget our little talk. I know I won't."

Shamus nodded his head and drove off.

Unknown to Benny, Sadie arrived at the hotel and parked. She'd seen the whole thing between Benny and Shamus. She got out of the car and walked over to him.

"I saw what you did to Earl, Benny."

"You did, huh?"

He could tell by the twinkle in her eye that what she'd seen was a tremendous turn on. He put his arms around her

225

waist and pulled her forward, then he kissed her forcefully.

Sadie found the strength of his embrace intoxicating. It had been so long since she was able to feel this good from an embrace. She liked Santino and he took care of her and their children, but she needed to be out with a man, if only to a hotel. Benny put his powerful hands around her small waist and lifted her onto the hood of his car. He kissed her again. Sadie could feel herself slipping deeper and deeper into the moment of their carnality. Having reached her point of surrender, she pulled away and said, "So, did you get a room?"

"Yeah, baby. I got a room."

"Then lead the way."

Chapter 60
"Amateur Night"

Lucas was eyeing the front door of the club all evening. The anticipation of seeing Johnnie had him fidgeting and on the edge of his seat. He had so much to tell her. Lucas had money in his pockets, new clothes on his back and a new job. In his mind, these were the necessary ingredients to get her to leave Earl, who was the only thing in the way of Lucas having Johnnie to himself. Soon, Earl would be out of the way too. Lucas looked at his new watch for about the hundredth time, then at the entrance again. Finally, she arrived. A broad smile flashed across his youthful face. He practically ran over to meet her. She was wearing a low-cut powder blue dress which showed off her hourglass shape, a pair of powder blue shoes with a matching purse and earrings.

"Hi, baby. I thought you'd never get here," Lucas said.

"I got here as quick as I could," Johnnie said. "You sure do look nice tonight. Is that a new suit?"

"Yeah. Just got it today."

"Where'd you get the money?"

"I got a job here. I'm working for Napoleon now."

"The owner?"

"Yeah. He's been tryin' to get me to work for him for

227

awhile. I refused until now."

"Why now?"

"Because I have you now, Johnnie. I gotta make some money or I'll lose you."

"Lucas, you don't have to ever worry about that. I'm yours. You have all of me."

"I do?"

"Yes. Don't you know that?"

"No, I don't know that. And I won't know that until Earl is outta yo' life for good."

"Now, Lucas, we discussed this already. You said you would trust me."

"And I do. But I don't want Earl around no longer than he has to be. You understand, don't you, baby?"

"Yes, I do."

"Well, listen, it's amateur night. I got us seats right up front so you can see everything."

"Oh, that's so sweet of you," Johnnie said and kissed him on the cheek.

The emcee of amateur night was a man called Fort Knox. His real name was Simon Young but nobody called him that. He lost most of his thirty-two teeth in barroom brawls. The rest rotted out.

Lucas grabbed Johnnie by the hand and led her to their table in front of the stage. As they approached their seats, Fort Knox saw Johnnie and nearly lost his mind.

"Oooooooh weeeeeeee," he said, his mouth glittering with gold. "We sho' do have a fine black woman comin' toward the stage tonight!"

Lucas, filled with pride, couldn't help smiling. Now, when Napoleon heard Fort Knox praising Johnnie, he looked toward the stage to see who the fresh meat was.

"Hey, house man," Fort Knox continued, "put the spotlight on her so the whole house can see the crown of

God's creation."

When the light hit her, Johnnie's bright smile lit up the room. Napoleon took one look at her and lust surged through his mind; his tool hardened and throbbed. He saw Lucas and remembered that he invited his girlfriend, who was only sixteen.

Bubbles, Napoleon's main enforcer, saw the look in his eyes. He'd seen it a hundred times in the years he'd known him. Bubbles knew that look could only lead to trouble.

"Boss, don't do this," Bubbles urged. His voice was like that of a deep bass singer.

"Don't do what?" Napoleon asked innocently.

"The kid is only seventeen and in love. What's gonna happen when he finds out you fucked his girl? I'll tell you what's gonna happen. He's gonna feel compelled to get even. Maybe try to kill you. In which case I will certainly have to kill him. If worse comes to worse and Chicago finds out that it was all over some sixteen-year-old kid, they'll come down here and take everybody out. Either scenario means trouble we don't need. And for what? Some pussy you can get anytime, anywhere? Besides, I like the kid. I'd hate to have to kill 'im over some stupid shit like this."

"You're right, old friend," Napoleon conceded. "It ain't worth it. Sho' would be nice, though."

"What's yo' name, young lady?" Fort Knox asked.

"Johnnie Wise."

"Well, Johnnie, this is amateur night. Can you sing?"

"Yes, I can."

"Well, come on up here and sing for us."

Johnnie was reluctant to go on stage, but Lucas encouraged her. She couldn't believe that her dream of singing in front of a live crowd was actually coming true.

"Go ahead and try, baby," Lucas said. "You never know. This could be your big break."

229

"You really think so?"

"Yeah, I do."

Nervously, Johnnie walked up the steps to the stage. It seemed like it was taking forever to get to the spot where Fort Knox was standing.

"Let's give her a warm Napoleon's Bayou welcome, y'all," Fort Knox said. "What are you going to sing for us?"

"Billie Holiday's 'God Bless the Child.' "

Fort Knox hugged her and whispered, "Knock 'em dead, kid."

Johnnie was nervous and exhilarated at the same time. There she was standing on stage, about to sing a song that a woman she admired had sung so sweetly. When she looked out into the audience, she saw only darkness. The room was quietly anticipating the sound of her voice. The music began and she opened her mouth to sing.

When Napoleon heard her voice, he knew then that no matter how wise it was to listen to Bubbles, he was going to have Johnnie, whatever the cost.

Chapter 61

"Let's finish this conversation in my office."

After being showered with thunderous applause,
Johnnie was hooked. She dreamed of this moment all of her
short life, but this was so unexpected. Now, it was
happening. As she returned to her seat, Johnnie wondered
what her chances were of winning the competition.

Lucas hugged her and held on tight. He kissed her and
said, "You were the best, baby. I think you're going to win."

"Lucas, my man, aren't you going to introduce me to
your girl?" Napoleon interrupted.

Both Lucas and Johnnie turned toward Napoleon. His
handsome face, his physique and his manner of dress
immediately impressed Johnnie. Napoleon could tell that
she found him attractive and started formulating his
strategy for the future conquest.

"I'm sorry, Napoleon," Lucas said. "I got so excited when
she arrived, I forgot all about introducing you."

"I can see how any man would forget such a miniscule
task when dating a beautiful creature like you," Napoleon
said, kissing Johnnie's hand while looking into her eyes for

any sign of prurience.

"Thank you," Johnnie said politely, showing no desire for him.

"It's going to take some time to figure out who won, but I think I can safely say you will be tonight's winner, and the patrons of Napoleon's Bayou are the richer for it. Thanks for coming tonight."

"You're welcome," Johnnie said. "And thanks for letting me sing. Maybe I can sing again sometime."

"Anytime." Napoleon smiled.

"Oh yeah, Johnnie," Lucas began. "Napoleon told me he can help us find out who killed your mother. Didn't you, Napoleon?"

"Yes, I did," Napoleon said, realizing that would be the best way to seduce her. "Shall we sit down and discuss it?"

"Yes," Johnnie said, suddenly serious. "I already know who did it."

"You do?" Lucas asked, surprised she hadn't told him sooner.

"I sure do."

"Who?" Napoleon asked.

"It was Richard Goode."

"The Klan leader?" Napoleon frowned.

"That's right, and Sheriff Tate knows all about it," Johnnie said. "He told us that no jury in the parish would convict him. He's so weak! I guess I can't blame him, though. Even if Sheriff Tate arrested him, they would let him get away with it."

As he listened, Napoleon didn't realize it, but he looked like the cat who swallowed the canary. *She likes strong men, huh? Well, baby, they don't come any stronger than me. It wouldn't be anything for me to kill a racist dog like him.*

"Sheriff Tate told you he knew Goode did it?" Napoleon asked.

"Not in so many words, but he knows they were seeing each other."

"Hold it," Napoleon said. "Let's finish this conversation in my office." He raised his hand for Bubbles to come over to the table.

Bubbles approached with a menacing stare in his eyes. He was angry because Napoleon had completely disregarded his advice. Now he was calling him over for an elaborate display of power that was specifically designed to win favor with Johnnie.

"Yeah, boss," Bubbles grumbled.

"Have Sheriff Tate meet me in my office in half an hour."

Chapter 62
"And that's exactly what you'll have."

"Where do you get off havin' this fuckin' jigaboo bangin' on my door in the middle of the night?" Tate demanded when he entered Napoleon's office.

"Who the fuck you callin' a jigaboo?" Bubbles shouted and slapped Tate upside the head.

Tate turned to retaliate, but Bubbles hit him in the stomach. When he doubled over, Bubbles grabbed the back of his shirt and tossed him face first into the wall like he was a rag doll. Then he threw a left-right combination to his kidneys. Tate groaned and leaned back, reaching for his bruised organs. Bubbles put his huge, mitten-like hands on the back of Tate's head and slammed his face into the wall three times. Dazed by the repeated blows, Tate staggered a few steps to the right and fell against the wall.

"Now get somewhere and sit yo' ass down," Bubbles shouted. "And if I hear that jigaboo shit again, I won't be so gentle."

"Now that that's settled," Napoleon said, finding it difficult not to laugh along with Lucas and Johnnie, "have a seat, Sheriff."

Still dazed, Tate stumbled over to a chair near Napoleon's desk. Bubbles, as was his custom, took out a

234

small bottle of bubbles and blew them in the direction of the debilitated sheriff. He always blew bubbles either before or after he killed or beat someone into submission. He chuckled.

"Tate, do you know this young lady?" Napoleon asked.

Tate had taken such a quick and fierce beating that he hadn't noticed anyone was in the room besides himself, Napoleon, and Bubbles. He looked at her.

"Yeah, I know her," Tate said. "She's a sweet girl. What's she doing here?"

Napoleon looked at Bubbles, giving him the signal to start the beating again.

"You just don't get it, do you, Tate?" Bubbles said and backhanded him. "You're here to answer our questions, not the other way around." He blew a few more bubbles at him.

"How did you know Richard Goode killed her mother?" Napoleon asked. "And Tate, spill it all. I'm in no mood to dance with you tonight. The first time I think you're lying, I'm going to turn Bubbles loose again."

"I ain't gon' be as nice as I was the first time." Bubbles smiled.

"I saw him do it," Tate confessed.

"You saw it?" Johnnie shouted. "You never said you saw it!"

"Yeah, I saw the whole thing," Tate continued. "It was a set-up from the word go. Apparently, Marguerite was attempting to blackmail Goode. When he got out of the car, he had a duffel bag with him. When she got out of her car, he showed it to her. Poor Marguerite must have thought she hit the jackpot. She didn't stop to think why they were on a quiet back road instead of their usual meeting place."

"So, what happened?" Johnnie asked, relieved to finally hear the truth.

"You saw her, Johnnie," Tate said. "He beat her like I

235

never saw nobody get beat in all my life. He took that German gun of his and beat her practically to death. Then he shot her in the head."

"And you just stood by and watched?" Bubbles asked incredulously.

"What the hell could I do?" Tate shouted. "You know how them people are. They cain't wait for an excuse for a uprisin'. Besides, I didn't know he was gonna kill her. I just thought he would beat her to scare her. I didn't know he was gonna kill her. I swear I didn't."

"Would you have done anything if you did know?" Bubbles asked sarcastically.

"Of course I would have. I wouldn't stand by and watch someone be killed. I am the sheriff."

"But you would stand by and watch someone being beat to death. Is that it, Sheriff?" Bubbles asked.

"Fuck you!" Tate shouted.

"Fuck me? Fuck me?" Bubbles repeated. "If we didn't need your sorry ass, I'd kill you just for the fun of it."

"All right, that's enough," Napoleon warned. "Show the sheriff to his car, Bubbles."

"Let's go, Tate," Bubbles commanded. "You served your purpose."

Napoleon waited for them to leave then he said, "Here's what I propose we do. We wait a few months until this blows over, then we kill him."

"I want him to suffer the way she suffered," Johnnie said. "I want you to take his gun and beat him with it first, then kill him. That's biblical justice, Napoleon. That's what I want. Biblical justice."

"And that's exactly what you'll have."

236

Chapter 63
"Vengeance is mine!"

The funeral was held at Mount Zion Holiness Church, at the corner of Waite and Henry Streets. As irony would have it, this was the same corner where Richard Goode picked Marguerite up for their regular meetings at the Savoy Hotel. The small white steeple church was overflowing with people; even the Negroes from Ashland Estates came. The atmosphere was significantly charged with the raw emotion of indignant colored people. Most of the people in the neighborhood considered Marguerite the white man's whore, but her death served as a vivid reminder of the fact that a white man could kill a colored person and get away with it, and it angered them.

Dressed in black, Johnnie sat in the first row of uncushioned pews with Lucas, Benny, and Brenda. As Johnnie watched the parade of people viewing the body, she could literally feel the contempt around her. She could hear the persistent murmuring, which was filled with an outrage ready to burst at the seams. Dennis Edwards shouted, "This is bullshit! How long we gon' put up with this?" Attorney

Ryan Robertson shouted, "What can we do? We don't even know who did it." Philip Collins, the barber said, "When a black man is accused of raping a white woman, do they care which black man did it? Hell no! Then why should we care which one of them did it? Let's just pick one and kill him." Without realizing it, the men were getting louder and more obnoxious as their anger boiled out of control.

If they keep talkin' like that, they gon' spoil the whole thing. Maybe even get more colored folk killed, Johnnie thought.

Napoleon Bentley, Marla, and Bubbles walked down the aisle. Suddenly there was quiet, yet the venom was still in the air. Everybody liked and accepted Napoleon, but right now, all they saw was a white man who had the nerve to barge in on their time of mourning.

One man stood up and said, "What the hell are you crackers doin' here?"

Before Napoleon could respond, Benny stood up and said forcefully, "This ain't the place and this ain't the time for this kinda talk. If y'all cain't respect the ceremony, at least respect us and let us bury our mother in peace."

Rahim Muhammad, of the Nation of Islam, owner and chief editor of the *Raven*, the Negro newspaper, stood up and said, "Brothas and sistahs, the brotha's right. Now isn't the time for retribution. But I say unto you that the time is coming when we will arm ourselves and defend to the death, if necessary, our women and children like any other man. A race riot is inevitable. The white man will come to destroy us again. This is what he does. Just as he destroyed the so-called American Indian, just as he enslaved us, just as he exploited the Chinese, just as he drove the Mexicans out of Texas, surely he will come to this place. We must prepare ourselves or we will die. If you doubt what I say, just remember the riots in Tulsa. Just as the police didn't save the people of Greenwood, the police won't save us. We must save ourselves."

The audience responded with loud applause and verbal acknowledgments of agreement.

Bubbles whispered to Napoleon, "We gon' hav'ta have a talk with the Muslim before he blows the plan to hell."

While everyone was completely captivated by the statements being hurled back and forth, Marla and Lucas were making eye contact. She looked good in that black dress and those dark shades. Lucas was so stiff he could be used as the bit for a jackhammer. *Well, just once more,* Lucas thought. *But this will be the last time I see Marla Bentley.*

"Vengeance is mine, saith the Lord," Reverend Staples shouted as he took the podium.

Silence filled the sanctuary when his words thundered in the small church. Dressed in a black robe with gold tassels, he looked out at the audience with righteous indignation.

"Jesus, when He saw the moneychangers in the temple, made a whip and beat them. And He told them, He said, 'Make not my Father's house a den of thieves.' Here, sister Marguerite Wise lays in preparation for her final resting place, and you people have lost your collective minds. You all are carrying on as if you've forgotten that we're here to celebrate the passing of a saint from this life to the next."

Someone shouted, "She done passed from this life to the next, that's fo' sho'. But a saint she ain't."

The congregation murmured in agreement.

"Now, you listen to me," Reverend Staples shouted. "All have sinned and fall short of the glory of God. Who are you to question the salvation of this sister? Need I remind you that Jesus had Rahab the whore in His lineage? And even if this woman fell short of God's salvation, I'm not here to

239

preach the gospel to her, but to you. The gospel is for the living, not the dead. It is for self-righteous people like you, whose only assurance of salvation is the known sins of others."

Johnnie listened attentively to Reverend Staples. While she knew what the Bible said about vengeance, she would see to it that Richard Goode got what was coming to him. God could have him when she was through with him.

Chapter 64
"The Reception"

Lee Shepard, Dennis Edwards' neighborhood mistress, entered the backyard of Johnnie's home, wearing a provocative dress and showing plenty of cleavage. She was tall, thin, and exceptionally good-looking. All the men at the reception found themselves staring at her, dazzled by her sassy persona as they watched her float across the manicured lawn. Even Reverend Staples stopped talking and stared mindlessly at the pompous vixen. As she walked by Dennis and Denise Edwards, she could hear an argument erupt between them. She smiled and began her trademark flirtations, which was how she seduced Dennis.

"Johnnie?" Johnny Wise said to the daughter he hadn't seen since she was five years old.

Not recognizing the voice, Johnnie turned around politely, expecting to see a guest who wished to express condolences. When she saw him, she knew intuitively that the man standing in front of her was her father. Johnny was a pretty man, tall, light-skinned and solidly built with thick, wavy hair that his daughter inherited. He was holding the hand of a beautiful black woman who Johnnie immediately knew was his wife.

"Daddy?" she managed to say.

241

"Yeah, little one." He smiled.

"I haven't heard that name in so long," Johnnie said, embracing him.

They took a couple steps backward and looked at each other admiringly. His wife cleared her throat to get his attention.

"Oh, I'm sorry. this is my family," he apologized. He introduced his wife, Jasmine; his son, John Jr., 10; and his twin daughters, Carla and Simone, 8.

Johnnie embraced her newly found brother and sisters. The sight of her father and the new family drowned the grief of the day. Johnnie embraced Jasmine, who stood there watching, unsure what to do, suddenly being a stepmother. To her surprise, Jasmine sensed no animosity.

"I'm so pleased to meet you," Jasmine bubbled. "I've been telling your father that we needed to come down here for years. I'm sorry we had to come under these circumstances."

"So am I," Johnnie said, remembering the terrible tragedy that brought her father home.

"Jaz, baby," Johnny interrupted, "do you mind if I speak with my daughter alone? It's been so long. We have a lot to talk about."

"Sure, honey." Jasmine understood. "Come on, kids. Let's get something to eat."

"Little one, is there someplace we can talk?"

"Yeah, let's go in the house."

Chapter 65

"You know what I mean."

The house seemed to have just as many people inside as outside. Benny saw his sister and Johnny, the only father he had ever known, walk in the kitchen through the back door. He and Brenda were sitting at the table eating their dinner. Excited to see him, Benny embraced Johnny and said, "Long time, no see. You and your family have to come out to the coast and see us sometime."

"We will, son," Johnny assured him. "Is this little Jericho?"

"Yeah," Brenda said. "You wanna hold him?"

"Yes," he said, taking the toddler in his arms. "How's your training comin', son?"

"Good. I'm in great shape," Benny told him. "Jack Wilkins is a tough son-of-a-bitch. Gotta be in the best shape of my life."

"Wish I could be there for you, son."

"Yeah, me too, Dad. So, how long y'all gon' be in town?" Benny asked him.

"A couple of days," Johnny answered.

"Yeah, me and Brenda gotta be goin' tonight. The fight's in Los Angeles. Long drive home, man."

"I know what you mean. Jasmine is a principal back in

East St. Louis. We gotta be gettin' back too." He handed the baby back to Brenda. "If y'all don't mind, I need to talk to my daughter, okay?"

"Sure, no problem," Benny said. "We understand. Y'all need to catch up."

"Come on, Daddy." Johnnie grabbed his hand. "I'll find a place for us to talk."

***

"How you doin', Lucas?" Marla asked. He was standing under a tall, leafy tree, trying to avoid the scorching rays of the sun. "You sure have changed your style of dress since the last time I saw you. That's a really nice suit. Did your girlfriend pick it out for you?"

"Thanks, Marla," Lucas said, looking around to see who was watching them, hoping Napoleon wouldn't put two and two together. "Yeah, she picked it out."

"So, have you been thinking about me since that last time we saw each other?" Marla asked. "'Cause I've been thinking about you a lot. The offer's still open. You do remember the offer, don't you, Lucas?"

"Yeah, I remember." Lucas tried not to smile. "So, where's Napoleon? Is he here?"

"Is that what you're worried about?" Marla wondered aloud. "He's here someplace, probably looking for your girlfriend."

Lucas frowned. "What do you mean?"

"You know what I mean." Marla smiled. "I know my husband, and I've seen your girlfriend. If you want to talk about it, you know where to find me." She walked away.

Lucas was about to follow her, but he got the feeling he was being watched. He looked over his shoulder and saw Bubbles staring at him. Bubbles raised his glass of Johnny

Walker Red and took a swallow. Lucas smiled nervously, wondering if Bubbles knew what was going on. He walked over to Bubbles to try to find out if Napoleon was having him watched.

Bubbles didn't suspect anything until he saw the guilty look on Lucas' face, like he had done or was about to do something he shouldn't. He'd seen that look many times. In fact, he too had once worn that look of guilt, that paranoia that came from wondering if anyone suspected that he'd had what didn't belong to him. If he was right, Bubbles thought, he would have to warn the kid without letting him know he suspected something. And if he suspected, others might too.

"So, where's Napoleon?" Lucas asked.

That confirmed it for Bubbles. Something was definitely going on between the kid and Marla. "He's around, kid," Bubbles admitted. "You never know when he's gonna show." He waited a few seconds to let his words sink in. When Bubbles saw the wheels in Lucas' mind start to churn, he quickly changed the subject. "Startin' Monday, I'm supposed to show you the ropes. You ready for this kind of life, kid?"

"Yeah, Bubbles, I'm ready."

Chapter 66

"You love me that much?"

It was dark outside and only a few guests remained. Lucas was sitting dutifully with Johnnie, but he couldn't stop thinking about what Marla had said about Napoleon. They were sitting under that same tree where Marla had approached Lucas. Except for the couple of hours she spent talking to her father, guests surrounded Johnnie the entire day, seeing to her wants and needs. And now, she wanted to tell Lucas what she and her father talked about.

"My father pretty much confirmed everything that Benny told me about my mother and Sheriff Tate," Johnnie was saying, but Lucas was somewhere else. "He told me he wanted . . ."

A few days ago, Marla told me that I can't trust Napoleon and that he doesn't have any friends. Now she's telling me he's got designs on Johnnie. Hmmm . . . he was kinda goin' outta his way to get in her good graces on amateur night. Is he really that eager to help us make Richard Goode pay for what he did to Johnnie's mother, or is he doing all of this because he wants my girl? But he had already promised to help me before he even met Johnnie. And he knew about Johnnie's mother being killed before I told him. Said he read it in the paper. Hmmm . . . I wonder.

Now Marla, she's a real sly one. She's trying to get me to see her again, and it doesn't even matter that we're at my girl's mother's funeral. Who the hell am I kiddin'? Yeah, she was tempting me here, but I had already made up my mind to fuck her before she even said anything. And what about Napoleon? Has he done anything but the right thing by me? I'm the one in the wrong. I wanna screw Marla, so do I wanna believe that if he wants to screw Johnnie, I'm justified?

Besides, what about her and Earl? I told her I don't like that shit. But does she stop? Hell naw! Trust me, she says. But I do love Johnnie. What's it going to hurt if I get a little from Marla? I mean, it's just one time. Hell, I didn't even stick it in last time. But she wants me to dip it. Shit! Who am I foolin'? I wanna dip it. I mean, she did say I could learn from an older woman. If I did it with her, it could make sex with Johnnie better.

Yeah, but what if we get caught? I'm a dead man. Maybe that's what Bubbles was sayin' without really sayin' anything at all. Fuck it! A piece of pussy ain't worth all that. I ain't gon' get killed over no pussy! Fuck that!

"What's on your mind, Lucas?" Johnnie asked.

"Huh?" Lucas said with a confused, vacant look on his face.

"I've been talking to you for about ten minutes." Johnnie frowned. "Are you even listening to me?"

"Yeah, you were tellin' me about the conversation you were havin' with your father."

Johnnie rolled her eyes. "You were not listening to me. You know it and I know it. Now, do you want to tell me what's on your mind? It's gotta be more interesting than what I'm telling you. You still worried you gon' lose me?"

Seeing a convenient way out of having to tell her what he was wrestling with—the enormous temptation of being with Marla, the dilemma of wondering if Napoleon wanted her and if Bubbles knew about it—he simply said, "Yes."

"Why can't you trust me, Lucas?" Johnnie asked. "I keep telling you that it's you I want to be with."

"Yeah, that's what you say," he said.

"You know, I can't believe you would do this today of all days. Why can't you just support me today, huh?"

"I'm here, ain't I? What more do you want?"

"I want your undivided attention when I'm talking to you, Lucas. Is that too much to ask?"

"Is it too much to ask to have the same freedom you have with Earl?"

Now Johnnie understood. She saw him talking to Marla from her bedroom window when she was pointing him out to her father. Talking to her seemed innocent enough, but Johnnie remembered the way they looked at each other at the funeral when they thought no one was paying attention. They were obviously attracted to each other, but Johnnie wasn't concerned about it until now.

"So, you want her?" Johnnie asked without malice.

Surprised that she would ask the question, Lucas frowned and tried to pretend he didn't know what she was referring to. "Who you talkin' about, Johnnie?"

She stared at him for about thirty seconds, narrowing her eyes and curling her lips the entire time. As she looked at him, the words of her mother echoed in her mind.

All men are like that. They all want what you got between your legs. Well, I see that she was right about Lucas too. But do I hold his weakness against him? He's been my only friend through all of this. I've asked a lot of him, and he said he would trust me. I guess I have to trust him now.

"Why you starin' at me like that?" Lucas asked

innocently.

Johnnie chuckled and forced a wry smile. "I'm not stupid, Lucas."

"I know that, Johnnie."

"Are you?"

"Am I what?" He frowned.

"Stupid." Johnnie paused for a moment. "Lucas, that's a white woman. And on top of that, she's married to a gangster who we know has no problem killing people. Is it worth dying over?"

Realizing he was caught before he even did anything with Marla, he just sat there shaking his head. *Damn, if Johnnie figured the shit out so quickly, I know for sure now that Bubbles was telling me he knew too. Is he going to tell Napoleon? Shit, I'm fucked and I didn't even do anything yet.*

"Well, is it?" Johnnie repeated. "Is it worth dying for?"

"No," he admitted.

"Now look, Lucas, if you feel it necessary to see other women, I'm not going to say anything. I don't like it, but what can I say at this point? Just don't be stupid about it. A white woman is instant death if you get caught." Then she seemed to have an afterthought. "Well, I guess about the only place in town that's safe is the Savoy Hotel. But you gotta realize that if Napoleon finds out about it, he'll kill you. And where's that going to leave me? I can't imagine going through what I'm going through and still end up without you in my life. I've already lost a mother, a father, and a brother. I couldn't bear to lose you too, Lucas. Just promise me you'll be careful, okay?"

"Johnnie, you've still got your father and your brother, and I promise you won't lose me."

"That's what I've been telling you. My father and his wife want me to move to East St. Louis, and my brother and his wife want me to move to San Francisco. But I want to stay here with you."

"Oh come on, Johnnie. Who you kiddin'?" he asked, shaking his head. "You have strong feelings for me. That I don't doubt. But the truth is you wanna keep what you've got going with Earl until you've completed your plan. If it wasn't for that, I'm sure you'd go with either your brother or your father."

Johnnie smiled. "Well, that's probably true, but I would want you to come with me."

"You would, huh?"

"Yes, I would."

"You love me that much?" he asked her.

"Yes, I do," Johnnie answered convincingly. "Just promise me this. If you gotta do somethin' with that white woman, go to the Savoy. You'll be safer there, okay?"

"Okay, but I won't be doing anything with her."

Chapter 67

"Yeah, we in love."

The following Monday, Bubbles, whose real name was George Grant, decided to take Lucas on what he called a road trip, which meant someone was going to be beaten to within an inch of his life. Bubbles could always count on someone to miss a payment and incur his wrath, which he dispensed with passion. This week's victim would be a longshoreman named Bruce Micheaux, who was behind on his payments.

Bubbles, born and raised on the mean streets of Chicago, enjoyed his work. He was tough, and loan sharking was his pride and joy. Napoleon promised to take care of him when they were released from prison. Bubbles saved Napoleon's life in prison, where Bentley was serving three to ten on a manslaughter conviction in an Illinois Federal Penitentiary some ten years earlier. Though Napoleon killed men before, he was innocent of the charges levied against him. He took the wrap for Vinnie Milano, one of Chicago Sam's chief capos. Sam told Napoleon that John Stefano, the boss of New Orleans, owed him a favor. If Napoleon was willing to relocate, he could have the Colored section when he got out.

While quietly serving his time, a riot broke out in the

prison cafeteria. Napoleon was about to be stabbed when Bubbles, who ran cell block E, subdued the would-be assassin and killed him in the struggle. Bubbles liked Napoleon. He wasn't like any white man he'd ever met. Napoleon didn't have an air of superiority like so many white men he'd known in prison. He found it strange that even in prison, white men thought they were somehow better than colored men were.

Later, Napoleon and Bubbles discovered that Vinnie Milano was the one who tried to have Napoleon killed in prison. The colored section of New Orleans was promised to Milano before he was implicated in a barroom shooting. Upon Napoleon's release, Chicago Sam kept his promise, and Napoleon moved to New Orleans, taking Bubbles with him.

As they drove down to the pier, Bubbles decided to give Lucas a warning without tipping his hand that he knew, or at least suspected, that something was going on between him and Marla.

"So kid, you and that girl of yours in love?" Bubbles asked.

"Yeah, we in love." Lucas smiled. "You ever been in love?"

"Once or twice, I guess," Bubbles admitted. "But the trouble with love is it can get all complicated and shit. You know what I mean?" He shot Lucas a menacing scowl. "Sometime people be in love, but they get a hunger for somethin' that don't belong to 'em. If they ain't careful, that hunger takes over, and they just gotta have what they set their hearts on havin'. Before you know it, somebody finds out and people end up dead."

Lucas realized that he was talking about Marla and himself. Fear shook his body. *Does Napoleon know?* He wanted to ask but was afraid.

252

"Sometimes all a man needs is a stern warnin', and that's enough for him to set his mind on other things. Things that won't get his ass killed over some pussy. I told Napoleon that very thing the other night at the club. I don't know if he heard me, though."

So, Marla was tellin' the truth. Napoleon's after Johnnie. But why is Bubbles warnin' me? Maybe he's warnin' us both. Maybe he senses what could happen and he doesn't want this thing to get out of hand. But what do I say? Do I just pretend like I don't know what he's talkin' about? Yeah, that's what I'll do. If I tell him I know what he's talkin' about, he'll have to tell Napoleon. So, that's what he meant. Okay, I take the warnin' and go on about my business. But what about Johnnie? What if Napoleon didn't take the warnin'? Will Johnnie betray me? Probably so. I mean, she just gave me permission to fuck Marla, didn't she? Me and Johnnie gotta talk about this shit before somebody gets killed.

"Well, I hope he heard you, Bubbles," Lucas finally said. "Sure would be stupid for a man to be warned and still end up dead over some pussy."

"Uh-huh," Bubbles grunted, satisfied he made his point.

It was 3 o'clock in the morning when they boarded the ship. Bubbles believed that the element of surprise was always the best approach. He preferred to catch them when they were in a deep sleep. "Nothing like wakin' a muthafucka outta his sleep and beatin' the shit outta him," he told Lucas with a ruthless smile.

Part 4
Murder in the Moonlight

Chapter 68
"There can be no doubt."

Meredith Shamus nervously entered the office of Tony Hatcher, the private investigator she hired to follow her husband. He was sitting at his desk, enjoying a cup of coffee. Hatcher followed Earl for nearly a month, which was when Meredith had first heard him whispering to a woman on the telephone. When she hired Hatcher, she told him she wasn't sure if Earl was seeing another woman or not. She told him about the telephone calls and what she'd heard. Hatcher told her that when a spouse suspects cheating, the spouse is usually right. Rarely were their suspicions unfounded.

Hatcher saw how uneasy she was and offered her a seat and a cup of coffee. In his experience, no matter how confident the spouse was of cheating, there was nothing like confirming their suspicions. He saw so many lives shattered by infidelity that he could often tell who could handle it and who couldn't. He knew which marriages would survive and which ones wouldn't. Eleven years of experience taught him that rich women like Meredith Shamus would be hurt but the marriage would go on.

He often wondered why they even bothered to find out. He decided to follow the rich wives to see if they had anything to hide, and most did. Affluent people often endured marriages of convenience, Hatcher discovered. Most of the women, he deduced, needed to feel justified when they fooled around. It was the only thing that made sense to him. Meredith Shamus didn't strike him as one who would fool around. She seemed wholesome, and he respected her for it.

Meredith took a sip of coffee and said, "Well, Mr. Hatcher, what do you have for me?"

"Your suspicions were true," he told her reluctantly.

Meredith sighed and looked almost relieved. "Do you have a name, pictures, tape recordings and things like that?"

"No recordings, but I do have a name and pictures. Are you sure you want to see them?"

Meredith took a deep breath and let it out slowly. "I suppose I shouldn't care, but I do. Yes. Let's see the pictures."

"Are you absolutely sure, Mrs. Shamus?"

"Yes, I'm quite sure. Don't worry, Mr. Hatcher. I won't fling myself out of your office window."

Hatcher looked at her for another second or two. He opened a desk drawer, took out a yellow packet of pictures and surveillance notes, and handed it to her.

"I have the negatives in a safe place, just in case something should happen to the pictures," he assured her.

Without a word, she cautiously opened the packet. Hatcher watched her closely, waiting to see how she would reacted to the photos. After seeing Johnnie for the first time, Meredith's heart shattered into a thousand pieces. She lowered her head and began to sob softly.

As though she couldn't believe what she was seeing, she said, "Earl's seeing a Negro?"

Hatcher wondered if he should tell everything he knew. Sometimes he hated his profession. It seemed like he was always the bearer of bad news. He felt like the grim reaper most of the time, holding a sickle, waiting for the most inappropriate time to lop someone's head off. But this was what he did. This was what he was good at. Besides, that's what she paid for, Hatcher thought.

"There's more, Mrs. Shamus," he said delicately.

"I want to know everything, Mr. Hatcher." She continued weeping. "Please, don't try to spare my feelings."

Hatcher took a deep breath and let it out slowly. "Not only is she a Negro, but she's only sixteen years old."

"What!" Meredith was astounded.

Hatcher walked around his desk and sat beside Meredith. She wanted to know everything, and he would tell her. He picked up the pictures and shuffled them until he came to the pictures of Johnnie getting out of Marguerite's car at the Savoy Hotel.

"This is where they met as recently as last week," Hatcher began. "When your husband went to Chicago, it gave me time to check her out. It turns out that he paid for her and her mother to stay at the Savoy for about a week."

"Her mother?" Meredith recoiled. "You mean he's seeing mother and daughter? Together?"

"I'm not sure what was going on between the three of them," he admitted. "I do know that your husband bought this young girl, Johnnie Wise is her name, a fifteen thousand dollar home in Ashland Estates."

"Are you absolutely sure about that, Mr. Hatcher?"

"There can be no doubt, Mrs. Shamus. None at all."

"And you say the mother and daughter both live there?"

"No, just the daughter."

"So, the mother approves of this?"

"That's the strange thing, Mrs. Shamus," Hatcher went on. "The mother and the daughter argued at the pool while they were staying at the Savoy. A few days later, the mother ends up dead. Beaten to death by an unknown assailant."

"And you think Earl did it?"

"Hard to say, but that's how it looks. The woman wasn't raped or robbed, just beaten to death. The question is, who wanted her dead?"

"Thank you, Mr. Hatcher. You'll keep this confidential, won't you?"

"Of course," Hatcher promised. "But what are you going to do with that information?"

"I'm not sure."

"Be careful, Mrs. Shamus," Hatcher warned. "If he did kill the mother, he's more dangerous now. He has nothing to lose. Do you understand?"

"Yes," she said, still not fully grasping the gravity of what Hatcher was trying to convey. "Well, I'll be going. I'll look at the rest of this later. Thanks for a fine job. I'll be sure to give you good references."

"Thank you. Let me see you to the door."

Tony Hatcher looked out of his twelfth floor office window. He watched as Meredith Shamus got into her Cadillac. "Poor broad," he muttered.

Chapter 69

"We would never do anything like that."

Seeing an ambulance and a crowd gathered in front of her home, Meredith's heart raced. She'd had her worst fears confirmed, and all she needed was more bad news. When she got out of the car, Meredith saw the coroner's wagon parked in front of her home. That could mean only one thing. Someone was dead. As she rushed to the house, Earl came out. He was crying. *Who's dead?* Then she saw her three daughters, Janet, Stacy, and Marjorie.

"Where have you been?" Earl asked.

Ignoring the question, Meredith asked with frayed nerves, "What's happened? Is everybody okay?"

No one said anything. They all just looked at her, hoping she would figure it out. Suddenly it hit her. Someone in her family was missing.

"Where's little Buck?" she forced herself to say.

No one answered. They just continued to stare at her with shell-shocked looks of grief on their faces.

"No. No. No. Oh, no . . . It isn't little Buck." Meredith screamed. Earl held her as she began to cry uncontrollably. "What happened, Earl? What happened? Tell me it isn't true. Tell me he's hurt real bad."

Earl wished he could tell her that, but he couldn't.

Meredith was shaking as Earl led her into the house and to the living room, where she saw the medical examiner and a couple of paramedics. Little Buck was on the sofa, covered from head to toe by a dark green blanket.

"I want to see him," Meredith managed to say through unrelenting tears.

The medical examiner pulled back the blanket and Meredith saw her son. It looked as though he was sleeping. Meredith felt her knees get weak from the raw emotion of the sight of him, but Earl held her up. She cried loudly saying, "No! God no! Not my little boy! Not my child! Not my baby!"

At that moment, West Buchanan stormed in. He saw Little Buck's body on the sofa. "What the hell happened?" he barked loudly.

"West," Earl, still brokenhearted, spoke. "It seems that Little Buck and the girls decided to climb the tree in the backyard and he fell and broke his neck."

West turned to the girls and yelled, "Why the fuck would you let him climb up in that goddamned tree?" Before the girls could answer, he turned to Meredith and yelled at her too. "And where the fuck were you? You're his mother, for God's sake!"

"Daddy, it wasn't anybody's fault," Meredith told him. "It was a terrible, terrible accident. Don't blame the girls."

"The hell it wasn't!" West shouted. "These three wenches hated that boy and you know it! How do you know they didn't lead him up there, knowing he would fall?"

"Daddy, they would never do anything like that," Meredith pleaded their case. "They loved little Buck. Didn't you, girls?"

"No, Grandpa. We would never do anything like that." Janet, the oldest, spoke for her sisters. "We loved our brother."

West was right. That's exactly what happened. They

didn't want him to die, but they hoped he would get hurt. Little Buck was still everybody's favorite, and they were treated like stepchildren. The girls were sorry little Buck died, but they were glad to see the anguish on their grandfather's face. As far as they were concerned, it served him right for treating them so badly. They knew that if Little Buck had never been born, they would still be living in relative squalor. Now that he was dead, it gave them all immense pleasure to know that their grandfather lost more than a grandson. All of his planning for little Buck was now a memory.

West shot an angry glare at Earl, knowing he would now have to keep him at the helm of Buchanan Mutual. He would have to start treating him like the son-in-law he was, if the company was to survive with a Buchanan male at the top, even if only by marriage. West had hoped Claire, his wife, would have a son when they found out she was pregnant. Throughout the pregnancy, he continually talked about how he would groom his son to take over the company some day, how his son would continue building what West began.

Unfortunately, the pregnancy was a difficult one for Claire. She died from complications after giving birth to Meredith. West's heart was broken. Not only had he lost his beloved wife, she didn't give birth to his beloved heir. West loved Meredith, but he didn't believe women could or should run businesses. Their job was to rear children and take care of the home. And now, because of his beliefs about women, he had to turn everything over to a man he despised. West shook his head objectionably and stormed out of the house.

Chapter 70

"I want you to stay on the case."

Later that night, Meredith followed Earl to Ashland Estates. She couldn't believe he would go to his Negro mistress at a time like this. She wondered if Earl told Johnnie Wise about her and their family. *Does he talk to her about things he couldn't talk to me about? Is that why he had to see her tonight? Is this how he copes with life?*

Meredith parked half a block away from Johnnie's house and watched Earl go to the front door. For a brief moment, she considered knocking on the door. There could be no denials if she did, but Meredith Shamus could never do that. She had too much pride to get into an ugly confrontation in public. She sat in the car and cried while she waited for Earl to come out. She toyed with the idea of confronting Johnnie but dismissed it.

Meredith picked up the file Hatcher gave her. For some strange reason, she had to see the photos again. As she shuffled through the pictures, she realized she hadn't seen all of them. She saw a strikingly handsome colored man talking to Earl. In the next still, the man was punching Earl. Meredith found herself staring at the man who had humbled her husband. He looked familiar. She shuffled the pictures until she came to a picture of Johnnie. She put the pictures side by side. The resemblance was uncanny.

Is this her father? No, it couldn't be. He looks to be only a few years older then her. How old did Mr. Hatcher say she was? Didn't he say she was sixteen? But she looks to be in her mid-to-late twenties. A brother then? Yes, her brother. But why didn't Mr. Hatcher tell me about him? Maybe there's something more in the packet.

Meredith reached inside the packet and pulled out a copy of the notes Hatcher took, which chronicled the dates and times Earl met with Johnnie. She read the notes rapidly, until she came to the night of the pictures at the Savoy Hotel. After reading through the notes, it occurred to Meredith that the notes and pictures were in perfect order. All she needed to do was put them back in their original order and she'd have the complete story.

From what she read, it was clear that the colored man was Johnnie's brother Benny. He and his wife Brenda were from California, according to the license plate on his car. They were there for the mother's funeral. The last entry under the Savoy Hotel said that Benny and Johnnie's next door neighbor rented a room at the Savoy.

Meredith started the car and pulled off. She decided to keep Tony Hatcher on the case. When she arrived at her home, she called Hatcher at his office.

"Hatcher," he said when he picked up the phone.

"Mr. Hatcher, this is Meredith Shamus."

"Yes, Mrs. Shamus. What can I do for you?"

"I want you to stay on the case. He's at the Negro woman's house right now. Can you get over there right away?"

"No problem, Mrs. Shamus. I'll get right on it."

Chapter 71
"I don't understand."

Freshly showered and smelling good, Lucas Matthews walked into the Bayou sharply dressed in a charcoal gray shirt and slacks with matching shoes, ready for work. Napoleon called him at his new apartment and told him to be at the Bayou at 10:00 that morning. He had a job for him. *He must have something special for me. Maybe we're finally going to take care of Richard Goode.* In the month that he worked with Bubbles, he'd learned how to shoot a pistol, how to use brass knuckles, how to brutalize a man without killing him, and why it was important to keep a debtor alive. "If we kill 'em," Bubbles explained, "we don't get paid."

Lucas saw Napoleon and Bubbles sitting at their usual table, having a bite to eat. He greeted them and took a seat.

"You look good, kid," Bubbles said. "Hard to remember that shabby bum that came in here a month ago."

"Thanks, man." Lucas smiled.

"Had a talk with Bubbles last night," Napoleon said. "Found out some interesting things about you, kid."

The comment made Lucas feel a little unsettled. *Did Bubbles say something about me and Marla?* "All good, I hope." Lucas pretended to be at ease with what he'd just heard.

"Bubbles said you're doing a great job and you're ready to go on your own. What do you think? You think you're ready?"

Relieved, Lucas regained his confidence. "Yeah, I'm ready."

"Great. You can start this week's pick-up by yourself. But I got a special favor I want you to do for me from time to time. You game?"

"Sure, Napoleon," Lucas said, excited. "What is it, man? You want me to start doin' the payoffs too?"

Bubbles smiled. "My, my, my. Aren't we an ambitious boy?"

"No, nothing like that." Napoleon smiled. "This is a little more personal. I want you to take my car and drive Marla wherever she wants to go."

Lucas' smile evaporated. "I thought you wanted me involved with the Richard Goode thing." He looked at Bubbles to see what he was thinking. Bubbles continued eating his breakfast, not even bothering to look at him. "Have Fort Knox or one of the other guys do it. I wanna be in on the Goode thing."

Bubbles stopped eating and looked at him, obviously aggravated by Lucas' arrogance. "Look, kid, do what the fuck he tells you! You got that?"

Lucas was surprised to hear Bubbles take Napoleon's side; especially after the two warnings he'd given him.

"I thought you and Marla got along, Lucas," Napoleon said.

"We got along fine, Napoleon."

"Then what's the problem?"

Lucas looked at Bubbles briefly. He had that same aggravated look on his face. *I guess he's coverin' his own ass.*

"It's no problem. But why me? Why don't she drive

265

herself?"

"Marla's afraid to drive. A couple of years ago, she was blind-sided by a truck haulin' moonshine. She's been reluctant to get behind the wheel ever since."

Lucas mumbled, "She ain't got no friends to drive her around?"

"Look, man, I told her I'd send someone. She doesn't like any of my other people and asked me to send you. Now, help me out here, man."

"Okay, Napoleon," Lucas said with resignation.

"Great. She's just got a few errands to run. It shouldn't take too long. Here's the keys to my car." He tossed them to Lucas. "That baby better not have a scratch on it when you bring it back."

"Don't worry. It won't," Lucas said. "Now, what about the other thing?"

"What other thing?"

"You know. The thing you promised Johnnie. She's been buggin' me about it."

The truth was, Johnnie hadn't said too much about it. She was surprisingly patient. Lucas knew Johnnie agreed with Napoleon. If they were going to get away with murder, they had to be patient.

"Didn't I promise to take care of it?" Napoleon asked Lucas.

"Yeah."

"Trust me then. We're already planning the thing, okay?"

"Okay, I'll tell Johnnie. Then maybe she'll get off my back," Lucas said. "So, what time do I pick up Marla?"

"Now."

"Now? I haven't even had breakfast yet."

"I'll call her and have her make something for you. It'll be ready by the time you get there."

"Okay. I'm gone," Lucas said and left. *This is just great.*

Napoleon is gonna end up killin' me over this shit. I haven't seen her since the funeral. And now, I gotta drive her around.

Bubbles waited until Lucas left the table then said, "Why you doin' this to the kid?"

"Because I can! Now, are you sure he got the message?"

"Yeah. I'm sure."

"Good. It's all coming together." Napoleon smiled.

"I don't understand," Bubbles said. "When you told me that you thought Marla liked the kid, I thought you should know that I already warned him about her. This is fucked up, man. A lotta good people are gonna die over some pussy, man."

"Men have always killed and died over pussy, Bubbles. And we'll continue to kill and die over it. That and money. And for the record, it's not all about fucking his woman. It's mainly about the money. But yeah, I'm gonna fuck Johnnie—at least once."

Bubble stared at Napoleon disapprovingly.

"Look, man, you don't need to understand everything right now. Just back me up like you've always done. And you're gonna make more money on this thing than you can possibly imagine, okay? Trust me on this."

"Okay, man. I just don't wanna kill the kid."

"We might have to, old friend."

Keith Lee Johnson

Chapter 72

"Go ahead and look."

"Hi, Lucas," Marla said, smiling from ear to ear. "Don't you look nice today."

"Thank you," he said shyly, almost embarrassed.

"Come on in. Breakfast is on the table. I hope you like hot cakes, eggs, bacon, and toast."

"Yeah." Lucas smiled. "I'm starvin' too."

"Well, there's plenty. If you want more, I'll be glad to make it for you."

As they walked to the kitchen, he couldn't help noticing how nice Marla smelled. Her perfume was intoxicating, and the way she smiled at him gave him a jackhammer erection. He'd seen Marla three times now. Each time he saw her he wanted her all the more. He fought the temptation to cop a feel of her shapely derriere, but stared hypnotically at it all the way into the kitchen.

"Lucas, I know you're staring at my ass." The tone of her voice was lighthearted and encouraging.

"Huh? No, I'm not," he said, wondering how she knew.

Marla looked over her shoulder and smiled approvingly. "Go ahead and look. I like the way it makes me feel when you look at me, Lucas. It makes me feel beautiful and desirable."

"I do?" he asked, more innocently than surprised.

268

"Ummm. It smells almost as good as you, Marla." *Shit! What the hell did I say that for?*

"Dig in."

"Ain't you gon' eat?" he asked, looking at a table full of food.

"No, it's all for you."

"Marla, I can't eat this much food," he told her with wide-eyed wonder.

"Nobody says you have to," Marla smiled. "Would you like some milk and O. J.?"

"Uh-huh," he said, pouring syrup on his pancakes.

Marla took two large glasses out of the cabinet and set them on the table. She watched Lucas devour the food as if he hadn't eaten in a month, and it pleased her.

"Say when," she said as she poured the beverages into the glasses, one container in each hand. She sat in the chair across from him and watched him eat. "So, are you afraid of me, or what?"

"What do you mean afraid?" Lucas asked, playing dumb.

"You know what I mean." Marla had a serious look on her face. "I know you enjoyed what I did for you the last time you were here. And I know you can't get it out of your mind, can you?"

Looking confused, he said, "What's the deal with you and Napoleon?"

"What do you mean?"

Lucas curled his lips and sucked his teeth. "You know what I mean. How come you and him don't get along? And how come y'all bothering with me and my girl? Are you tryin' to get back at him, or what?"

"If I tell you, will you answer my question?" Marla bartered.

"Yeah, but you go first."

"Well, Napoleon and I have been together for twenty

269

years. I married him right out of high school. We've had good times and bad. Mostly bad, relationshipwise. As far as material things, I've had it pretty good, never wanted for anything. Even when he went to prison, he saw to it that me and the children were well taken care of. I don't fault him for that. I guess our relationship started to disintegrate when we moved down here to New Orleans."

"What happened when y'all moved down here?" Lucas asked, listening to every word, still shoveling food into his mouth.

"You know, as much as I'd like to put the blame squarely on his shoulders, the truth is I was just as much to blame as him. It's never just one person when a marriage goes bad. It takes two to tango. Anyway, I guess we just lost interest in each other. At first, we had sex all the time. Anywhere, anytime."

Lucas blushed from the open sex talk. Like most men, he thought that women basically had sex with men because men wanted them to. If a woman were the aggressor, she was a whore. Marla sensed what he was thinking and said, "I can see you've been brainwashed."

"Brainwashed? What do you mean brainwashed?" he asked, dumbfounded.

"Basically, it means to continuously fill a person's mind with information that you want them to believe. Pretty soon, whatever information was in their brain is replaced by the newer information, even if the new information is bogus. Understand?"

"Yeah, but why do you say I'm brainwashed?"

"Tell me something. Have you ever heard the cliché 'good girls don't put out' ?'"

"Yeah. I've heard it."

"Do you believe it?"

"Yeah. I guess."

"Why do you believe that?"

"I don't know. I just do."

"That's my point exactly," Marla said forcefully. "Somebody told you that, and now you believe it, yet you don't know why. That's how brainwashing works. The victim never knows what's happened to him."

"Well, my mother is one of the people I heard it from."

"No offense, Lucas," Marla said sincerely. "I'm not putting your mother down, but women have been brainwashed too. You see how this thing perpetuates itself? Women tend to put each other down for doing the very thing they fantasize about." Lucas sat there listening, amazed at her candor. "Do you remember me asking you if you've ever had a woman and not some teenage girl who doesn't know her own sexuality yet?"

"Yeah, I remember."

"Good. What I didn't tell you was that often women don't really blossom sexually until they're around thirty-two or so. That's when we have sex on our minds all the time. Kinda like you do now."

Frowning, he said, "I don't have—"

"Don't even bother denying it. I know that sex is almost always on your mind. You don't have to admit it for it to be true. The bottom line is when a woman reaches a certain age, being a good girl loses a lot of its luster. We become more like a teenage male in our thinking."

Lucas blushed again. "So, you sayin' women your age want to do it as much as men do at my age?"

"Uh-huh. Hard to believe, huh?"

"Yeah. And why are you tellin' me this?"

"I'm trying to teach you something about women. For example, you ever notice how women call each other sluts and whores and the like?"

"Yeah."

271

"Because we've be socialized to only want sex when it's socially acceptable. But at the same time, when we go to a rock and roll concert, we scream our heads off and often throw our panties on the stage. Why? Because the performer's bigger than life. But if the same guy we saw on stage was just another guy walking down the street and women chased him, that wouldn't be socially acceptable—hence the brainwashing. Understand?"

"Man, Marla. You smart." Lucas grinned, feeling a little more relaxed, dropping his guard. "You know a lotta big words. Did you learn how to talk like that in college?"

"No. I learned to talk like that by reading books like *Lady Chatterley's Lover*. It's one of D. H. Lawrence's best. It's been banned in the United States as pornographic, but through some of Napoleon's Chicago connections, I was able to procure a copy."

Having no idea what she'd said, Lucas nodded.

"Books help shape your thinking," she went on.

"You mean brainwashing?"

Marla laughed. "Kinda, but different. Reading opens your mind to different views. In other words, when you read, you get to determine what goes in your brain. You basically brainwash yourself with ideas you never thought about until you picked up a book and started reading. Understand?"

"Not really. But it sho' do sound good when you say it."

Marla laughed again. "Are you finished eating?"

"Yeah. I'm full, thanks. It was delicious."

Marla cleared the table then asked, "Is your girlfriend a good girl?"

"Yes. A great girl."

"Have you had sex with her?"

"Well . . . yeah."

"And she's still a good girl?"

272

"Yeah. I think so."

"Okay. Are you her first and only?"

Lucas frowned. He thought about Earl and how he agreed to put up with their sexual liaisons. Anger began to mount and it showed on his face.

"Judging by the look on your face," Marla continued, "you're not, are you?"

"No, I'm not," he grudgingly admitted.

"Well, is she still a good girl?"

Lucas hesitated. "Yeah. I guess so."

"Why is she still a good girl?"

"I don't know. I guess because I like her."

"So, let me get this straight. Your girlfriend can have two lovers or more and still be a good girl?"

"Well, I guess two or three is okay, but not many more."

"Okay, so is five too many?"

"That's pushin' it, but okay. Five and that's it."

Marla smiled. "So, anything less than five lovers and you won't consider your girlfriend a whore. Is that a fair statement?"

"Yeah. Five or less is fair."

"Okay. Well, I've had less than five men. Am I a whore?"

"How did we get on this subject anyway?" Lucas asked, exasperated.

"Answer the question, Lucas. Would you consider me a whore if I've had less than five lovers?"

"I couldn't say you're a whore if both of you had less than five men."

"So, then I'm a good girl too, right?"

"Right," he said with a laugh. "Are you happy now?"

"I'm not finished with my questions. After I finish, maybe then I'll be happy."

Lucas shook his head. "Ain't we supposed to be runnin' some errands?"

273

"Don't worry. We'll get to that or we won't," Marla told him. "Now, when you first did it with your girlfriend, who was the aggressor?"

"You mean who made the first move?"

"Uh-huh."

"I did," he said.

"So, you seduced her?"

"Huh?"

"You know. Got her in the mood and she surrendered?"

"If you mean did I make her wanna give it up, I sho' did."

Marla laughed. "Yeah, that's what I mean. You did what was necessary to get what you wanted, right?"

"Yep."

"So, what's wrong with a woman doing the same to achieve the desired result?"

"Marla, you sho' do talk pretty."

Feeling in control of the situation, she said, "Come here, Lucas." When he didn't move, she went over to him and kissed him. "You like that?"

"Yes," he heard himself saying, and the jackhammer came alive again.

Chapter 73

"My dark Adonis."

Marla kissed him again, but deeper and more passionately than the first time. "Did you like that?"

"Yes, but—"

Marla kissed him again, and this time Lucas kissed her back. Then he stood up, still kissing her passionately. They felt themselves being pulled further into their carnality. As they pulled and tugged at each other's clothing, they staggered around the kitchen, bumping into the stove and refrigerator.

With his shirt off and tossed on the floor, Marla looked up at the man-child towering over her. His rippling muscles excited her. When she touched him, his skin felt like velvet.

"My dark Adonis," she heard herself whisper just before he picked her up and laid her on the kitchen table.

As he unsnapped his pants, he looked down at Marla. Her skirt was up, exposing the blonde pubic hair covering her inviting vagina. His mouth watered with anticipation. Lucas avoided her because he knew he couldn't resist this temptation, but now, here he was, right where he didn't want to be, sent by the man who gave him a job and promised a better future than the one he had. But none of that mattered now. Not only did he want her, but he needed to be inside her. It was the only way to get past the lust he felt every time he saw her.

With her legs spread wide, Lucas guided himself inside her. To his surprise, he had no trouble getting in. He lifted her legs up onto his shoulders and ease forward until all of him was in her. He leaned forward, placing both palms on the table and pounded her into an orgasm.

"Lucas," Marla said softly. "I think I would be more comfortable if we used the chair."

"Okay," he said dryly.

A few seconds later, Marla was sliding up and down his pole like a toy horse on a merry-go-round. She rode his greased stallion like a cowboy busting a bronco. With each stroke, she seemed to hit just the right spot. Soon, Lucas found himself moaning uncontrollably. He felt himself on the verge of release and craved it all the more. Marla could sense the eruption and quickened her pace.

Then it came. The suddenness of it brought a smile to her face. She slowed down, feeling like the bronco was busted and now under her control. Lucas licked her erect nipples slowly. Marla allowed her head to fall back and enjoyed the sensation of his warm tongue. He grabbed a hunk of her blonde hair and kissed her mouth hard. Before long, they were grunting and groaning again.

Chapter 74

"He's dead!"

"Are you sure it doesn't bother you that me and your brother had a thing together while he was in town?" Sadie asked Johnnie. They were in Johnnie's kitchen, having some pie.

"Yeah, I'm sure," Johnnie told her. "I know how men are now, and my brother ain't no different."

"Isn't any different," Sadie corrected. "There's no such word as *ain't* in the English language, Johnnie. When you go to work for the Beauregards, Ethel will constantly correct your English until she's satisfied she's properly educated you."

"I know, Sadie, but I'll remember that's how she is. Can you tell me anything more about the Beauregards?"

"Well, if you can get through the first couple of months or so, you'll have it made," Sadie assured her. "Ethel Beauregard wants to be treated like the fucking Queen of England. That's why her last maid quit. Betty Jean got sick and tired of Ethel constantly putting her down because her English wasn't up to Ethel's standards." Sadie laughed a little, then went on. "That damned Ethel still doesn't understand why Betty Jean quit a perfectly good and respectable job for a colored woman, as she called it, to work

277

in a restaurant that paid less money. It wasn't just dealing with her. It was also dealing with the constant advances from Eric, her husband. When you start working for them, be on the lookout. The man has a thing for black women. He's been after me for years, and Betty Jean just couldn't take it anymore. Poor Ethel. She thinks the world of Eric. To her, he's the perfect southern gentlemen."

"You know what, Sadie? I think I'm related to them."

"What? How?"

"I'm pretty sure that Eric's father is my grandfather."

"What? Are you sure?"

"No, I'm not sure. But I intend to find out when I start working for them. Do you know if there is a Nathaniel Beauregard related to them?"

"I don't know, but Betty Jean told me they have pictures of family members dating back to the early 1800s. If he's in their family, that's where you'll find him."

The telephone rang. As Johnnie answered it, she said, "I'll be sure to check it out." Before she picked up the receiver, she said, "I bet this ain't—I mean, I bet this isn't anyone but Earl. She put the phone to her ear. "Hello."

"Johnnie, I got great news," Earl told her with unfamiliar excitement.

"Yeah, Earl. What is it?" Johnnie looked at Sadie, who was laughing silently.

"He's dead! The old bastard is deader than a doornail!"

Confused, Johnnie asked, "What are you talking about? Who's dead?"

"West is dead! The mangy old fart got drunk and wrapped his Rolls Royce around a tree."

Johnnie frowned. "How can you be happy about something like that, Earl? The man is dead."

"Fuck him! Have you forgotten that he was moving me out of the company just a few weeks ago?"

"No, I haven't forgotten. But to be happy about someone's death? That's sick."

"I suppose you wouldn't be happy if someone killed the man who killed your mother."

"That's different."

"How is that any different?"

"The difference is your father-in-law didn't kill anybody."

"Yeah, well, moving me out of the company would have killed me, if only symbolically."

"Whatever you say, Earl. Whatever you say."

"I thought you would be happy about this. It means that you can have anything you want now. Meredith is at his lawyer's office now, finding out how he divided up his fortune. I can see him telling Seymour Collins to leave Meredith the money, but leaving me in charge of the business. That's the only way things could have gone. What else could he do? I know he's not going to let her run Buchanan Mutual. He's too much of a misogynist for that. It probably killed him, but when little Buck died, he didn't have any choice." He laughed.

"Sounds like you got everything figured out, Earl."

"I do. And from now on, it's everything first class. We're going to move into that big mansion of his. I'm going to have his cars, his money, his company, everything."

"I guess this is the end for us then. You don't need me anymore. You can have any woman you want now, Earl."

"I know that, but I want you. Don't worry. I'm going to take care of you for the rest of your life. You won't have to worry about anything, ever. You can go to college if you want. I'll pay for it. Whatever you want. I can afford it now."

"Whatever I want?"

"I promise. Whatever."

"Okay, I'll remember that. Listen, Sadie is here, so I gotta go, okay?"

279

"Yeah, I'm at the office. I have to catch up on everything. I've been so busy since he died. There were so many things he hadn't shown me about the business. It's been a crash course. That's why I didn't go with Meredith. A lot has happened all of sudden, you know what I mean?"

"Yeah, I know. A little while ago, my mother and I were at the Savoy sipping iced tea at the pool. Now she's been savagely killed and the police haven't done anything about it."

"Johnnie, is there anything I can do? Just name it."

"Thanks, but I don't think the killer will ever be found. He's white, you know?"

Earl was quiet for a second or two then said, "Okay, well, I gotta go. I'll call you, okay?"

"Okay," she said and hung up the phone.

"So, that was Earl, huh?" Sadie asked.

"Uh-huh." The doorbell rang. "I'll be right back. Let me see who this is. It's probably Lucas."

Johnnie looked through the peephole. She frowned when she saw Napoleon Bentley. Instantly, she knew why he was there. He was going to hit on her again, and she was glad Sadie was there. That way, she could make just about any excuse to get rid of him.

Chapter 75
"That doesn't bother you?"

"Sorry to come over uninvited, Johnnie, but I have a couple of things to discuss with you. Is it a bad time?"

"Well, I have company, Napoleon. My next door neighbor is here. We were in the kitchen having some sweet potato pie. Would you like a slice?"

"Don't mind if I do." He smiled. "But what I have to talk to you about is of a delicate nature. It's about Richard Goode and another matter."

Johnnie's eyes widened with excitement. *Finally, the day of reckoning is here. I'll get rid of Sadie so we can discuss this thing in private.*

Napoleon followed her into the kitchen where he saw Sadie sitting at the table, putting her last piece of pie into her mouth.

"Sadie, you know Napoleon, don't you?"
"Yes, of course. Who doesn't know Napoleon?"

"Napoleon, this is Sadie, my neighbor and best friend."

"Charmed, I'm sure," Napoleon said, kissing her hand.

"I don't mean to be rude, Sadie, but we have some

business to discuss," Johnnie told her. "Can I catch up with you later?"

"Sure, no problem," Sadie said and left quietly.

"Have a seat, Napoleon," Johnnie said, cutting him a slice of the pie. "So, are we ready? Are we ready to get him?"

"Yes, we're ready," Napoleon told her eagerly. He pulled the German Luger out and placed it on the table. "This is it, the gun that he killed your mother with."

Johnnie stared at the weapon closely, almost afraid of it. "Can I hold it?"

"Sure, go ahead. It ain't loaded."

Johnnie picked up the Luger and rubbed her fingers over the barrel. "It's heavy," she said.

Napoleon watched her look the gun over for a few moments while deciding what his next move would be. He had to be careful. If he said the wrong thing, it could ruin his plans for bedding her.

"How did you get the gun, Napoleon?"

"We just followed him around for a while to learn his habits. After dropping his wife at the train station, Goode and his crony Joseph King went out drinkin' last night. We knew the wife was outta town. That's when we went into his house and took the pistol. Nothin' to it. He probably won't even miss it, at least not before the deed is done."

Excited, she asked, "When are you gonna do it? And remember, you promised that I could be there to see it."

"Yeah, I remember," Napoleon said with a twisted smile. "We're going to take care of it this weekend. Saturday night. He's preached his last sermon."

A smirk suddenly appeared at the corners of her mouth. It was pure joy to know that Richard Goode would be dead in just three short days.

Seeing the merriment in her eyes, Napoleon decided to tell her the other reason he was there. "Johnnie, there's another matter we need to discuss too," he said, becoming deathly serious all of a sudden.

Noticing the change in attitude, Johnnie became serious also. "What's wrong, Napoleon?"

"Do you know what it's like to be betrayed, Johnnie?"

"Yes," she said almost inaudibly. "I know that feeling all too well. Why do you ask?"

"I guess there's no other way to say this, other than coming out with it. Lucas is having a thing with Marla, my wife. A man in my position can't afford to allow that to go on without an immediate response. I'm going to have to kill him."

What are you up to now? You come in here talking about betrayal, talking about Lucas and your slut of a wife. Have you forgotten all the moves you've made on me?

"I saw them in my pool one day," Napoleon continued, "splashing around like a couple of school kids with the hots for each other, but didn't think anything of it. He's so much younger than her."

Yeah, but that didn't stop you from approaching me. I'm only sixteen, you hypocrite.

While Napoleon was talking to her, it occurred to him that she wasn't surprised. She wasn't hurt like he thought she would be. He was planning to use her emotions as a means to get her into bed. Now he had to try something else.

"That doesn't bother you?"

"No, and I'm not surprised the way she was all over him. You know how Marla is. She's your wife. And you of all people know how men are. Did you really expect him not to? Ya know, Napoleon, I'm surprised you would even try this. Coming to my house in the middle of the afternoon when you know Lucas won't be here. You know I'm devoted to him, no matter what. For all I know, you set this whole thing up to trap me into sleeping with you. The way Lucas tells it, you and Marla don't even have that great of a marriage." The doorbell rang. "I swear this place is busier than the Quarter during Mardi Gras today. Hold on for a second."

Stunned by her revelations, Napoleon took a bite of his pie and decided to kill Lucas. Johnnie's resistance made bedding her more desirable. His mind was made up. He was going to have Johnnie, and if killing Lucas was the price, so be it.

I'm well within my rights. You don't fuck a man's wife and expect to get away with that shit. On top of that, I'm a made man. I have to do something. I don't give a damn if I did set him up. I didn't make him fuck her. He did that on his own.

Johnnie opened the door and saw an expensive-looking white woman standing on the porch with a leather briefcase in her hand, wearing a black suit and pumps and a black veiled bonnet.

"Ms. Wise, I'm Meredith Shamus. I need to speak with you immediately."

Chapter 76
"Keep that in mind."

"Uh, uh, uh." That was all Johnnie managed to say, surprised by the brazen appearance of her lover's wife.

Seymour Collins had offered to speak on her behalf, but Meredith felt she needed to confront Johnnie herself. This would be the first time Meredith ever confronted anyone for any reason. Incredibly nervous but determined, she pulled the screen door open and walked into the house, hoping to appear strong in her attempt to persuade the young teenager to let her husband go.

Johnnie, still in shock, was powerless to stop her. Her mind raced, wondering what she was going to say to Earl's wife, who obviously knew about the affair and had come to confront her.

"I'll make this quick, Ms. Wise," Meredith began again, feeling in control for the first time in her life. "You've been having an affair with my husband and it's going to end— today." She didn't bother to wait on a response. She continued. "I haven't been able to find out what sort of hold you have on him, but have no illusions. No matter what the cost, I'm willing to pay you or blackmail you to get you out of his life. You think Earl killed your mother, don't you?"

Johnnie frowned. *What are you talking about?*

"I assure you, Earl isn't the type of man that would kill anyone. He has many faults, but he's my husband and the father of my children. I will do just about anything to keep my family together. So, how much is it going to cost me?"

"Huh?" Johnnie frowned.

"Ten thousand?"

Still confused, Johnnie said, "What are you talking about?"

"Twenty thousand," Meredith said firmly.

"Mrs. Shamus, I'm confused. Are you going to actually give me twenty thousand dollars to leave your husband alone?"

"Yes. I'm sure Earl has told you about the tragic death of our son. And my father is recently deceased also. All I have is what's left of my family, and as I said, I'm determined to keep my family intact."

Johnnie turned her back to hide her thoughts. *I wonder how much I can get outta her. I mean, if she thinks I love Earl, she's outta her mind. I've been wanting to get rid of him for a long time. Let's see just how important her family is to her.* Johnnie faced her again. "So, you want him back? Well, twenty thousand isn't quite the figure I had in mind. I was thinking more like fifty." Johnnie's heart thundered in her chest when she heard herself say the excessive amount.

"What makes you think I'll pay you fifty when I'm only offering you twenty as good faith money? What do you think Earl is going to do when I tell him about you and Martin Winters?" Meredith waited to see how much damage the revelation did before she continued the barrage. "That's right. I know all about your tryst with him too. What do you think he's going to say when he finds out you've been sleeping with Martin, one of his best friends? Oh . . . and how could I forget about your football player friend, Lucas Matthews? I understand he spends his nights in your bed as well. I wonder how he'll feel when I tell him that you're opening your legs to not one, but two white men. To be just sixteen, you've been a naughty little girl. But it's all over."

Deflated, Johnnie sat down on the couch and tried to figure out what her next move would be. Meredith finally said, "Ms. Wise, I'm going to pay you the fifty, but here's what you're going to do. You're going to break it off with Earl—permanently. You're going to do that for free. That's not going to cost me a dime. I'll pay you the fifty thousand to keep our family name out of this murder business with your mother. That's the deal. It is a one-time offer. Take it or leave it."

"I'll take it," Johnnie said.

Meredith opened the briefcase and took out fifty thousand dollars. She placed it on the cocktail table then she opened the door to leave. "Oh, and Ms. Wise, if you decide to renege on the deal, know this: My father left everything to me—his fortune, his company, everything. If I can't persuade Earl to stay with me and his family, I will let him leave, but he'll be penniless. I know Earl bought you this house and has embezzled money from the company— money that you've invested with Martin. You've done well for yourself. Take some of that money and educate yourself. Don't let your skin color be an excuse for the things you do any longer. I've been very generous, but I will be equally ruthless if you break our agreement. Keep that in mind as well."

With that, Meredith left quietly.

Chapter 77

"I'm gonna enjoy this."

"So, you've got a thing goin' with two other men besides Lucas," Napoleon said with a laugh. "No wonder you're not bothered by Lucas fooling around on you."

Meredith Shamus had so swiftly blown in and out like a hurricane that Johnnie had forgotten Napoleon was there. When she turned around to face him, he was leaning against the entrance to the kitchen, smiling like he was about to devour his unwitting prey.

"Lucas knows all about Earl! So what?"

"Yeah, but I bet he doesn't know about Martin Winters, does he? How do you think he's going to feel when I tell him?"

"Napoleon, don't do that. I love Lucas. Please don't do that."

"Don't worry. I won't say a word, as long as we have an understanding." He smiled.

"No, Napoleon. I won't do that."

"Sure you will. You'll do it because you know I'll tell him. You'll do it because if you don't, I'll kill him. And you'll do it because it makes sense. I've been wanting to fuck you since the first time I laid eyes on you. What's another fuck going to hurt? You've fucked so many already. I just want my piece, and you can stay with Lucas for all I care."

Johnnie turned her back to him so she could think. *Lucas fought for me. He trusts me. He stole for me. He got a job for me. And he even put up with me havin' sex for money. Do I wanna take the chance on losing the only person that ever cared for me? I can't let him find out that I'm doin' it with three men. He thinks I'm a good girl. I don't want him to change his opinion of me. I am a good girl and I'm gonna prove it to him now that Earl is outta my life. I guess one more man isn't gonna kill me.* She faced Napoleon. "So, I just gotta do it once?"

"Yeah, just one time. I'm not greedy," Napoleon told the young-minded teenager, feeling triumphant. "Just one elegant night at the Bel Glades Hotel and your secret will be safe."

"One time and that's it?"

"Yep. One time. I swear."

"And what about Lucas?"

"What Lucas doesn't know won't hurt him."

"What about him and Marla? What are you going to do about that?"

"Nothin'. I don't give a damn what she does or who with. Let them fuck each other if that's what they want."

"Let's go upstairs then," Johnnie said, believing that it would be quick and painless—no more than five minutes. She could live with that because it would be almost like not doing it at all. And since it would only happen once, she could even forget it happened. "We don't have to go to the Bel Glades. They won't let me in there anyway."

"They'll let you in if I tell 'em to."

"Why can't we just get it over with right now since that's all you want?"

"Because I want to wine and dine you first."

"Fine. When is this supposed to take place?"

"This Friday. The night before we take care of the preacher."

"What about Lucas? We usually see a movie or something on Friday night."

"Lucas will be busy this Friday. I'll see to it. I want you and Lucas at the Bayou tonight to finalize the plans for Goode," Napoleon told her. He placed his arms around her tiny waist and kissed her. It felt good and made him hard. He placed both hands on her tight ass and squeezed. "I'm gonna enjoy this. I can't wait until Friday."

"Then let's take care of it now," Johnnie urged.

"There's something to be said for anticipation," Napoleon said with a smile. "See ya later tonight."

Chapter 78

"How is that bad news?"

After Napoleon left, Johnnie called Martin Winters. She wanted to invest the fifty thousand she'd received from Meredith. While the telephone rang, she wondered how Earl was going to feel when his wife told him that she was going to be the boss from now on. She laughed a little when she thought about it.

"Martin Winters' office, Cynthia speaking."

"Cynthia, this is Johnnic Wise. Is Martin in?"

"Yes, but he's not taking your calls any longer," she said, sounding almost sorry there wouldn't be any more verbal potshots between them.

"What? Why?"

"I'm not sure why, but he told me to give you to Sharon Trudeau. Hold on. I'll put you through."

Johnnie tried to say something, but Cynthia was already gonc. While she waited to be transferred to Sharon, Sadie came back over.

"Girl, you sure have a lot of guests today." Sadie laughed.

"Yeah, I wonder who gon' show up next," Johnnie said, putting up her forefinger.

"Ms. Wise, Sharon Trudeau. I understand you used to be Martin's client?"

"Yes, Ms. Trudeau. Do you know what happened? Do you know why he's not taking my calls?"

"Well, I'm not supposed to say, but the word is his wife found out about you two."

"I see." Johnnie laughed. "So, I'm supposed to work with you now?"

"That's entirely up to you, Ms. Wise. But just because I'm a woman is no reason to think I can't handle your portfolio just as well as Martin, if not better. All I ask for is the opportunity. And please, call me Sharon."

"Did he tell you I'm a black woman, Sharon?"

"He didn't have to. We all saw you that first day you came in. It was the buzz of the office for a while."

"Really?"

"Really. When can you come in so we can discuss some ideas I have to increase your net worth?"

"How about tomorrow afternoon?"

"Sure. How about one o'clock?"

"I'll be there."

"See you tomorrow at one," Sharon said and hung up the phone.

When Johnnie looked at Sadie, her attitude seemed chipper, as if she was anticipating good news. Unable to contain her curiosity, Sadie asked, "So, what are you so peppy about?"

"Guess what?"

"What?"

"It's a great day!"

"It is? Why?"

"Because everything in my life is coming together. You'll

never guess who paid me a visit."

"Who?"

"Meredith Shamus."

"Earl's wife? What did she want? I mean what happened?" Sadie asked excitedly.

Johnnie poured them both a cup of coffee and sat down. Relishing every moment, she looked at Sadie and shook her head. "I almost don't believe it myself. I think I need to pinch myself to see if I'm dreaming."

"Well, what happened?"

"I don't know where to start, but Napoleon had come over here, as you know, to discuss some business. I'll tell you about that later. When I opened the door, I didn't know who it was. But when she told me who she was, I was scared. I didn't know what she was going to do. Then she started talking about me leaving Earl alone, as if I wanted him or something. She even offered me money if I would let him go. And for some stupid reason, she thinks Earl might have something to do with my mother's death."

"Well, did you tell her he had nothing to do with it?"

"No. Why would I do that? She was throwing money around to get me to leave him and to keep her family's name out of the murder, so I took it. I mean, wouldn't you? If you could get rid of the thorn in your side and make money to do it, would you do it, Sadie?"

"Hell yeah!"

"Like I said, at first I was scared, but when she came in here like she knew everything there was to know and only knew part of the story, I thought, well, fine. I can get rid of Earl now. I no longer need him with the money she paid me. I'm thinking, with my investments and working for the Beauregards, I'll be okay money-wise."

"How much did she pay you?"

"A lot."

293

"Okay," Sadie said with a laugh. "You don't have to tell me."

"There's more. Not only did she know about Earl, but she also knew about Martin."

"Your stockbroker?"

"Yep. But he's no longer my stockbroker. She told his wife about our thing together. So, he's gone too. I guess the thing that I like about it is I didn't have to break it off with either of them. I think it would have been messy if I had. And eventually I would have to. This way it's clean, and I can't be blamed for it."

"Yeah, that's true. Leaving a man can be hazardous if he's not ready for it to be over. Earl will have a hard time with this."

"Too bad. I could care less. If it wasn't for him and what he did to me, I wouldn't be like this. I say good riddance." Johnnie frowned. "I can't wait to tell him it's over when he calls. It's just a good thing I got this house in my name, otherwise I would be looking for someplace else to live."

"You sure would," Sadie agreed. "You were smart to do that. I wish I had thought of it. See, that's how a man keeps you around. As long as he has the money and you don't, you're at his mercy."

"Now for the best news. Napoleon told me they were ready to get that Klansman preacher," Johnnie said, suddenly serious. "They're gonna do it Saturday night, and I get to watch."

"You sure you wanna be there?"

"Yeah. If it were your mother, wouldn't you want to be there? I mean, if he were executed for his crime, I'd get to be there then, wouldn't I? So, why not now?"

"I was just checking to make sure. That's all, honey."

"Okay, but the bad news is, Napoleon overheard Earl's wife mention the thing with Martin Winters."

"How is that bad news?"

"You know he's been trying to get into my drawers since we met."

"So, what does that have to do with anything?"

"He told me that if I didn't sleep with him, he would tell Lucas. I don't want Lucas to know what was going on between me and Martin. I wanted to learn about the stock market and Martin was teaching me. I had what he wanted and he had what I wanted. It was only a few times. Based on what I learned, it was worth it. Don't you ever what to be rich, Sadie? Don't you ever want to have your own money? Don't you ever want to do what you wanna do and not have to worry about what it's going to cost?"

"Honey, you don't have to justify yourself to me. Who am I to judge you? You know my situation. I just wish I was as smart as you are."

"But I feel like a tramp, selling myself to men to get where I wanna go in life."

"Johnnie, at some point you're going to realize that this is a dog-eat-dog world. People do all sorts of evil to each other to meet their own selfish ends. Men have used women for centuries. It's time we got ours."

"Yeah, you right. You right."

"So, are you going to do it?"

"You mean sleep with Napoleon? Yeah. It's just one time."

"That's what he told you?"

"Yeah, that was the deal."

"What if he likes it and wants to continue seeing you? Ever thought about that?"

"No, but I don't think he'll do that."

"Do be so naïve, Johnnie. Why wouldn't he? Shit, he'll want to do it again just because it's fresh. Why would you believe a man who would stoop low enough to blackmail a

295

sixteen-year-old for some pussy? Does that make any sense to you?"

"You got a point. I just don't want Lucas finding out about Martin."

"Well, that's a chance you might have to take. But if you sleep with Napoleon, he'll keep on trying to see you. He's obviously obsessed with you. Any time a man has to resort to blackmailing a woman for some pussy rather than plain ol' seduction, he's desperate. If he's desperate, he's capable of anything. Don't trust him."

"Okay, Sadie, I won't."

Chapter 79

"Come on. Let's eat."

Napoleon convinced Johnnie to keep their rendezvous at the chic Bel Glades Hotel. He reserved the honeymoon suite. The suite was filled with long-stemmed red roses and candles, giving the room a romantic ambiance. He knew Johnnie would be apprehensive and cold. To her, it was only a chore she had to complete. Like ironing clothes, it was something that had to be done but no pleasure was derived from it.

Napoleon didn't want an unemotional, detached romp. He wanted her to take an active part in the interlude. He wanted her to be reckless, to throw herself into the night and be liberated from her sense of loyalty to Lucas. In short, he wanted her to want him as much as he wanted her. To him, that was the only way sex could be truly enjoyed.

Johnnie was afraid to be seen riding in his car, and agreed to meet Napoleon in the parking lot of the hotel. She remembered what it was like to ride through her old neighborhood with Earl when Billy Logan yelled "Ya whore!" at her as they rode down the street. She felt bad enough that she was betraying Lucas, but she also disregarded Sadie's sisterly advice, which was another reason she didn't want Napoleon to pick her up.

Johnnie was astonished by the luxurious hotel's marbled floors and massive pillars, which stretched up to the ceiling. Without thinking, she said, "Wow."

When Napoleon heard her, he knew she had just lowered her guard, if only a little. It was what he hoped would happen. As far as he was concerned, all women craved power, riches, and beautiful things. It was like a sweet pastry to them—hard to resist. His tool stiffened, and an almost invisible victorious smile appeared.

When the employees spoke to him using his first name, suddenly Johnnie felt like a piece of meat on a very expensive hook. Johnnie's attitude changed and Napoleon could feel the vibe.

Stepping into the elevator, Napoleon said, "What's wrong? Don't you like the hotel?"

"It's okay," she said dryly.

Napoleon fell silent as he considered what just happened. He could tell by the sullen look on her face that she was upset because she no longer felt special. They exited the elevator on the top floor and entered the honeymoon suite, complete with his and hers bathrooms.

Johnnie gasped when she saw that the luxurious suite was full of roses. The sweet scent filled the room and she inhaled deeply. Although she didn't want to be, Johnnie was impressed.

"Make yourself at home," Napoleon said in a low, romantic voice. "We have all night."

She scanned the room and was taken in by the picture window. From where she was standing, she could see the city lights of her native New Orleans. "The city is beautiful at night," she heard herself say.

"Yes, it is," he agreed. "Would you like to see it from the terrace, Johnnie?"

"Yeah. Why not?"

Just before walking out to the terrace, she noticed the enticing aroma of the dinner he'd ordered for them. She wondered what they were going to have—it smelled marvelous. When he opened the terrace door, a cool breeze swirled around them. The breeze was the perfect antidote to the blistering August night. New Orleans was usually an inferno in late summer.

"Johnnie," Napoleon called to her softly. "I'm not going to bullshit you, okay? I love women, and black women in particular. Sure, I've had other women here. I'm not going to lie about that. But none more gracious, none more lovely, none more stylish than you."

"Is that supposed to make me feel better about what I'm doing?" she said disapprovingly.

"Well, it's supposed to make you feel better about me. In the business I'm in, I don't meet a lot of honest people."

"What makes me so special, Napoleon?"

"Your innocence," he said sincerely.

"What do you mean?"

"You have an innocent way about you that hasn't been corrupted, even though you've done some not so innocent things. It's hard to explain, but it's your innocence that attracts me, not just your beauty."

Johnnie looked over the cement baluster to see what the street looked like from the fiftieth floor. "Everything looks so small from here," she said.

"See, that's what I mean, Johnnie."

"What?" she asked naïvely.

"You say that like you didn't realize things would appear smaller from this height. It's like you don't know these things or something."

"Well, I'm only sixteen," Johnnie said, feeling the need to defend herself.

"Yeah, but you look like a woman," he said, turning a

deaf ear to her youth. "You act like a woman. And that's the attraction, don't you see? You have the face and body of a woman and the innocence of a child. Men are going to want to protect you. That's what we enjoy."

"Protect me from what?" Johnnie asked, still looking at the street.

He turned her around to face him, then gently lifted her chin so that he could look into her eyes. When she looked at him, she could feel his powerful aura. "Anything and everything. All the evil of this world." And with that, he kissed her. "Come on. Let's eat."

Chapter 80

"I'm not willing, Napoleon."

Napoleon escorted Johnnie to the dining room table and held her chair until she was comfortable. Then he lit all the candles on the table. He smiled at her when he turned off the lights and took his seat at the other end of the table.

For the first time that night, Johnnie smiled and relaxed. After bowing her head, she said a short prayer of thanksgiving, then anxiously lifted the lid and looked at the food that smelled so wonderful. Their dinner consisted of honeyed pot roast, turnips, sweet potatoes, macaroni and cheese, fried jumbo shrimp, lobster, fried perch, greens, and a German chocolate cake.

"Why did you order so much food, Napoleon?"

"I didn't order it from the hotel. I had it brought here, just for you. I didn't know what you would want, so I ordered a lot. I can get more if you want."

"No, this is enough. Can I take some with me when I leave?"

Napoleon laughed. "Sure, take as much as you like." He sat quietly, watching her fill her plate, enjoying the view. She was almost finished before she realized he hadn't eaten anything.

"Aren't you going to eat something?"

Napoleon popped the cork on a bottle of white wine and poured some in her wineglass, then he sat in the seat next to her. "Sure, I'm going to eat something tonight. I was just hoping it would be you." He grinned and picked up one of the shrimp. "Here, try one of these."

Johnnie opened her mouth and allowed him to feed her the shrimp, then washed it down with a swallow of white wine. She choked on the wine a little.

"Is this your first time having wine?" he asked her.

"Yes."

"You have so much to learn, Johnnie. I would love to open a whole new world for you, if you let me."

She took another sip of her wine and said, "Well, I hope you can show it to me tonight, because that's all you get. Remember?"

"I was hoping to change that agreement, if you're willing, of course."

"I'm not willing, Napoleon. You wanted me for one night. That's all I'm giving you. As a matter of fact, I'm finished eating. Let's get to it so I can go home. Where's the bathroom so I can change?"

"It's right behind you."

She turned around and looked through the darkened suite, spotting her bathroom. She drained the rest of her wine then left the table to change. Turning on the light, she saw four dozen roses on the wall to wall counter. A smile emerged. She undressed and looked at her naked body in the full-length mirror on the bathroom door, then put on a sheer red negligee. When she opened the door to leave, she had a real appreciation for all the candles in the room for the first time.

Napoleon had rearranged the candles while Johnnie was in the bathroom changing, creating a path to the bed, where he waited for her. He watched her approaching the bed, his lust ever growing as her silhouette became more and more clear. When he stood up to greet Johnnie, her eyes immediately dropped to his penis.

She gasped slightly when she saw how big he was. Her experiences with Earl and Martin led her to believe that all white men had small penises.

"Don't worry, baby," he beamed. "Napoleon ain't gon' hurt you with the snake. It don't bite."

Nervously, she walked up three steps and crawled into the king-sized bed. They were in the darkest part of the room until Napoleon lit the candles on the headboard. "Don't be nervous, Johnnie," he said.

"I'm not," she answered.

He knew she was lying, but didn't care. "I promise I won't hurt you, okay?"

"Okay," she said, determined to get through it as quickly as possible so she could go home.

Sliding over to her, Napoleon felt the warmth of her youthful body and the irritating fabric of the negligee. "Take this off," he whispered.

With both hands, she pulled the garment over her head and lay motionless next to him. Napoleon took a long, admiring look at her incredibly developed body. His desire to be inside her became almost unbearable, but he knew he had to put a leash on his lust. Being the ladies' man that he was, he knew that kissing was the one aspect of foreplay that most women couldn't resist. Diving in with both lips, he kissed her inviting, thick mouth. He felt her body reject his touch and ignored it. The wine would kick in soon, he thought.

His persistent kissing paid off. After about twenty minutes, she was kissing him back. Feeling like he had the green light to touch her, he did. Napoleon slid his hand down her side, around her wide hips, and down to her naturally muscular thighs. She flinched slightly. He ignored it and continued his approach to the land of gold—the only human organ in the world that relieved stress and gave indescribable pleasure at the same time.

Gently, he touched her forbidden zone and felt her sticky fluid. The sensation he felt at the moment had to be fought. His lust begged him to enter her, but his goal demanded patience, so he waited. He continued to stroke her there, softly, and her body betrayed her. Knowing she was letting go, he encouraged her by continuing to do the thing she enjoyed.

"Just do it," she begged, "so I can go."

"Not yet, baby. Not yet. This is my only night. Let me enjoy it."

"But I gotta go, Napoleon," she pleaded.

"Shhhhhhhhh," he said, taking one of her sizable nipples into his mouth while continuing to stroke her.

"Don't do that, Napoleon. Please don't do that," she beseeched.

"Why not?" he asked, coming up for air.

"'Cause it feels too good."

"You think that feels good? This is just the beginning of what I have in store for you."

With his tongue, he made circles around her nipples and began the long trek to the land of gold. After reaching it, he lapped for what seemed like an eternity, letting her sensitivity be his guide.

Johnnie tried, but her body demanded liberation and she gave into it. She began to scream and she didn't care. It felt that good. With her legs on his shoulders, Napoleon began to impale her with his long tongue. Having lost any semblance of control, Johnnie pumped him in the face until she came—loudly. Then he slid his tongue back up to her breasts and licked them until she moaned.

"Stick it in me now," she demanded. "I want it now!"

Positioning himself to enter, he did it with ferocity. They pumped hard and steady. Johnnie could feel herself on the verge of another orgasm and pumped faster. They slammed their bodies together so savagely that each time they touched, the smacking of their bellies could be heard over their moans.

Napoleon was digging all nine inches into her with no problem, and it turned him on even more. Suddenly, he felt her nails in his back. He could tell she was close now. The bedsprings howled and the headboard banged against the wall. Napoleon could hear a constant thud over and over again; the bed coming off the floor, then slamming down again. Finally, they came together. Exhausted, he heaved heavily.

"That was great, wasn't it, baby?" he asked her. Hearing no response, he found the strength to raise his head. He looked down at her. He could see that she was still breathing, but Johnnie had passed out from the intensity of the orgasm.

Chapter 81

"Can you bring my purse?"

It was 4 o'clock in the morning when Johnnie woke up. She opened her eyes, expecting to see Napoleon, but he was gone. He had blown out the candles before he left, leaving the room completely dark. She rolled over onto her back and began to consider just what had happened that night.

She felt terrible for giving herself to Napoleon and even worse for enjoying it so much. To date, Napoleon was definitely the best lover of the four men she'd known. She thought about their sexual encounter and without intending to, began to relive it. As she imagined everything that happened between them, she grew angry at Napoleon for making her beg him to enter her. The last thing she wanted to do was have him inside her, but to actually beg for it? She hated him. Although she was glad it was over, a small part of her wanted it to happen again; that angered her too.

Johnnie swung her legs over the side of the bed. She decided to take a shower and get home as soon as she could. When she turned on the light in the bathroom, she saw a note from Napoleon that read:

> *Good morning, Johnnie,*
> *I enjoyed our time together. Don't worry, I won't be bothering you again. Meet me at the Bayou tonight around ten o'clock. I'm expecting a call from Bubbles and Lucas. They should know exactly where our boy is. Tonight is your night. Are you ready for it? I am. I will deliver everything I promised you.*
>
> *Yours truly,*
Napoleon
>
> *P.S. Lucas is a lucky man. You saved his life tonight.*

Johnnie folded the note and put it in her purse, then climbed into the shower.

***

"Where the fuck you been?" Johnnie heard Lucas ask when she entered the house.

Startled, she recoiled and said, "Lucas, you scared me to death. How did you get in?"

"Through the window over the kitchen sink. I broke your plant coming in."

Johnnie looked at the window and tossed her purse on the counter. The poinsettia was missing. She went over to the window and locked it. "I thought I locked this window," she said, buying time to think of just the right answer.

"So, where you been?" he repeated.

"Well, at least you asked me without being profane this time" She frowned. "Why do you ask questions that you really don't want to know the answers to?"

"So, you was with Earl again?" he asked rhetorically. "When you gon' leave that white man alone?"

"This was the last time," she said, grateful he had supplied his own answer. "His wife found out about it and put a stop to it. Apparently her father was killed in an accident and left everything, including Buchanan Mutual, to her."

"So, this was one last fuck, huh?" Lucas said more than asked.

"Since you won't respect me, I'll ask you the same question. Did you fuck Marla yet?"

"No."

Johnnie rolled her eyes. "Don't lie, Lucas. I know you did."

"How?"

"A woman knows these things about her man," she said, still frowning. "What do you think is going to happen if certain people find out what you did? You could get killed. Did you ever think about that? That you could be killed for what you did?"

"Yeah, I thought about it," he said, lowering his eyes.

"So, you did do it with her," she confirmed. "Well, you better stop."

"Why you so worried about it, Johnnie? Do you know something I don't?"

"I know you're the typical male that has trouble turning down pussy. I know that."

Lucas walked over to her and took her in his arms. "I love you, baby."

"Would you do anything for me? Would you do anything to keep me safe, to keep me from being killed? Would you sacrifice yourself for me, Lucas? I would sacrifice myself for you. I would do anything to keep something bad from

happening to you. Anything at all. I love you that much. Do
you understand that? Do you? Please tell me you do."

"I understand, baby. But what's this all about? Did Earl
find out about me or what?"

"No. And we don't have to worry about him anymore,"
she said, thinking of a convenient way to change the subject.
"Guess what? Not only is Earl outta the picture, I got some
money outta the deal."

"Oh yeah? How much?" he asked, raising an eyebrow.

"Just a few thousand."

"A few thousand, huh?"

"Yeah, a few. And Earl is gone forever."

"Forever, huh?" he said, smiling for the first time. "So,
it's just you and me now, right?"

"Uh-huh."

"Let's go upstairs and celebrate then," Lucas said. "I
know you ain't tired from being with a white man. It was just
the regular thirty-second deal, I'll bet. Cain't no white man
put it on you the way I do. Ain't that right, baby?"

"That's right," Johnnie said without hesitation.

"Why don't you go on upstairs and get ready for me? I
wanna get something to drink."

"Okay, I'll be waiting," she said and went upstairs.

Lucas opened the refrigerator and took out the orange
juice. He opened the cabinet door to get a glass and saw
Johnnie's purse. He poured himself some juice and drank it
straight down, he rinsed the glass, then turned to go
upstairs. But his curiosity got the better of him. He was
warned by his mother to never go into a woman's purse, just
as he was told to never go into the girls' restroom in school.
He had to see what they kept in those little bags that was so
important.

He went back to the counter and picked up the purse,
then looked back at the door to make sure Johnnie hadn't

come back. He opened the purse and looked inside. At first glance, there was nothing worth hiding in there; just some keys, some money, a makeup kit and a few other odds and ends. He reached inside and grabbed the money to see how much she had. When he pulled it out, the note from Napoleon came out with the money. After reading the note, it all became clear. She was telling him that if she hadn't slept with Napoleon, he might be dead now.

How could she do it? How could she fuck him? Marla was right. He doesn't have any friends. He knows I love Johnnie and he fucked her anyway. And he had to threaten her to do it. Maybe she thought she was doing me a favor. Napoleon don't scare me. I can take care of myself. The bastard! I'll kill him before he kills me.

"Is everything okay down there, Lucas?" Johnnie shouted.

"Yeah. I'm on my way up," he said, putting everything back in the purse.

"Can you bring my purse?"

Chapter 82

"Hurt my feelings how?"

Napoleon was sitting behind his desk when Johnnie, escorted by Fort Knox, entered his office. He gestured for her to sit down while he finished the conversation. She stared at him, wondering if he was going to bring up the previous night's diversion, but he never looked at her. She thought all day about what happened between them, just as Napoleon knew she would. It was all a part of his plan to take her from Lucas. When she passed out, he thought it all out. Johnnie was young and beautiful, just the sort of woman he wanted on the side.

Too bad she's only sixteen. What the hell? Age is only a number.

He wanted to kill Lucas, but that would make it impossible for her to be with him. Something more sinister must be done with him.

"So, he's there right now?" Napoleon asked, looking at a picture of a nude black woman on the wall, determined to acknowledge Johnnie only when absolutely necessary. "Okay, we're on our way. We'll meet you in the parking lot."

He hung up the phone and looked at Johnnie. She was absolutely gorgeous, even when she wasn't dressed up. She was wearing a pair of dark slacks and a dark blouse.

Napoleon could tell she'd made the effort to downplay her looks, so he played it cool—like nothing ever happened between them.

"Let's go. They're waiting for us in the parking lot of the Savoy."

They rode in silence the entire way. Napoleon knew she was expecting him to hit on her again, so he didn't. His plan required him to keep his word to her. That way, when Lucas was out of the picture, she'd have the freedom to choose him. When they pulled into the parking lot of the Savoy, Johnnie said, "Napoleon, I hope you know nothing is going to happen between us after tonight."

"I know. And I'm glad."

"You are?" she asked, surprised at what he'd told her.

"Yeah. It was a mistake. I feel bad that I even put you in that sorta position. Besides, it wasn't exactly the way I thought it would be."

Confused, Johnnie asked, "What do you mean by that?"

"I don't wanna hurt your feelings, kid."

"Hurt my feelings? Hurt my feelings how? And I'm not a kid anymore."

"Well, it wasn't that great. You know how you want something really bad and when you get it, it ain't what you think it's going to be?"

"So, I wasn't good enough for you?"

"No, sorry," he said, smiling within.

"Well, what did I do wrong? I thought you enjoyed it."

"Look, there they are. Let's go," he said and got out of the car.

Perfect timing. She'll be thinking about what I said all night. It's all coming together.

"Napoleon," Bubbles began, pointing at the exit that Johnnie had come out of a few times. "His car is right over there. All we gotta do is wait."

Looking at him now, Napoleon seemed more dashing to Johnnie than he ever had. He appeared to have everything in control. She stared at him, totally unaware that Lucas was watching her, quietly seething. A crooked smile escaped her lust-filled mind and etched itself on her unsuspecting face. From his black alligator shoes to the white sports coat that hugged his muscled shoulders, she studied him as though he was a book to be absorbed.

Lucas' anger was boiling over. He was about to lose control when Napoleon said, "Okay, Bubbles, you ride with me. Lucas, you and your girl can ride together."

Oh, now I'm his girl all of a sudden. Last night it was, "Johnnie I would show you the world if you let me." Now I'm just Lucas' girl. Can't you even say my name? I'm a real person, not a ghost.

"Okay, Napoleon," Lucas said, trying hard not to let on that he knew about them. "Johnnie, Bubbles' car is way over there—outta sight."

"Here you go, kid," Bubbles said, tossing him the keys.

Lucas caught them, grabbed Johnnie's hand, snapping her out of the lustful trance, and practically dragged her over to Bubbles' car. He opened the door for her then slammed it when she got in.

"What's the matter, baby?" Johnnie asked when he got in the car.

"You fucked Napoleon, that's what's wrong!"

"Huh?" she said, shocked that he knew. "What are you talking about?"

Lucas backhanded her. "You know what the fuck I'm talkin' about, Johnnie! I'm not stupid!"

313

Chapter 83
"Say what?"

Watching the exit door from the front seat of Napoleon's car, Bubbles asked, "So, are you satisfied now?" referring to his romp with Johnnie.

"Naw. I ain't satisfied," Napoleon replied. "I'm a long way from being satisfied. Gonna have to get rid of the kid."

"Why? You got what you wanted," Bubbles said. His heart went out to Lucas.

"Well, I want some more. A lot more."

"Napoleon, that girl ain't but sixteen years old." Bubbles scowled. "What the fuck are you thinkin', man?"

"I'm thinkin' I found a glittering jewel in a land where jewels don't come along very often."

"Don't tell me you in love with her."

"No, old friend. Love it ain't, but there's a lot I can teach her."

"You mean to tell me some sixteen-year-old girl's pussy is that good?"

"It's more than that. Look, Bubbles, I'm not going to explain myself to you. You'd never understand."

"So, tell me about it. What happened?"

"We fucked and it was good."

"You mean she gave it up willingly?"

"You damn right. Begged for it, as a matter of fact."

"What did you do, eat her out?"

"Uh-huh. I ate the pussy like it was the nectar of a Georgia peach. You ever eat a pussy, Bubbles?"

"Naw. Thought about tryin' it out, though. When I was in the joint, I kept hearing the white boys talk about eatin' pussy. That's all they talked about. Like it was better than dickin' a bitch."

"Black women say black men won't eat pussy. Is that right?"

"Cain't speak for other men. I just know I don't. Never had to. My dick has always been good enough."

"That's what you say. But I've eaten many black women who had men with big dicks, and they love it. You think it's just the nine inches I put on 'em that keeps 'em comin' back? No. It's the way I ate that pussy. I eat pussy like its goin' outta style."

"That's how you ate her last night, huh?" Bubbles laughed.

"Yeah, man. I ate her so long that all she could do was coo like an infant. Then I fucked her like she's never been fucked. I fucked her so good that she passed out."

"Say what?"

"Yeah. She passed right the fuck out she came so hard."

"So, did she blow you too?"

"No, but she will."

"Sure she will."

"Bubbles, let me tell you something. When you eat a woman's pussy right, you won't have to ask her to blow you. She'll do it because she wants to."

"Bullshit! It's hard to get a black woman to suck my dick. She might slobber around for a minute or two, but that's it."

"Then she tells you it's too big or her jaws hurt, right?"

315

"Yeah."

"She's just playing to your ego. Try this. Stop asking her to suck you, and you start eating her. I don't mean for a second or two, either. I mean put your face in that muthafucka.   Eat that muthafucka like you eatin' a watermelon. No offense."

Bubbles laughed.

Chapter 84

"Look! Here he comes!"

Johnnie's face felt like it was vibrating from the sting of the slap. She held her hand to her jaw, trying to figure out how Lucas found out so quickly.

"First it was Earl, now it's Napoleon! Who else you fuckin'? Maybe you are a whore!"

With that, tears streamed down her face. To be called a whore, even in question form, cut her to the center of her being. It was different being called a whore by Lucas. He was the one person who never looked at her that way. He always respected her, and now even he was referring to her in those terms.

"Marla was right. He was after you," Lucas continued. "That's the real reason he sent me and Bubbles to watch Goode all night. Just so he could get some from you. Ain't it?"

"I did it for you, Lucas," Johnnie said desperately. "He knows about you and Marla. He told me he was going to kill you. He said if I did it with him, he would let you live."

"I know. I read the letter last night."

"You knew, and you did it with me last night anyway?"

"Yeah, so what? He's white. How good could he be in bed? That's what I thought last night until I saw the way you was lookin' at him a few minutes ago."

"It didn't bother you last night, but it bothers you now?"

"Yeah. And last night I needed some."

Johnnie was quiet as she contemplated what he said. *All men are like that,* she heard her mother saying. *They all want what you got between yo' legs. Don't hold their weakness against them.*

I guess she was right—even about Lucas. What am I going to do now? I feel so alone. Who do I trust now? She was even right about how men react when we do the same things they do. He fucked Marla, but I'm the whore.

"So, what does this mean for us?" Johnnie asked. "Are we finished? Don't you want me anymore?"

"I'll think about it," he said gruffly. "You need to be thinkin' about whether you want me the way you was lookin' at him."

"I do want you, Lucas. Why do you think I've done all that I've done? Just because I wanted to do it? I want a better life. Don't you?"

"Yeah. Why do you think I'm working for Napoleon?"

"Then we both have done things we didn't necessarily want to do, right?"

"But you enjoyed it with him, didn't you?"

"No, I didn't. It was something I had to do. It was business, that's all. I swear. I won't do it again. Can you say the same thing about Marla? Can you tell me you won't do it with her again? You had an excuse before. Now that Earl's gone, we can be together like you wanted. Isn't that what you said? You wanted him out of the picture. Well, he's out now. Let's put the past behind us, baby, and move forward, okay?"

"That's easy for you to say. You're a woman. You're supposed to understand how men like to have a variety of women. It don't mean I don't love you, though."

Johnnie folded her arms. "So in other words, you're gonna keep fuckin' Marla, even after what I did to save your life. You're gonna go back and do it again, aren't you? Marla must be better than me if you can't give it up. That's all I gotta say. I mean, if you know he'll kill you over this and you still go back, it must be made of gold or something."

"No. I'm not gonna do it with her again," he told her, but he was lying. He wanted Marla one last time, then he'd leave it alone—he was sure this time. "Look! Here he comes!"

Chapter 85
"The day of reckoning is here."

Richard Goode didn't realize he was being followed until he was halfway across the Lake Pontchartrain Causeway. Thoughts about his new demimonde distracted him, having finally found a black prostitute willing to do all the things Marguerite used to do. His preoccupation with black whores caused him many sleepless nights. Being a preacher with such thoughts about women, especially black women, produced a moral battle within him.

He fought long and hard against his flesh, but in the end, his flesh won out more times than he'd like to remember. Recalling that the Apostle Paul was known to beat his body to bring it into submission was an idea that would surely work for him. In his twisted mind, he needed to be severely beaten for being who he was—the Grand Wizard of the Ku Klux Klan. Who better to punish him for his bisexual tendencies than a black woman who he swore never to bed? Besides, no self-respecting white woman would do such things, even if she were a whore. However, another problem arose.

At some point, he began to enjoy the beating. In fact, the idea of being beaten with a riding crop appealed to his latent homosexuality. Before long, he gave into that as well.

Soon, he accepted who he was—a hedonistic bisexual whose political beliefs mirrored those of Adolf Hitler.

He decided to wait until he was off the twenty-nine mile bridge before he made a run for it. The plan was to get home and get his shotgun. Exiting the bridge, he immediately turned off the headlights and floored it. Constantly looking in his rearview mirror, he could see dust flying everywhere. It wasn't long before he saw the Cajun restaurant where he met Marguerite. Whoever was following him, they were gaining ground, he thought.

Up ahead, he saw the lights of his farm about three miles away. Seconds later, Bubbles pulled up right next to him. Something inside Goode compelled him to see who was chasing him. He looked over and saw Napoleon and Bubbles; both were smiling. Instantly, Napoleon pulled out the German Luger and pointed it at him. Fear gripped Goode and he swerved off the road into a ditch. Goode managed to get out of the wrecked car and ran through the cornfields toward his house.

"He's heading for the house!" Bubbles shouted. "Lucas, drive up there and we'll run him right to you."

Lucas' tires spun, throwing dirt and gravel. His adrenaline flowed and he found the excitement intoxicating. Goode was only about thirty yards ahead of Bubbles and Napoleon, but he was running for his life. His only chance was to get to the barn before they caught up with him. His heart beat like kettle drums, but he was almost there, almost safe. Goode was just about to run into the barn when Lucas, running at full speed, tackled him with the ferociousness of a Lawrence Taylor sack.

Goode screamed when several of his ribs almost gave way to Lucas' broad shoulder. The timing of the hit was executed perfectly. Lucas stood over his victim and said,

"Now, that's how you hit a muthafucka. Eat your heart out, Grambling."

Just then, Napoleon and Bubbles arrived, panting and sweating profusely.

"Let's finish this bastard!" Lucas shouted, kicking him in the ribs.

"Wait," Napoleon commanded. "Let me catch my breath."

Johnnie watched what was happening from the car, taking it all in. She needed to see him. She needed to look into his face and see this evil man who killed her mother.

"What's going on, fellas?" Goode finally said, catching his breath. "What did I ever do to you?"

Goode heard the car door slam shut and heard footsteps coming toward him. As the person came closer, he could tell it was a woman.

Johnnie looked down at him with a disgusted look on her face. "The day of reckoning is here, preacher," she said.

Narrowing his eyes, Goode began to recognize the woman. "I know you," he said, "You're Marguerite's daughter."

Bubbles grabbed Goode by the lapels and snatched him to his feet. "Stand up when you address a lady."

Goode laughed. "A lady? Ha! I bet she's a whore just like her bitch of a mother was before I put her outta her misery." He laughed again. Lucas hit him in the nose, then in the body.

"All right," Napoleon said. "Let's get this over with. Johnnie, you got anything you wanna say to this worthless piece of shit?"

"Yeah. I wanna know why you did it. Why did you kill my mother?"

"Because the black bitch tried to blackmail me, that's why! She threatened to go to the *Sentinel* about our arrangement. Wanted me to buy her a house in niggertown so she could be near you. The dumb bitch actually believed me when I agreed to do it." He laughed. "If you sow to the wind, you reap the whirlwind. She got what was coming to her, and I'm gonna get what's comin' to me, and I don't regret a damned thing. Now, let's get it over with."

"Anything else, Johnnie?" Bubbles asked.

"No, nothing," she said sadly, realizing that her good fortune had in some way caused the death of her mother.

"You're just like her," Goode shouted just before the beating began. "You're a good for nothin' black nigger whore! Don't forget that! You can't change what you are!"

From the car, she watched the professional beating. The first blow to the nose with the German Luger was difficult to watch. His blood sprayed like a mist when the gun connected. Lucas and Bubbles took turns beating him mercilessly with brass knuckles and the Luger. The repeated blows to the face nauseated her, but Johnnie found the strength to continue watching—she owed it to her mother. Surprisingly, Goode never cried out, never begged for his life. With each blow, he looked at her and smiled. Is he enjoying this, Johnnie wondered?

It's true. What Richard Simmons told me is true. She was beating him in that hotel room. Am I just like her? Or am I worse? I don't know anymore.

"Is that enough, Johnnie?" Napoleon asked after taking a drag of a cigarette.

Johnnie snapped out her moment of introspection. She looked at Goode, who still had a superior grin on his pulverized face. "I want him to feel what she felt. I don't want him smiling before he dies."

"This sick son-of-a-bitch ain't gon' ever feel like that, Johnnie," Bubbles said. "He loves this shit. I'm gettin' tired of whipping his ass."

"Lucas, take his pants off," Napoleon ordered. "We're gonna cut the muthafucka's nuts off."

"No!" Goode shouted, suddenly gripped by fear. "Don't cut my balls off."

"Oh, you afraid now, huh?" Bubbles asked sarcastically.

"No! Don't do it. Please don't do it," Goode pleaded.

Bubbles and Lucas held the half-naked man down while Napoleon castrated him. "Aaaagh!" Goode screamed when he felt the sharp blade cut into his flesh.

Johnnie had seen enough. She could no longer watch the mutilation. She turned away and covering her ears. Even with them covered, she could hear his screams. "Enough!" Johnnie shouted, still looking away. "Just do it." And with that, Bubbles put the Luger to the Klansman's head and fired.

Chapter 86
"What have I done?"

A few days later, Johnnie kept hearing Goode's screams in her head. Day after day, the images of his beating would come to her from nowhere. This wasn't the way justice was supposed to work, she thought. Justice was supposed to feel good. After all, he got what he deserved, didn't he? Nevertheless, she regretted what she'd done. On top of that, Lucas was still hurt. He knew Johnnie enjoyed that one night with Napoleon, but she believed he'd get over it eventually.

Sitting at the kitchen table, Johnnie sipped her morning coffee and read the previous day's *Sentinel* while she waited for Sadie to come over for their usual gossip session. The article was about Richard Goode's brutal death, stating that his wounds and injuries were similar to Marguerite's. She turned the page to the opinion section and saw an article by the paper's editor. Her hand started to shake uncontrollably when she began reading the it.

The circumstances and deaths of Richard Goode and Marguerite Wise are too similar to ignore. According to the autopsies, they both had almost identical wounds and bruises. Both victims had broken noses, a broken jaw, missing teeth, broken ribs, and a punctured lung. A police official confirms that both victims had sustained lacerations from the same weapon—a German Luger, found at the scene with Goode's blood on it. The most shocking aspect of this whole episode is that the Luger belonged to Goode. The killer or killers must have taken it from him.

This bit of information leads one to think that Goode must have been involved in the death of Marguerite Wise. Did Goode kill Marguerite that night a couple of months back? If so, was his death a revenge killing? It's no secret that Goode is the Grand Wizard of the Ku Klux Klan. But if he killed Marguerite Wise, what was his motive? According to the police, Marguerite was a known Sable Parish prostitute. Was Goode seeing her secretly? If so, what happened? Did she threaten him in some way? All of these questions need answers. But the most troubling question is what will the Klan do now that their leader has been murdered?

It is conceivable that Goode killed Marguerite Wise. Marguerite's killer was never brought to justice. As a matter of fact, no one was even arrested. Therefore, it's possible that Goode's death was an act of vengeance. If it was, the city has bigger problems. Vigilantism cannot be condoned for any reason. This is why we have laws and a court system. The untold numbers of victims who have been lynched because someone thought they were guilty are far too numerous. When a group of people decide to work in concert to kill another human being on suspicion alone, none of us are safe. With the death toll at two, will it stop here? In all likelihood, it will not.

Johnnie's hand shook even more when she finished the article. She hadn't counted on this happening. Napoleon was supposed to be an expert at this sort of thing. It was just a matter of time before the New Orleans police would come to talk to her, she thought.

What am I going to do now? It's not going to matter what my reasons were. Goode is white and I'm black. They're going to kill me for sure. I gotta get outta here.

Johnnie recoiled when she heard the rapid tapping on her back door. She looked up in horror, scared to death it was the police, forgetting that Sadie was coming over. When their eyes met, mutual fear could be felt as well as seen.

"Come on in," Johnnie called out.

"Have you read Rahim Muhammad's article in the *Raven* today?" Sadie asked, almost in a state of panic. "That nigga gon' get us all killed."

"No. Have you read yesterday's *Sentinel?*" Johnnie queried with equal consternation.

"What did it say?" they asked in unison then exchanged papers.

"Oh no," Johnnie mumbled as she read the article.

Shame on the Sentinel *for publishing the work of totally irresponsible journalists, stirring up the white population with unsubstantiated theories about Richard Goode and Marguerite Wise. And for what reason? To outsell the* Tribune *and the* Times, *their chief competitors? Didn't they know an article like that could cause a race riot? We haven't had a race riot in New Orleans since the late 1800s. There hasn't even been a Klan uprising in nearly fifteen years. Well, let me be the first to say that the Negro isn't going to take it this time. We will not stand by idly and watch angry Whites destroy what we've built for no other reason than jealousy and blind rage over our prosperity. Just as the black Tulsans defended themselves and their property in 1921 against white rage and aggression, so shall we if it comes to that.*

The Sentinel *does, however, make a compelling argument for what happened to Marguerite Wise. And if they're right in their supposition, justice has been done. The black people of New Orleans didn't know who killed Marguerite Wise before yesterday's article appeared. But as far as we're concerned, this is divine justice. Whoever killed Goode did so with the same ferocity he himself meted out. As the article so vividly stated, his wounds were reminiscent of what the* Sentinel *presumes he did to his victim. As for the castration, we ask only this: Has he ever castrated anyone? The Ku Klux Klan is known for castrating Negro men. The question that begs to be asked is this: Were Richard Goode and Marguerite having relations?*

According to the Sentinel, *they were. Assuming their conjecture is correct, maybe Goode did kill her. Maybe she was going to reveal that a Klan leader, of all people, was frequenting black prostitutes on a regular basis. That information would have destroyed his standing with the Klan, would it not? And for that very reason, we say again that justice has been served in this city. Let us lay aside our anger and continue on, lest we destroy our city and ourselves along with it. Let there be no further bloodshed in this sordid matter. I appeal to the white community with sobriety of thought and sincere forbearance of spirit. But I also say this: If Whites will not lay aside their anger, neither will we lay aside ours.*

They finished their respective articles at precisely the same time. Then Johnnie, with a heavy heart said, "What have I done?"

Chapter 87

"That's the idea, you dumb nigger."

The riot started on Main Street at 9:30 that same night. It was nearly a hundred degrees, and tempers flared with in the white community, aided by Joseph King, Richard Goode's fiery acolyte, who learned of the piece in the *Raven* when a Negro tried to explain that Rahim Muhammad didn't speak for all Negroes in the parish. King convinced Whites to join his cause to right the wrong perpetrated by the black heathens, who were just waiting for an opportunity like this to rape their wives and daughters. His passionate lies led even the decent white men and women, along with their children, to join the volatile mob.

Nearly five thousand Whites armed with rifles, knives, clubs, and torches swarmed into Sable Parish and completely plundered it, hanging men, women, and children, who weren't prepared for the assault. The rampage went on for nearly three hours and fueled their ever-growing thirst for blood. Having conquered Sable with relatively no resistance, they proceeded on to Baroque Parish, where they planned to sack the town the way the Romans demolished their enemies.

From nearly a mile away, the black citizenry of Baroque Parish could hear horns and a cacophony of endless, mindless banter. The angry mob started the riot by throwing a brick through the window of Philip Collins' barbershop, and the looting began. From every quarter, shattered glass could be heard. Then from the rooftops, shots rang out and Whites began to fall to the ground, their bodies having been pierced by bullets. Pow! Pow! Pow! They took cover and returned fire. The shooting went on until the black citizens ran out of bullets. That was when the pillaging went into overdrive.

The wrathful mob looted Dennis Edwards' clothing store, Addison's bakery, the Baroque Parish Bank, the grocer, restaurants, and anything else in sight. They hanged the captured men on light poles and raped the women—even the little girls. It was when they reached the Savoy and saw the mixed couples that they decided to torch the community for vengeance.

Richard Simmons and his employees did their best to defend the historic building, but in the end, there were just too many of them, even though many would-be assailants had been wounded or killed. Simmons was forced to watch the Savoy burn to the ground and witness Trudy's rape before they tied him to a telephone pole and set him on fire. White men, women, and children watched him burn alive, listening to his gut-wrenching screams as if his death was a delectable treat.

From there, they went to the *Raven* and destroyed the printing presses before setting it ablaze. Growing ever confident, they proceeded to the library where Reverend Staples, wearing his clergy garb, sat on the concrete steps waiting for them. When they approached him, he stood up and said, "Men and women of New Orleans, fear God! Take your children home! This is madness! Surely you won't destroy this building. It is rich in culture and serves as our only means of history. Please, leave us our library and our school, lest we perish as a people."

"That's the idea, you dumb nigger," Joseph King shouted from the massive crowd as he fired his rifle. Reverend Staples looked surprised when the bullet pierced his forehead. He dropped to his knees and fell face forward on the hot concrete. "Come on, boys!" King shouted. "Let's burn the school too."

Chapter 88

"It's suicide to try."

Having ransacked Main Street, the volatile mob proceeded to Ashland Estates, where they planned to burn the homes of the affluent Negroes. "Why should they live so good?" one man shouted. "A nigger is a nigger, no matter how much money he's got," another shouted. "They all deserve to die for what they did to Richard Goode," a policeman dressed as a civilian said. "No white man should ever have his balls cut off."

Napoleon, being white, easily mixed in with the mob and waited until they left Main Street before he called Bubbles to let him know the mob was on its way. The men of Ashland Estates knew they couldn't defend Sable Parish or Main Street. They planned to give token resistance to the rioters, hoping they would be overconfident by the time they reached Ashland Estates, where fifteen hundred Negro men were waiting, armed to the teeth, along with a hundred or so white men who had families there. The plan was to let them in then close the door behind them, leaving no avenues of escape. The Negroes were outnumbered three to one, even with the Whites who joined them.

When Sadie told Santino Mancini, her benefactor and the father of her children about the coming riot, he started a chain of calls to all the white men who had families in Ashland Estates. Mancini called Sheriff Tate and the police for assistance, but got no satisfaction. That's when they decided to use their considerable wealth and resources to defend their women and children, even at the risk of being found out by their wives. The white men stood shoulder to shoulder with the black men, determined to be victorious in this battle.

In the distance, they could see the headlights and torches. A moment or two later, they could hear the angry mob. Their approach was swift, completely unaware that they were in the crossfire of well-armed black men who were willing to die rather than see any more destruction of their property on that blistering night in August.

"That's far enough!" Mancini shouted from behind a barricade of sand-filled sacks. The men of Ashland Estates decided to let a white man assume the position of leadership, hoping the mob would listen to him before more people were killed. "There's been enough killing tonight. You all just go on back home and cool off!"

"We ain't leavin' 'til we burn this place to the ground," Joseph King shouted. "And no nigger-lovin' white man is gonna stop us. We got you outnumbered. No way you can stop us from coming in there."

"Maybe not," Mancini shouted. "But we're prepared to die trying. Besides that, you all are surrounded. Look around you." The black men came out of the shadows like ghosts. "It's suicide to try. Now, go on back home and cool off!"

The mob heard numerous rifles and shotguns being cocked. They looked around and began to assess their chances of survival with all those rifles cocked and aimed at them.

"I see women and children in the crowd," Mancini began again. "We don't want to kill anybody, let alone women and children, but you leave us no choice, sir. I beg of you, leave this place in peace and don't come back."

The mob began to murmur among themselves, shaking their heads.

"They killed and mutilated a white man," King said to the crowd, who had lost their desire to continue after seeing so many well-armed Negroes. "We can't let them get away with that. If we let them get away with it, they'll rape our wives and daughters next."

"Isn't that what you just did?" Lucas shouted. He was standing next to Bubbles with his rifle aimed at the leader.

The murmuring grew louder. A different voice from the crowd interjected, "I'm taking my family home. It ain't worth it." Another voice shouted the same thing—then another and another. Several had already turned to leave when Rahim Muhammad shot Joseph King in the forehead. Suddenly everybody was shooting; Blacks and Whites alike fell. So many bullets were fired that the air was filled with smoke and the smell of sulfur. When the hail of bullets finally ceased, amazingly only two hundred men, women, and children were dead, with two thousand wounded—but the homes in Ashland Estates were saved.

Chapter 89

"I've got everything under control."

With Marshall Law declared and the presence of the National Guard to keep the peace, racial tension eventually subsided. J. Edgar Hoover sent a team of FBI agents into the area under the pretense of investigating the riot, when in actuality they were investigating the local rackets. When news of the riot reached Chicago Sam, he decided to discuss it with John Stefano, the boss of New Orleans. Sam and Vinnie Milano, his chief capo and Napoleon's archenemy, were picked up at the airport by one of Stefano's men. They were driven straight to the Stefano mansion where they would discuss what happened.

On the way there, the driver spotted the FBI tailing them. When they pulled into the driveway, they saw several more FBI agents in dark suits snapping pictures. The driver pulled into the garage and closed it before opening the door for Sam and Vinnie. They were led through the mammoth residence to the den, where Stefano and his bodyguard were waiting for them, smoking sweet-smelling Cuban cigars.

Stefano stood up when Sam and Vinnie walked in. They kissed each other on the cheek. The bodyguard offered them a cigar and a seat then closed the door. Sam sat down, but Vinnie was on duty, as was Stefano's bodyguard. They

335

watched each other, wondering how good the other was at doing his job.

After lighting his cigar, Stefano said, "Here's what we found out, Sam. The Klansman killed the spade just like the *Sentinel* said. Napoleon Bentley, the cocksucker, decided to kill the Klansmen because he's bangin' the daughter of the murdered broad."

Though he was seething, Sam concealed his anger and said, "You think he loves this woman?"

"Woman my ass, Sam," Stefano foamed. "The daughter's only sixteen fuckin' years old. I don't mind her being a nigger. Who gives a fuck about that? I've had my share of nigger and spic women. They're fuckin' beautiful. But when it affects my business, that's where I draw the fuckin' line. You never, never let a fuckin' woman affect business, Sam! Never! He's gotta go! I got the fuckin' FBI lookin' up my ass with a microscope. The sons-of-bitches are every fuckin' where. It's fuckin' embarrassin', Sam. But more important, it's affecting business."

"Calm yourself, John," Sam said nonchalantly. "I'll have a talk with him."

"Are you fuckin' kiddin' me?" Stefano said with renewed fury. "The Spaniard's gotta go. I'm losing money with the fuckin' Feebees everywhere, taking pictures and following our every move. The locals are in line, but Feds—you know how fuckin' Hoover is."

"Relax. He's just makin' it look good, John," Sam said confidently. "We've got the dirt on Hoover. Don't worry. I've got everything under control."

Chapter 90
"I'm gonna kill you, you dago bastard."

Napoleon knew trouble was on the horizon when he saw Sam and Vinnie come into the Bayou. Rarely did a boss go into another boss's territory without permission. The only time that happened was when the visiting boss was taking over. Since Sam didn't bother to tell him he was coming to town, Napoleon knew his ultimate plan to take over all of New Orleans had finally arrived. When he looked at Vinnie Milano, he could tell that Vinnie still wanted the action in the Colored part of town. It was worth three million dollars a year. The way Vinnie saw it, that money was rightfully his.

Sam and Napoleon smiled when they greeted each other with a kiss. He shook hands with Vinnie Milano; both men were stone-faced. *I'm gonna kill you, you dago bastard,* Napoleon thought.

Bubbles watched the exchange between Vinnie and Napoleon from a distance. He walked over and spoke respectfully to Sam and Vinnie. He knew this day would come the night Napoleon met Johnnie. Everything that happened after that was inevitable, and it was all Napoleon's fault. Now they were both dead men, and nothing was going to change that. Not now. Not after seeing Sam in a nigger joint. It was already settled. It was just a matter of time.

337

They sat down at Napoleon's table and Sam said, "You really fucked up this time. I mean you really blew it with Stefano. It's a good thing for you I'm on your side. You got the fuckin' FBI lookin' into our business because you decided that a nigger bitch is more important than business." Sam looked at Bubbles for a reaction, but he didn't reveal his emotion. He just listened stoically.

"Stefano wants you dead, but I said no," Sam continued. "Everybody deserves a second chance, I told him. I gave him my word that I'd talk to you, and I have. Me and Vinnie are taking the next plane back to Chicago. But remember, you're only here because John Stefano owes me and I owed you. You fuck up again and you're on your own."

"Thanks, Sam," Napoleon said. "I guess we're even now."

"Don't guess, Napoleon," Sam said. "I won't warn you again. Vinnie, let's get outta this dump."

Vinnie grinned when they stood up. The smile alone was evidence that this wasn't the end of it as far as Napoleon was concerned. He knew they were planning to come back when the heat was off, but by then, Napoleon would own New Orleans.

Chapter 91

"But what about the police?"

The presence of the National Guard brought sanity back to New Orleans. Sable Parish was destroyed, Main Street was a heap of rubble but much of Baroque Parish remained intact. Johnnie was supposed to start the Beauregard job a week ago but it was postponed because of the riot. With the curfew lifted during daylight hours, citizens were allowed to go to their jobs and places of business—at least those businesses that weren't located in what was once a thriving suburb, now a charred wasteland.

The Beauregards lived at 1619 Harmony Street in the Garden District. *The Sunday Times* reported that the curfew would be lifted Monday. Ethel called Johnnie and told her she wanted her to start at 8:00. After being restricted to her home for a week, Johnnie had no idea how much damage was done by the riot until she saw what was left of the school. She pulled over to the nearest curb and cried.

It's all my fault. If only I hadn't talked Earl into buying me that stupid house, Mama would be alive and there wouldn't have been a riot. People are dead because of me. How can decent people behave this way?

She wiped her eyes, put the car in first gear and pulled away slowly, looking at all the burned-out buildings on Main

Street. Broken glass, bricks, furniture, and clothes were strewn about haphazardly. As she drove past what was left of the library, she saw a huge dark spot on the steps. *That's where they did it. That's where they killed Reverend Staples.* Business owners were everywhere, trying to pick up the pieces. They seemed to be determined to rebuild; that's what Dennis Edwards said to a reporter from the *Times*.

Bernard Coleman, the architect, when interviewed said, "We intend to rebuild our community and go on with business as usual." With all the damage, Coleman stood to make a fortune in rebuilding costs alone.

Continuing slowly, she saw many of Baroque's business owners, along with their children cleaning their shops. Philip Collins and his sons were hauling barber chairs back into the shop. When he saw the sad look on her face, he called out, "Don't be sad, Johnnie. We whipped the white man's ass for a change. We gon' be all right! Don't you worry your pretty little head none. We gon' be all right." He wiped the sweat off his brow with his arm and went back to work.

Johnnie was surprised he knew her name, and wondered if he knew she was the reason for all of this. If he did, he certainly didn't blame her; at least he didn't act like he did. Continuing down Main Street, she saw Bernard Coleman and Michael Nagel, both wearing hard hats. They were looking over some plans sprawled out over Nagel's pickup truck. When they saw her, they smiled and nodded approvingly.

Something's strange. Everybody's smiling at me like nothing happened. They gotta know I was involved with Richard Goode's death. There's a lady going into the bookstore. I'll ask her.

Johnnie pulled over to the curb. "Excuse me, Miss," she began. "What's going on? Why are people so happy today?"

"Because we approve of what you did, Johnnie," she said after walking over to the car.

"Uh, what did I do?" Johnnie asked with a confused look on her face. "And how do you know my name?"

"I'm sorry. I'm Lisa Cambridge," she said, shaking, her hand. "I own Cambridge Books and Publishing. This is a small town. Everybody knows you, but no one blames you. If the police would have done their jobs, none of this would've happened."

"But what about your businesses? They were destroyed."

"We've got insurance, dear. Buchanan Mutual is paying for all of this. At the most, we've lost money from daily sales, but that's about it. Bernard says he can make Main Street better than before. We're all excited about that."

"But what about the police? Aren't they going to arrest somebody sooner or later?"

"I doubt it. Ryan Robertson slapped the city with a ten million dollar lawsuit this morning. The police never came to stop the rioting. He says they'll probably make a deal and he'll drop the suit. But more important, them crackers know not to come here again."

"Who is Ryan Robertson?"

"Just one of New Orleans' finest attorneys. You oughta meet Ryan and Anita. They're really nice people. One day, when you and Sadie come outta the house, I'll have to introduce you to your neighbors."

"Okay, well, I gotta go. I gotta get to work," Johnnie told her, even though she hadn't decided if she was going to take the job. She mainly wanted to see if there was a picture of Nathaniel Beauregard. That would tell her if she was related to them or not. "I'm supposed to start a new job today."

"Okay, take care. Call me some time. I'm in the book."

"I will," Johnnie promised and pulled away.

Chapter 92
"Why would good white people start a riot?"

Johnnie drove to the Garden District with a sense of relief, like the weight of the world was suddenly lifted from her shoulders. It was 8:30 when she reached the Beauregard Mansion. Ethel made it very clear that she wanted her there by 8:00 sharp. Johnnie opened her car door and stepped into the blaring heat. Ethel was standing in the foyer watching her as she came up the long walk. The twenty-six room mansion was certainly impressive, Johnnie thought. *I wonder how much work there is to do.*

Ethel opened the door. She was petite with high cheekbones—probably a nice-looking woman when she was younger. Her smile was as bright as the yellow dress she was wearing.

"You must be Johnnie," Ethel said with an accent that seemed to be a cross between New York and the Mississippi delta. "Y'all must really learn to get here on time."

"Yes, ma'am," Johnnie said and attempted to enter the house.

Ethel said, "Remember your place."

Johnnie frowned. "Huh?"

"Go around to the back."

Johnnie stared at her for about ten seconds then dutifully walked around to the back of the mansion, where Ethel was waiting for her in the kitchen.

"I'll show you around," Ethel said. "Normally I don't open my own door, but our butler was injured in that awful riot your people started. I swear to God that I don't know why no one's been arrested. All those white people dead and not a single Colored in jail. Does that make sense to you, young lady?"

"How do you know Coloreds started it, ma'am?" Johnnie asked, ignoring her question.

"Don't be silly," Ethel said with a laugh. "Why would good white people start a riot?"

"This is a big house, Mrs. Beauregard," Johnnie said, ignoring that question too. "This seems like a lot of work."

"Don't tell me you're afraid of a little work."

"No, I'm not afraid of work." *You've got a lotta nerve. You seem to be in perfect health. You can clean this house yourself, but you hire a maid and ask me if I'm afraid of work?* "It's just that I was told you have a really big library here. From what I can tell, all the rooms are really big. You have a basement too, right?"

"Yes, but Sadie led me to believe that you were taking the job."

"I'm sorry she told you that, Mrs. Beauregard, but I'm thinking about going to night school, and I don't know if I can handle the extra work."

"I see," Ethel said, scowling.

"I'll tell you what. Let me see how big the library is, and then I'll know if I want the job or not."

"I hope you'll work for me. I really need someone. It's been months since Betty Jean left me high and dry. She didn't even give me a reason. She just left."

343

Ethel slid the French doors of the library open and they entered. The first thing Johnnie noticed were the portraits on the walls. It took every bit of strength she had not to run over to the paintings and search frantically for her grandfather.

"If you worked here, you could use this library to study," Ethel said, trying to sweeten the offer. "And I'll pay you more than what I paid Betty Jean. How does that sound?"

"Who are the people in these pictures?" Johnnie asked, hoping to hear the one name she would recognize. "Are these the men in your family?"

"Yes, they are," Ethel said. "The women are on the other side of the room."

"Do you mind if I look at them?"

"Sure. Go ahead. Their names are inscribed on the frames," Ethel told her.

Johnnie went from one picture to the next, barely looking at the figure in each portrait. As she read each name, anxiety began to build. Then finally, she saw his name. Nathaniel Beauregard. *Grandpa! It's you!*

"I'll take the job," Johnnie beamed. She was thrilled at the opportunity to get to know them, even though the Ethel Beauregard had no idea Johnnie was a blood relative. *I'll get to know my family, and if they're nice people, I'll leave after a few months and never let them know who I am. But if not, I'll bring shame on them all and ruin the entire family.*

Book Club Discussion Questions

1. What was Johnnie's main character flaw?
2. Why do you think Johnnie didn't run to the altar when she knew she should? What do you think held her back?
3. Was Marguerite really looking out for Johnnie's best interests as she claimed?
4. Was Marguerite right about black men?
5. Why do you think the author didn't give much of a description of Earl Shamus and Richard Goode?
6. Was Marguerite right in her assessment of the ongoing problems between black women and white women? If wrong, why don't these women like each other? If right, what if anything can be done to change the attitudes of both races?
7. How did you feel when the girls at church laughed at Johnnie?
8. Did Earl love Johnnie? Explain your answer.
9. When Johnnie didn't understand "big words," she bought a dictionary. What do you do? Do you pretend like you understand, or do you ask the person the meaning of the words?
10. Was Johnnie a lady, a whore, or both? Explain your answer.
11. "How could you do it with the white man?" Billy Logan yelled. Was this a legitimate question? Should the races be segregated again? Why or why not?
12. Was Coach Mitchell right when he refused to endorse a letter to Grambling University for Lucas Matthews?

13. Did you like Lucas? Why or why not?

14. If Marguerite had not come home early, would something have happened between Johnnie and Lucas?

15. In 1952, prior to Affirmative Action, Baroque Parish's black businesses were thriving. What happened between then and now? Why aren't there more black businesses like they had back then? Is it because Blacks are being held back? Or is there another possibility? If so, discuss some of the possibilities.

16. In Fletcher's Funeral Home, there is a plaque with a quote from Frederick Douglass. What is the quote? There are two onyx figurines on his desk. Who are these men, and why did the author select those two historical figures for that scene?

17. Napoleon Bentley: Would you date him? Why or why not?

18. At the Savoy, Marguerite told Johnnie she could still be an evangelist. Why didn't Johnnie stop selling herself and go back to the Lord?

19. Why didn't Lucas and Napoleon listen to Bubbles' advice on love and sex?

20. Johnnie is only sixteen when the novel ends. What do you think will happen with her life?

IN STORES NOW

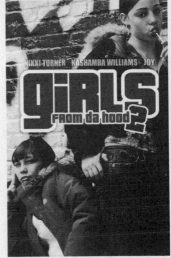

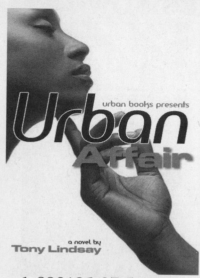

urban books presents

Urban Affair

a novel by
Tony Lindsay

1-893196-27-5

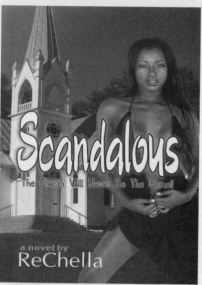

Scandalous

The Church Will Never Be The Same!

a novel by
ReChella

1893196-30-5

URBAN BOOKS PRESENTS

PAYBACK

a street saga by
roy glenn

FEBRUARY 2006
1-893196-37-2

URBAN BOOKS presents

HARLEM CONFIDENTIAL

COLE RILEY

FEBRUARY 2006
1-893196-41-0

MARCH 2006
1-893196-32-1

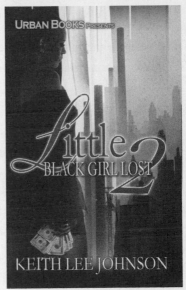

FEBRUARY 2006
1-893196-39-9

MARCH 2006
1-893196-33-X

APRIL 2006
1-893196-34-8

OTHER URBAN BOOKS TITLES

Title	Author	Quantity	Cost
Drama Queen	LaJill Hunt		$14.95
No More Drama	LaJill Hunt		$14.95
Shoulda Woulda Coulda	LaJill Hunt		$14.95
Is It A Crime	Roy Glenn		$14.95
MOB	Roy Glenn		$14.95
Drug Related	Roy Glenn		$14.95
Lovin' You Is Wrong	Alisha Yvonne		$14.95
Bulletproof Soul	Michelle Buckley		$14.95
You Wrong For That	Toschia		$14.95
A Gangster's girl	Chunichi		$14.95
Married To The Game	Chunichi		$14.95
Sex In The Hood	White Chocalate		$14.95
Little Black Girl Lost	Keith Lee Johnson		$14.95
Sister Girls	Angel M. Hunter		$14.95
Driven	KaShamba Williams		$14.95
Street Life	Jihad		$14.95
Baby Girl	Jihad		$14.95
A Thug's Life	Thomas Long		$14.95
Cash Rules	Thomas Long		$14.95
The Womanizers	Dwayne S. Joseph		$14.95
Never Say Never	Dwayne S. Joseph		$14.95
She's Got Issues	Stephanie Johnson		$14.95
Rockin' Robin	Stephanie Johnson		$14.95
Sins Of The Father	Felicia Madlock		$14.95
Back On The Block	Felicia Madlock		$14.95
Chasin' It	Tony Lindsey		$14.95
Street Possession	Tony Lindsey		$14.95
Around The Way Girls	LaJill Hunt		$14.95
Around The Way Girls 2	LaJill Hunt		$14.95
Girls From Da Hood	Nikki Turner		$14.95

Girls from Da Hood 2	Nikki Turner		$14.95
Dirty Money	Ashley JaQuavis		$14.95
Mixed Messages	LaTonya Y. Williams		$14.95
Don't Hate The Player	Brandie		$14.95
Payback	Roy Glenn		$14.95
Scandalous	ReChella		$14.95
Urban Affair	Tony Lindsey		$14.95
Harlem Confidential	Cole Riley		$14.95

Urban Books
74 Andrews Ave.
Wheatley Heights, NY 11798
Subtotal: _____
Postage:_____ Calculate postage and handling as follows: Add
$2.50 for the first item and $1.25 for each additional item
Total: _____
Name: _____
Address:_____
City: _____ State: _____ Zip: _____
Telephone: (   ) _____
Type of Payment (Check: ___   Money Order: ___)
All orders must be prepaid by check or money order drawn on an American bank.
Books may sometimes be out of stock. In that instance, please select your alternate choices below.

Alternate Choices:

1._____

2._____

PLEASE ALLOW 4-6 WEEKS FOR SHIPPING